The MISSING DIARY

Tasmin TURNER

CRIME SCENE KOSOVO BOOK 1

Copyright © 2023 Tasmin Turner

Tasmin Turner asserts the moral right to be identified as the author of this work.

EBOOK ISBN 978-1-9911924-0-0

All rights reserved. No part of this book may be reproduced, stored in a retrieval system, or transmitted in any form or by any electronic or mechanical means including photocopying, recording, information storage and retrieval systems, or otherwise, without prior permission in writing from the author, with the exception of a book reviewer, who may quote short excerpts in a review.

This book is a work of fiction. Unless otherwise indicated, all the names, characters, organizations, places, events and incidents in this book are either the product of the author's imagination or used in a fictitious manner and are not to be construed as real. Any resemblance to actual events or persons, living or dead, or organizations, is fictionalized or coincidental.

For any inquiries regarding this book, please email:
joann@dreamlifenz.com

Also available as a print on demand book
ISBN 978-1-9911924-1-7

For more information see www.wish-books.com

Cover Design by ebooklaunch.com

Wish Books

People

Angela Keys, Office Assistant, OIDC (the Organization for International Development and Coordination)

Caitlin (Kit) Chase, lawyer from New Zealand working in the Office of the Chief International Prosecutor in OIDC, Pristina, Kosovo

Dasham Raco, boss of an organized crime group running guns, drugs and extortion rackets in Kosovo

Don Edgson, canine-unit leader and general dog handler, US military officer on secondment to EUFOR

Enver Raco, Dasham Raco's nephew and accomplice

Eva Refazo, chief international prosecutor, OIDC

Frank Stanton, US Ambassador to Kosovo

Gregor Petri, a major from the Romanian military on secondment to EUFOR

Jacob Mueller, former German ambassador, heading the Organization for International Development and Coordination in Kosovo, the OIDC

Jyoti Prabhu, International Coroner, Pristina

Matthew (Matt) Hackman, major in the Special Investigations Branch, British Military Police, EUFOR

Merita Shala, a former Kosovo policewoman and associate of Dasham Raco

Miloš Mandić, representative from the National Assembly in Belgrade

Owen Reese, sergeant in Special Investigations Branch of the British Military Police with EUFOR

Rosalyn Chase, Kit's mother in New Zealand

Sergei Sokolov, attaché with the Russian Liaison Office, Pristina

Vasha Blaku, confidential informant in criminal investigations

Vernon Chase, Kit's estranged father. who moved to Australia for a position as a defense contractor.

Visar Dreshaj, Pristina politician, Foreign Minister, and former commander in the Kosovo Liberation Army

Xander Willis, Kit's fiancé in New Zealand

Animals

Bambino, Eva's terrier cross rescue dog

Max, Belgium Tervuren canine unit member

Places

All Gem Hotel, a luxury hotel, Pristina, Kosovo

Belgrade, capital city of the Republic of Serbia

Black and White Café, a café in mid-town Pristina

The Boom Boom Room, a Pristina night club

Camp Prizren, German military base with a medical center

Club Europa 50, a sophisticated Pristina club bar

Dragodan Steps, steps from the center of Pristina

Dubrovic, a historic city in Croatia

Gërmia Park, a Pristina park at the wooded lower foothills of the Rhodope mountains

Pristina, the capital city of Kosovo

Prizren, a historical town in Kosovo

Saint Heliers, Auckland, New Zealand, Kit's upmarket home suburb by the sea

Staro Dorbi, the rural community where several Serbian farmers were killed.

Sunny Hill, a suburb of Pristina where Matt Hackman lives

Trepča, the site of a large precious metals mine, spanning Kosovo and Serbia

Organizations

European military and police force, EUFOR, engaged in law enforcement in Kosovo during the post-conflict period

Kosovo Liberation Army (KLA), an ethnic Albanian separatist militia that sought the separation of Kosovo from the Federal Republic of Yugoslavia and Serbia

The Organization for International Development and Coordination in Kosovo (OIDC), an international organization assisting with the administration of Kosovo during the post-conflict period

Khash, a philosophical system based on applying lessons from the game of chess to life

Task Force Capture, EUFOR task force working to solve the crimes at Staro Dorbi

Task Force Eagle Eye, an informal crime-solving task force

Background

During the 1998–1999 Kosovo conflict, ethnic Albanians opposed the Serbian Government of the former Yugoslavia in Belgrade. Kosovo broke away and sought to set up an independent state, which Serbia did not recognize. NATO allied forces drove Serbian forces back following a humanitarian crisis. International organizations stepped in to support the government in Kosovo. This story is set in a fictionalized post-conflict Kosovo. Further information is provided in the author's note at the end of the book.

Prologue

Written by a woman in love with two men.

When did my love for my two brother warriors begin? Only weeks or months ago, but it seems that I have known them forever. These lovers have made prisoners of my heart and drawn blood. Peace and war, love and hatred are closer than I ever dreamed possible. God only knows where this story will end. Only writing consoles me.

My two sacred brothers of the blood I call by their nicknames, their *noms de guerre*: Razor and Vuk 'the Wolf'. I met Razor while I was still working for the Kosovo Police. Wolf I met later on a mission up north. They each showed me something different about the relationship between a man and a woman.

Merita's diary, 16 June 2000

CHAPTER ONE

St Heliers
Auckland, New Zealand

"You can't be serious," said Xander as he tossed the letter down. The blue logo smacked of it being official. His normally relaxed features were taut. "You're not going."

"Don't tell me what to do." Caitlin's bright blue eyes blazed. "This is my big opportunity," she said, desperate for a new role now she no longer worked as an associate at the Crown Law Prosecutor. "I won't get another chance to be an international prosecutor."

"*Assistant* prosecutor," Xander corrected as he placed the coffee maker on the stove. His large brown eyes with long lashes, magnified by the glasses he wore, watched his fiancée Caitlin, better known as Kit, with caution.

"This could be my only opportunity to work abroad. Maybe get a major war crimes prosecution under my belt. They won't offer a position like this again."

"It's too dangerous." He pointed towards her, seeing ambition in her eyes. "And you know it."

"I'll be fine," she replied dismissively. "I'm always fine." She looked away from Xander and studied the letter again.

The Missing Diary

Seeing Kosovo appear on a TV news item, Xander picked up the remote control, and sound burst into the room.

"During the 1998–1999 Kosovo conflict, ethnic Albanians opposed the ethnic Serbian government of the former Yugoslavia in Belgrade. Kosovo broke away and sought to set up an independent state, which Serbia did not recognize. Allied forces drove Serbian forces back following a humanitarian crisis. The bombing stopped in June 1999. But a year later, there's still much for international organizations to do here."

Images flashed over the screen of derelict, bombed-out buildings and refugees streaming out of Kosovo. Grim women and children traipsed along country roads with what luggage they could carry. Groups of men accompanied them, carrying weapons and belongings, their faces bitten by the harsh weather. The screen switched to other images of fighters masked in balaclavas and special forces uniforms and toting automatic weapons. Another scene showed a convoy of tanks rolling into Kosovo.

"What did I just say?" said Xander. "It's not safe."

Kit remained by the kitchen table, where light streamed in through the large glass doors leading to the patio, watching the news segment.

"Jacob Mueller, former German ambassador, now heads the Organization for International Development and Coordination in Kosovo, the OIDC." The TV anchor turned to a dignified older man, his features set in a concerned expression.

"Mr. Mueller, as head of the OIDC in Kosovo, can you tell our viewers about the challenges you face?"

Mueller fixed the interviewer with an appraising look. "The OIDC is here to end the humanitarian emergency and put Kosovo on the road to development. We're doing this with the help of the European military and police force, EUFOR. Strategic infrastructure projects are essential to help get Kosovo back on its feet. We support peace by coordinating with the United Nations, the Organization for Security and Cooperation in Europe, and other partners."

The pair watched until the programme moved to another topic, and Kit muted the television again.

"You've never been to a war zone," Xander argued. "You have no idea what you're letting yourself in for, let alone the crime and violence in Kosovo." He wiped his hands and came closer to her.

"Nah," Kit said. "All that's exaggerated. Anyway, it can't be much worse than working in a downtown law firm. You should have seen the bloodshed around the water cooler," she added with a smirk. "Professional reputations were on the line because of office gossip."

Frustrated by her indifference to the dangers, he tempered his approach. "I realise you didn't enjoy working there, but this could be even worse, honey," he pleaded as he rubbed her shoulders.

Xander was right. She hadn't enjoyed her job, but otherwise life was pretty good if she was honest. House-sitting her aunt's restored Victorian villa, which had been in the family for three generations, while she cruised the South Pacific also gave Kit time to enjoy sailing in Auckland's generous coastal waters. But with Xander only working mornings at a suburban accounting firm while studying part-time for his master's in business administration, it'd be ages before they could afford a place of their own.

"I need you here with me." He kissed her neck above the camouflage T-shirt she wore.

Still damp from her evening exercise, she pulled away, her auburn ponytail swinging. She felt energised after her part self-defense, part aerobics. and part street fighting class she took to learn Krav Maga, with a military veteran, to keep fit and focussed.

"It's only for a short time. The letter says the contract is for three months with the possibility of extension. And the job pays well. This'll help us save for the deposit on a house of our own. I haven't been able to find work for months. This is my chance to prove myself."

Trying to avoid a full-blown fight, he reached out again to stroke her hair, lifted a handful to his face, and inhaled. It smelled of candied violets blended with vanilla that lingered from her fragrance. "Foxy lady, don't be upset with me," he pleaded as he softened his voice.

She turned to face him. "I'm not upset with you, but I have to do this. I wish you wouldn't call me that, by the way."

She remembered when they first met. He'd been at the same yacht regatta in the lead-up to the America's Cup sailing off the New Zealand coast. In his early thirties, Xander Willis looked the epitome of the boy next door: round face, dimpled chin, and a wide, friendly smile framed by a full head of glossy chestnut curls. He'd seemed the perfect fit. Then.

"I don't understand how you could walk away from the grand lifestyle we have here to go somewhere like Kosovo," he said in a voice that had hardened.

"Perhaps life is too easy here," she said, looking around at the antique-silver tea service that sat on the embroidered-lace tablecloth. A bunch of pink and white peonies graced a large crystal vase on the table.

"What do you mean?"

"Do you ever feel you have to make a difference? To be connected with what's going on in the world? And feel like it matters?"

"I already know what's going on out there, and I don't want to connect to it. You shouldn't either." He paused and thought for a moment. "What does your mother think?"

"I haven't told her yet, but I expect her to support me."

Kit's mother Rosalyn had brought up the Kit and her sister single-handed. Rosalyn had persuaded the court that their father, Vernon Chase, should not have unsupervised access to the girls. He lost interest in their family after that, and they heard he had moved to Australia for a position as a defense contractor.

"You've inherited your father's craziness," he snapped.

Kit glared at Xander as he sat down on the couch and turned up the sound on the news. It was showing airstrikes in the Balkans again. She grasped the envelope and marched out of the living room. "I'm going to look at flights," she said. "They need me in Pristina as soon as possible."

Xander was startled when he heard hissing on the stove. The coffee pot had boiled over, leaving spilt coffee sizzling on the glowing element.

Chapter Two

My beloved's nickname is Razor because he likes to cut people and occasionally himself. He can kill with the flick of the blade, a touch they barely feel until it's too late. He makes a good living from his skills. Wolf likes to give orders, including in the bedroom. It amuses me to obey him sometimes.

Merita's diary, 1 July 2000

Even though her eyes were gritty from jet lag as her flight approached Kosovo, she was eager to see her first glimpses of the Balkan Mountains. As it emerged from swathes of dark clouds, the countryside stretched out beneath her like a rough patchwork quilt overlaid with villages and roads.

The passengers disembarked quickly from the aircraft. Kit followed them and the signs, which were helpfully in English and Albanian, to passport control.

"You're from New Zealand," the immigration official said as he scrutinized Kit. "We don't see many of these passports here. But New Zealand is a friend of Kosovo, so welcome to Pristina." He stamped her passport firmly with a flourish and waved her through.

A throng of people were waiting for passengers to emerge. Kit recognized her new colleague, Angela, from the emails they had exchanged. Her fair hair and friendly face drew Kit's attention amid the sea of bearded men with crew cuts who were waiting for passengers. A blonde woman in a fitted blue jacket and slacks held up a sheet of paper with Caitlin Chase written on it. Kit's casual clothing, auburn braid, sea-blue eyes, and light makeup gave her away as an international in a place where women were more likely to wear full makeup and carefully coordinated outfits.

"I'm Angela Keys from OIDC. You must be Caitlin," the woman said in a Yorkshire accent.

"Hi," Kit replied, smiling broadly. "Yes, but most people call me Kit."

"Welcome to Kosovo, Kit. You can call me Angel. Let's get out of here. The jeep is across the car park."

Kit followed Angel out of the airport building and waited on the sidewalk while she brought a white, four-wheel-drive jeep with OIDC plates. As she waited, Kit looked around. She was in a European country, but it wasn't the Europe she knew. A cold wind cut into her body, which was weary from the lengthy flight. The chill was uncomfortable but woke her up as she observed her surroundings. The people had an expression of determination that she had only seen rarely in New Zealand. The sharp sound of a horn drew her attention back to the road. Angela had pulled up in the jeep, ready to load the luggage.

Kit steadied herself by gripping the sides of her seat as the vehicle bounced over the pot-holed road. No one had cut the grass and shrubs beside the road for a long time. Recent rain hadn't fully drained away and had left muddy patches in the countryside.

"First time in the Balkans?" Angel asked.

"Yes. I was wondering why the immigration official welcomed me when I said I was from New Zealand."

"They do that. If you were from a non-recognizing country, such as Spain or India, for example—don't even mention Russia—they might not have let you in without a visa. That would have made things more complicated. We would have issued you with international ID and got you in with that. As it was, we were lucky. New Zealand is a recognizer."

"I know I should've studied all this before I came. But what do you mean by a recognizer?" All of a sudden, she felt unprepared for the complexities of the new world she had stepped into.

"A country that recognizes Kosovo as an independent state. Quite a few countries don't. Serbia still claims that Kosovo is a part of its territory, supported by Russia and quite a few others such as China and India. Even several European countries who are part of the Western Alliance and helped Kosovo don't recognize its independence. Probably because they have their own renegade groups who would like to claim independence."

"Like the Basque separatists."

Angel nodded. "Many states of the former Yugoslavia have become independent from Serbia. Except Kosovo. Serbia calls Kosovo and Metohija the spiritual heart of Serbia, and it won't let go."

"I'm not sure I understand what you mean by that."

"You and me both," Angel said as she swerved to avoid a pothole. "One of these days, when you've settled in, I'll take you to one of their monasteries and you can better understand."

"Sounds amazing. I'd love to."

"The local Albanians are mainly Muslim, the same as they are in Turkey, and they have their mosques."

"Wow, that's different to what I'm used to in New Zealand."

"This will be an eye-opener for you."

"I'm not sure what to expect," Kit said as she held her handbag to her body with an arm as a swimmer might clutch a life-saving ring.

"That's simple," Angel said. "Expect the unexpected."

At that moment they hit a pothole, and the large bump jarred Kit. She gripped the seat again and tried to smile.

"Another piece of advice a local taxi driver gave me which turned out to be useful," Angel continued, "he said we should always have a plan B and a plan C, in case plan A doesn't work out."

Kit laughed. "I'll try to remember that."

"In fact," Angel said as she shifted down a gear, "we'll use plan B now because the main road looks closed."

Kit noticed the roadblock ahead as they turned onto an uneven, gravel road.

"What's it like living in Kosovo? I mean apart from being unpredictable."

"How's your Albanian?" Angel glanced at Kit and then into the rear-view mirror.

"Nonexistent," Kit replied. "I studied French at school, so I could speak it in French Polynesia and New Caledonia. That's about it."

THE MISSING DIARY

"You could get by with basic German at a pinch," Angel said. "After the conflict, a lot of people took advantage of the gray or black market to survive, without worrying too much about whether it was illegal or not—drugs, weapons trafficking, and corruption. And reputedly trafficking in organs. Kosovo falls between the cracks. It's a territory, and no one's really in charge."

"I thought *we* were," Kit said.

"On paper, yes, OIDC and EUFOR keep the Kosovars and Serbians from killing each other. The Kosovo Liberation Army honchos took control of the local politics. They do their best to keep things under control, but rumors are rife."

"Rumors?"

"Who can be bought," Angel said. "But on the bright side, even though they're recovering from a war, the locals are generally friendly. They're curious about people from abroad. Kosovo's off the beaten track in Europe, so you can impress your friends by telling them you're living somewhere exotic. A lot of people think it's like the Wild West." Angel laughed.

"Before the war, a lot of people in New Zealand didn't even know where Kosovo was. When I left, they seemed worried about my safety here."

"Life is pretty safe for internationals as long we follow reasonable precautions. Like, let someone in the office know when you're going somewhere unusual by yourself. We can always call OIDC security for backup if we need to."

"I'd better make of note of the important phone numbers," Kit said.

"You'll get a briefing on all that. Best of all, the cost of living is low."

"Perfect for saving money then." Kit laughed and patted her handbag.

"You have to try the local food too—there are plenty of fresh vegetables and seasonal fruit. The savory pastry, *burek*, served with yogurt is the best. I'll show you some good local cafés and restaurants. You might need to dodge the odd bullet, though—mainly from happy shooting."

"What's that?"

"When the locals are celebrating, they fire their guns into the air. What goes up must come down—so there are often injuries when people get hit by bullets coming down. And many are still armed."

Kit looked alarmed.

"Don't worry, you'll be fine," Angel assured her. She picked up a heavy, black radio telephone and turned it on. "Sierra base, this is Charlie Lima One, over."

The device crackled into life. "Charlie Lima One, this is Sierra base, you are loud and clear, over."

"Sierra base, I've collected the new staff member Caitlin Chase from the airport. We're heading to mission HQ along route B. Over."

"Roger that. Be advised that a military convoy is traveling on a road from the airport. It might slow down traffic. See you when you arrive. Over."

"Copy that."

Kit watched, fascinated but bewildered. It was the first time she had seen a radio telephone.

"Do all these vehicles have radio sets?" she asked.

"Yes. You'll get one too. They're useful to notify HQ where you are if the telecoms network goes out."

As they reached a bend in the road, Kit saw a convoy of trucks carrying soldiers under camouflage-colored covers. EUFOR was spelt out in large letters on the side. Kit gripped the seat a little harder when she saw they were carrying rifles.

"So," Angel said, "I'm taking you to HQ. You'll meet our boss, Eva. Then I'll take you to your hotel."

"Where is it?"

"We've reserved a room for you in the Grand Hotel for a week while you settle in and find an apartment."

"Okay, thanks," Kit said. "I'm looking forward to meeting the team."

"You'll like Eva. She gets the job done, but she isn't a stickler for rules. Do you have a family?"

"My fiancé's in Auckland and so's my mom. Family and friends."

"Pristina isn't a family duty station—the organization doesn't make it easy for family to come here. Unfortunately."

Kit wondered if it really was unfortunate that Xander couldn't be with her. "I don't know. I'm kind of looking forward to the adventure by myself, at least for a while. Besides, Xander's busy with his work back in Auckland. I'll be checking in regularly with my mom."

"People often end up extending their contracts. The money's good and life is okay in Pristina," Angel said.

"I'll see how things go." Kit watched the landscape slide past. Several houses were severely damaged or burned-out ruins. A jet passed close overhead and Kit shivered, sensing for the first time that she was in a conflict zone.

Angel looked at her out the corner of her eye. "Don't worry, you'll get used to it."

They drove through an industrial area on the outskirts of Pristina and eventually pulled into a driveway. A security barrier blocked access to the compound, while security officers scrutinized them through the window of the sentry house. One emerged and signaled to Angel to turn off the engine so he could look underneath the car with a mirror. "Checking for explosives," Angel said matter-of-factly as she showed her badge and signed Kit in. The guard issued Kit a temporary ground pass before Angel eased the vehicle through the gate and into the OIDC compound.

Many offices were located in basic, white container buildings, while an older, more established building stood in the middle of the compound. They swung into the car park, and the two women got out. A few spaces down, Kit noticed a slim, elegantly dressed woman in her early fifties who was struggling to take a pile of files out of her vehicle. As she lifted them out, she dropped pages and scrambled to collect them, while a small, black terrier-cross pawed at her hand and stood on the typed documents.

"Stop it, Bambino!" she shouted as she pushed the dog away and tried to put her sheets back in order. She was dressed in a smart taupe pencil skirt and matching jacket, with a high-necked blouse. She bent down awkwardly in her high-heeled black pumps. Her dark blonde hair, threaded with silver, was pulled into a careless bun, and tendrils fell around her face.

Angel tilted her head in the direction of the woman. "That's the boss, Eva Refazo," she whispered as she walked over to the woman. "Hey, Eva, can I help?" Angel bent down to pet the dog. "Hi, Bambino."

"*Buongiorno*, Angel," Eva said. "I'm just about done, thanks." She gathered the documents into a pile and stood up, bracing against the car unsteadily. Angel extended her hands and took the pile of papers. Eva smoothed down her skirt and grabbed her bag.

"I've brought our new staff member. You remember that Caitlin Chase is arriving today?"

Eva squinted over her dark glasses in Kit's direction. "*Si*. Yes, of course. Tell her to come inside and join me in my office in five minutes."

Kit watched from a distance and enjoyed the drama. This was not what she had expected from her first meeting with the high-powered international prosecutor, Eva Refazo. Eva looked disorganized, hardly the fine legal mind that Kit imagined when she'd read her academic articles on international criminal law.

Eva pushed the car door closed with her foot and took the documents from Angel. She called the black-and-white dog who trotted behind her toward the squat, grey, four-story building behind her.

Angel returned to Kit. "You'll like her," she reassured Kit. "She's a brilliant lawyer and a good sport. A bit absent-minded sometimes, but at other times she has a mind like a steel trap. She has a soft spot for rescue dogs. There are quite a few wild dogs in Pristina. EUFOR culls them, but there are always more."

Kit nodded. "What should I do with my luggage?"

"Leave your bags in the jeep," Angel said. "After I've introduced you to Eva, we'll go to your hotel. Over the coming days, you'll check in with the admin people, meet our colleagues, get a security briefing, get your phone and computer set up, things like that. We'll get you an ID card and you'll be legal." Angel smiled.

It was noon, and in the distance, Kit heard a plaintive prayer. "That might take me a while to get used to."

"The call to prayer at the local mosque? They do it five times a day."

Kit blushed, feeling naïve and inexperienced. Although she had traveled in the Pacific and Western Europe, she had not spent much time in countries with large Muslim populations.

"It doesn't seem like a Muslim country on the surface from the little I've seen. In general, the women aren't veiled," she said. "People are dressed like other Europeans."

"They have a pragmatic approach, the same as in our countries. Most people go about their daily lives as best they can. You notice it more during the month of Ramadan when quite a few people fast. Also, you might see more women covering their heads in Prizren, for example, than in Pristina."

When she thought about Islam, she thought about television reports of people on pilgrimage to Mecca, not going about their everyday lives in Europe.

"We'll arrange for you to get a briefing on the overall situation and the history of Kosovo. The Serbian community is Orthodox Christian, while most of the local Kosovo Albanians are Muslim. Kosovo was under Turkish rule for five hundred years, and then it was socialist under the former Yugoslavia. Even though society is mainly secular, the cultural and ethnic divisions include religion."

"A briefing would be good. I should have studied up on this more before I came," Kit said.

"Don't worry. I didn't know about these things when I arrived either, but you'll learn. Let's get you inside and you can have a word with Eva."

Angel steered Kit toward the broad steps leading up to the entrance. "This building used to belong to a manufacturing firm," she said. "The international community occupied quite a few properties around Kosovo to set up their base for operations."

She ushered Kit into a large corner office where she found Eva sitting at her desk with files piled high on either side of her. Bambino, the rescue dog, was lapping fresh water from a bowl in the corner.

"Excuse me, Eva. This is Caitlin Chase, our new staff member," Angel said.

Eva looked up. "Welcome to the team, Caitlin. Did you fly direct from New Zealand?"

"Yes, ma'am," Kit said. She knew that Eva had lead the first prosecutions for war crimes in Rwanda and was known in Europe for lobbying to extend universal jurisdiction against war crimes.

"Would you like me to bring coffee?" Angel asked Eva.

"Yes, please. We've got instant—or *Nes* as they call it here—Caitlin. No espresso in the office, sorry. I hope that's okay." Eva indicated that Kit should take a seat on the leather couch.

"So, when did you arrive?" Eva asked.

"About an hour ago. Angel collected me."

"We've had a few New Zealanders with the organization. You can settle in over the next few days before you start work." Eva indicated the files piled atop the desk with a sweep of her hand. "We have a lot of work, and it's increasing."

Angel brought a tray with instant coffee, creamer, sugar, and two mugs.

Eva poured the coffee and pushed a mug toward Kit. "So, how do you feel coming to work in a place like Kosovo?" she asked.

Kit sipped her coffee, then placed the cup on the table and took a deep breath. "I did well at law school in criminal law and thought I'd have a career in New Zealand representing defendants in criminal cases. But after I worked in a couple of central city law firms, I realized it wasn't for me. I am excited about having the chance to work with an international law team."

"I always found it more rewarding to be on the prosecution side. My parents are Italian diplomats, so we moved around a lot, and I did my doctorate in jurisprudence in Rome."

"I've heard about your professional reputation. I was thrilled at the chance to work with you."

"I hope you won't be disappointed." Eva smiled. She motioned to Bambino, who trotted over to her to receive a pat.

"I'm sure I'll learn a lot from you," Kit said. "I'm thrilled to be working in Kosovo. I found the daily grind of the Auckland law firm was wearing me down. But I'm fascinated by international criminal law, and the chance to work for an global organization such as OIDC is fantastic."

"Well," Eva said as she stirred a heaped teaspoon of sugar into her coffee, "if you're looking for the cutting edge, you've found it. What about family?"

"I'm single. I have a boyfriend back home, but he's cool about spending time apart."

"Good. You'll get regular breaks for R & R. Perhaps you could meet him halfway between Kosovo and New Zealand."

"Yeah, maybe," Kit said. "I've stopped off in Thailand before when I've flown between New Zealand and Europe."

Eva put down her coffee cup. "When you've settled in, I'll give you a couple of files. The first is a high-profile, sexual violence case. I need someone to sit in on the interviews and keep an overview of evidence collection. A woman lawyer can reassure the victim who, by the way, is called Vasha Blaku, and witnesses. We work with the EUFOR Criminal Intelligence Unit on the investigations."

"In New Zealand, it's unusual for a prosecutor to be involved early on in a case," Kit said.

"It's not unusual here. Have you worked on sexual violence cases before?"

"Not directly, although I did research for one of the partners in my law firm."

"Are you okay with the file?" Eva asked. "Several of the facts are traumatic, although all these cases are, in their own different ways."

Kit thought for a moment. Although the knot in her stomach said otherwise, she nodded. "Sure."

"Conflict-related sexual violence is underreported in Kosovo because of the social stigma for victims. The paternity of babies born after a rape is open to question. This is used as a weapon of war to demoralize a population and impact its ethnic composition."

Kit held her mug on her lap between her hands. Although it was instant, it tasted okay as they discussed the unpleasant topic.

"This case has a number of unusual elements," Eva continued. "Most of the reported incidents were between Serbs and Albanians. When Serb forces drove ethnic Albanians away from their homes, they often looted and burned the houses. After that, further crimes, such as rape or murder, were committed by rogue elements within the Serbian forces. We're not talking about *normal* conflict between military forces, but rather crimes committed against the civilian population. In this instance, a Kosovo Albanian woman, Vasha Blaku, was abducted and sexually abused—by another Albanian—for weeks before being released. Dasham Raco is known as the 'Machine Gun Kelly' of Kosovo because he's the boss of an organized crime group running guns, drugs, and extortion rackets."

"Machine Gun Kelly?" Kit asked. "Wasn't he an Irish American gangster whose favorite weapon was a submachine gun? I'm part Irish."

"That's the one," Eva said. "Good that you know your own criminal history. The Cosa Nostra come from my part of the world."

"I thought you said many of the crimes have an ethnic element," Kit said.

"They considered Blaku a Serb collaborator. Because she was romantically linked to a prominent Serb politician, they used the kidnapping to punish her and provoke the Serbs. She could also be a useful witness for our organized crime investigations into Raco."

"I see," Kit said. "It sounds complicated."

"You'll find that most things are here. We have other allegations of rape, but too often the family cover it up because it's a stain on family honor. They threw out some of our earlier cases when witnesses refused to testify. Without evidence, there isn't much we can do to prosecute the offenders. It would be helpful if you're there when Blaku's interviewed to check that the evidence being collected is admissible in court."

"Sure, I'd be happy to help out. It sounds very interesting," Kit said, nervous all of a sudden. This was why she had come to Kosovo, wasn't it?

"Don't worry," Eva said. "I'll be here if you need advice, and I've assigned Angel to help you."

"Who else is on the team?" Kit asked.

"While we work independently, our office is under the head of the OIDC Mission for administrative purposes. I'll take you to meet him soon. You'll report to me as my assistant prosecutor. Angel will take you to meet the others."

"Great."

"One more thing, and then we're done for the day. There's a conference I'd like you to go to tomorrow. This'll help you to hit the ground running and learn about the major players here. Did we get Caitlin on the list of participants, Angel?"

"We did."

"Angel will fill you in. I want you to be a fly on the wall and listen to the discussions. Introduce yourself to people during the coffee breaks if you get the chance, but say nothing during the proceedings. We try to stay out of local politics and keep a low profile."

"Will do," Kit said. "As a lot of Kiwis do, I'm good at keeping a low profile."

The next morning, Kit walked up Mother Teresa Boulevard from her room at the gray, socialist-style Grand Hotel to the All Gem Hotel. Her briefcase contained notepaper, pens, and pencils. It was mid-July, on average the warmest month in Kosovo, and temperatures were already climbing toward the early eighties.

Kit walked with a spring in her step among the bustling café culture. By ten o'clock, the cafés were full of people smoking, chatting, and drinking strong, hot coffee. She stopped off at the Black and White Café and picked up a double espresso to go, juggling it with her bag and jacket. She stopped for a moment to rearrange her things, caught her heel on the uneven pavement, and almost dropped the coffee.

"Can I help you?" a voice said from behind.

Kit was startled and glanced over her shoulder. "No thanks," she said, but at that moment she dropped her briefcase, which broke open and spilled its contents.

"Allow me," he said as he bent down and scooped up the contents of her briefcase and handed them back to her.

She found herself face to face with a man whose dark eyes and brows were startling against his fair skin and short, amber-blond hair. He wore a gray suit, which emphasized his broad shoulders, with a crisp white shirt and silk tie. His English was perfect but had an Eastern European inflection that Kit couldn't immediately identify.

There was something catlike about his manner, his head tilting to one side as he surveyed Kit and their surroundings. He seemed to be a man who was aware of everything going on around him.

"No, I'm fine," she said.

"Perhaps we're heading in the same direction," he persisted. "I'm going up the boulevard to the All Gem Hotel. How about you?"

"Yes, I am. How did you know?"

"Well, I wasn't sure … but I'm walking that way. Have I seen you around here before?" he added.

"That's unlikely. I only arrived yesterday."

The Missing Diary

"Welcome to Pristina," he said and smiled. "Allow me to introduce myself. I'm Sergei Sokolov from the Russian Liaison Office. Can I carry your bag while you drink your coffee?"

They set off along the street. Kit accepted his offer and allowed him to carry her bag while she sipped her coffee.

Once they arrived at the imposing facade of the All Gem Hotel, she dropped her coffee into a bin and retrieved her bag.

He nodded and clicked his heels together in a gesture that was at the same time charming and ridiculous. "I'll leave you for now. Here's my card." It bore his name, position as attaché at the Russian Liaison Office, phone number, and email. "And your name was …?"

"Caitlin, Caitlin Chase," Kit said. "I'm with the Chief Prosecutor's Office at OIDC. I started work there yesterday, so I haven't got business cards printed yet."

"No matter. I'm familiar with your office. Allow me to invite you for a coffee one day soon."

She didn't answer but gave an almost imperceptible nod.

"I'll be in touch," he said as he turned and took the marble steps two at a time before disappearing into the hotel.

She wondered whether it was by chance that he had helped her this morning, or could it have been part of a more elaborate pattern to gather intelligence? She knew Russia was a close ally to Serbia, and that it had been forced out of Kosovo by the Western allied air strikes a short time ago. She tucked away his card for future reference. There was no Russian Embassy here because

Russia considered Kosovo a rogue Serbian province. Embassies were only for other nation states, but the Russian Liaison Office served similar functions.

By the time Kit found the conference room upstairs, the meeting had already started. The mezzanine floor was traditional European style—a lot of marble, flower arrangements, oil paintings, and red carpet. An attendant at a table by the entrance to the room checked her off the list and gave her a name badge. Kit slipped through the door. The lights had been dimmed in a room of about one hundred people, which was furnished with carved wooden chairs covered with green velvet upholstery. She took a seat in a row at the back of the room and pulled out her notebook.

Five men sat behind their name plates at a table at the front of the room. In the middle sat the head of the OIDC mission, Jacob Mueller. She had seen him on TV a few times. He spoke with a crisp German accent as he called the meeting to order. She had the impression that he was someone who commanded respect but was short on affection. The foreign minister, Visar Dreshaj, who represented Kosovo, flanked him. The ambassador from the United States and the Russian representative were also at the table.

Jacob Mueller welcomed the panelists and conference participants as Kit settled into her seat. "At this first meeting after the peace conference, we are here to acknowledge the great strides made by both Belgrade and Pristina toward peace, and also the international contact group, which has worked so closely with them. Miloš Mandić is joining us from the National Assembly in Belgrade via a video conference link, while Visar Dreshaj from Pristina is with us today. I would like to welcome the senior members of the diplomatic community, especially Frank Stanton, US Ambassador, and His Excellency, the representative of the Russian Federation. I give the floor to Ambassador Robert Stanton."

A well-groomed, middle-aged man with silver-gray hair and sporting aviator glasses nodded to Mueller in response to his introduction.

The ambassador took a mouthful of water from the bottle on the table as he surveyed the room. Kit felt that he noticed her presence, even though they hadn't met, as he scanned the room.

"As you know, supporting Kosovo is my top priority. And by that I mean helping to strengthen the institutions of Kosovo and helping the country to recover from the terrible conflict," he said with an educated east-coast accent. "The United States is a strong supporter of human rights and development in Kosovo. Our focus is on enhancing accountability, transparency, and efficiency in the political and economic systems. This event gathers a unique blend of political and diplomatic leaders, as well as legal practitioners and industry leaders. Together, we have a chance today to acknowledge recent progress in strengthening Kosovo's progress and institutions. We should use this opportunity to address deficits in the system."

The conference continued. At the end of the morning session, Mueller, as chair of the meeting, opened the floor for questions. Kit had been thinking about what Eva had said about unreported, conflict-related sexual violence. She was still jet-lagged and had forgotten Eva's directive to keep a low profile. She put up her hand. When Mueller nodded in her direction, she stood up. "Maybe this conference should discuss what's being done about the high levels of sexual violence in Kosovo," she said in a loud voice.

There was silence. The panel members looked at her. No one replied. Instead there was a quiet rustling as everyone turned to stare at her.

"I mean, er, isn't there a lot of unreported conflict-related sexual violence? Against men too, for all we know."

When there was still no response, the silence became more awkward.

"I'm sorry, could you please tell us the organization you represent?" Mueller said at length.

"I work for OIDC," she replied.

He raised his eyebrows and continued. "This topic is not on our agenda for discussion, although the question is, of course, important. I suggest we move on to another topic our panel is better prepared to discuss, such as economic development in the region and the path to EU candidacy."

Kit sat down. Her stomach was churning. Her impulsive question had not made the good impression she'd hoped. She collected her things and slipped out of the conference room before she embarrassed herself more. What a first day at work this was. Perhaps now would be a good time to contact the real estate agent Angel had referred her to and check out apartments before she headed back to work.

Chapter Three

My beloved has disappeared without telling me where he's gone. I can only guess that he's on a mission somewhere doing something he thinks I shouldn't know about. My other warrior brother is asking a lot of questions, which I can't answer.

Merita's diary, 10 July 2000

Kit mounted the white marble stairs of the OIDC headquarters. Her legs were tired after having climbed a number of staircases as she viewed several apartments with the real estate agent. She planned to take Angel to check out a couple that looked suitable. A second opinion was always good.

"What the hell did you think you were doing?" Eva exclaimed.

Kit was jolted back to the present. Eva was waiting for her at the top of the stairs with her hands on her hips.

"What do you mean?" Kit asked, although she had a good idea.

"What were you doing talking about sexual assault at the conference and in front of everyone, including our boss?"

"You said it was an issue."

"Yes, I did, but that was between us. I told you to be a fly on the wall, for goodness' sake."

"I thought it was something that needed to be addressed."

"That's not the point. This is an extremely sensitive issue and has to be treated as such, not trumpeted all over town by someone who has been in Kosovo all of twenty-four hours. I want to make this clear, straight up. You do not make public statements without my say-so. Is that understood?"

"Okay," Kit said. She looked down, and her face flushed.

"Maybe I shouldn't have sent you to a high-level conference on your first day. Although I thought you would have the good sense to keep quiet and observe. I'm going to cut you some slack. But I don't want to hear about anything like this happening again."

Kit's face was now bright red. She wished the floor would open and swallow her. "I'm sorry about my poor judgment. You probably want to put me on a flight back to New Zealand."

"I was called to Mueller's office an hour ago to explain why my latest recruit was making provocative statements on an ultra-sensitive topic at this conference, causing him and the organization embarrassment."

"I apologize. I should have thought before I spoke."

"Yes, you should have. I was going to introduce you to the head of mission today, but after your performance this morning, I think you'd better keep a low profile for a while." Eva took a deep breath and exhaled. Her shoulders dropped as she indicated with a nod that Kit should accompany her to her office. "Come with me. There's someone I want you to meet."

Eva led her past the anteroom, where Angel sat working on a computer. Angel smiled at Kit with encouragement once Eva had gone past. Kit grinned back, reassured by her gesture.

A powerfully built man in his mid-forties stood up from the couch as they entered Eva's office. He was wearing khaki trousers over heavy, lace-up military boots. Major Matthew Hackman had a strong, angular face with a determined set to his jaw. His easy smile sent crow's feet fanning out from his eyes. His regular features were marked by a scar on his left temple and a slightly irregular set to his nose, as if it had been broken and healed not quite straight. His curly brown hair was cut short and parted to the side. His clean and freshly laundered army fatigues smelt of mint and were worn with a green shirt that matched his eyes. His gaze was shrewd, yet calm. Kit noticed his tan, as if he spent a lot of time outdoors, unlike the legal types she was used to working with.

"Caitlin, I'd like you to meet Major Matt Hackman from the Special Investigations Branch of the British Military Police with EUFOR. He's assisted by Sergeant Owen Reese."

"How do you do, Caitlin," Hackman said as he extended his hand. She had to look up to meet his eyes. He stood over six feet tall and towered above her, even though she was in high heels. He was accompanied by a younger man, shorter with broad shoulders and of stocky build, whose blue eyes sparkled as he extended his hand to Kit.

"Sergeant Reese has joined us from Wales," Hackman said.

"Guilty as charged," Owen said in a warm Welsh accent. "It's a pleasure," he added.

"Major Hackman has requested our assistance to take a statement from the sexual assault victim and asked us to coordinate the collection of evidence," Eva said to Kit. "I'd like you to assist him. This is strictly confidential. Is that understood?"

"Understood."

"The name of the witness is Vasha Blaku. She was abducted and detained by crime boss Dasham Raco for three weeks, during which time she was sexually assaulted. We have reason to believe that she may have heard or seen some things that might help us solve other crimes perpetrated by the group," the major said. "Part of the motivation for the abduction seems to be as a punishment for Vashu Blaku, a Kosovo Albanian woman, and her lover, Miloš Mandić, a Serbian politician. Collaboration with the Serbian Government is viewed very dimly by the Kosovo/Albanian community."

Kit found all this confusing and thought a briefing would help her better understand the complexities of the ethnic tensions in the region, but after her black mark from this morning, it didn't seem the time to ask for special treatment. The names sounded exotic and were difficult to remember, but the name of the Serbian politician sounded familiar from the morning. She'd understand the context better eventually.

"Miloš Mandić, isn't he in the Serbian National Assembly?" Kit asked.

"Yes," Eva replied.

"So why did Raco release Vasha? He could easily have killed her," Kit said.

"In this society, however unfairly, rape is considered a deep stain on a woman's honor and that of her family. It's often seen, literally, as a fate worse than death for a woman."

"How far has the investigation gone?" Kit asked.

"It's still in the early stages," Matt said. "Blaku has complained about her unlawful detention by Raco and the others, but not about the sexual assault."

"Was she examined by a doctor?" Kit asked.

"No," Matt said. "She refused medical attention."

"That could make it more difficult to prove rape. How long ago did she report the crime?"

"Two days ago," Matt replied.

"It could be worthwhile if she was examined. There still could be evidence of sexual assault," Eva said. "Kit, you should try to persuade her to see the doctor."

"And what do we know about this Miloš Mandić?" Kit asked.

"Well, that's another story," Eva said. "He's been accused of war crimes. He was a commander in the Yugoslav Army for a while and was said to have ordered ethnic cleansing by driving people out of their villages. Some say his troops were guilty of rape in this process."

"Hence a kind of eye-for-an-eye sense of justice," Kit said.

"It would appear so," Matt replied. "Frankly, however, it's not so much the allegations of sexual assault during Blaku's detention that concerns us. It's her value as a witness concerning the activities of an organized crime group headed by Dasham Raco."

"Machine Gun Kelly of Kosovo?" Kit asked.

"One and the same," Eva said. "She was locked in his apartment where the group held a lot of their meetings. We think she might have seen or heard things that could help with inquiries."

"So, what's the priority—the kidnapping and sexual assault charges, or the organized crime charges?" Kit asked.

Eva and Matt spoke at the same time. "Yes."

"Organized crime," Matt said.

"We can't just overlook those serious offenses," Eva said, looking squarely at Matt.

"Not overlook." Matt shrugged. "They're just not as high a priority. It's an offense against one woman, while organized crime affects the whole community."

"You see what we're up against," Eva said as she looked at Kit. "If criminal investigators don't take sexual violence seriously, no one will."

"I do take it seriously," Matt corrected. "It's just not as high a priority as some other crimes."

"You know what," Eva said grimly, "maybe you were not wrong with your remarks this morning, Kit."

Kit took a deep breath as she felt a sense of vindication. Even if she had barged in where angels feared to tread, Eva had acknowledged that she had a point. "I'd like to sit in on the interview with Blaku, if you don't mind. Let's take it from there. Perhaps there'll be enough evidence for us to get all the convictions coming to Raco."

"That's fine with me." Matt rose to his feet. "Blaku's coming into the station in about an hour. If you like, Sergeant Reese can take both of us and then bring you back after."

The Missing Diary

Kit stood up. She felt her feet had hardly touched the ground since she had arrived. "I'll just freshen up and be with you in a moment."

Kit walked out to the lobby and into the ladies' bathroom. She looked at herself critically in the mirror. The overhead lights were harsh, and the old Yugoslavian-era bathroom looked like something from the 1970s, not the 1980s, and eggshell-blue paint was flaking in the corners. Kit pulled out her compact and retouched her lipstick, Sandstorm by Revlon. A warm, reddish-brown shade with shimmer, it said on the end. Under the harsh light, Kit didn't like who she saw today in the unforgiving mirror. Her red hair was pulled into a high ponytail and looked straw-like. Dark rings around her normally bright-blue eyes made her look like a woman in her mid-forties rather than her early thirties. She was probably still suffering from jet lag. She dabbed powder on her nose and ran a comb through her bangs and briefly through her ponytail; her hair was still sun-streaked from summertime in New Zealand.

For just a moment she had a flashback to the time when one of the partners in the law firm where she worked told her she had to leave, that the firm was downsizing and restructuring. It had taken her a couple of months to admit that she was suffering from anxiety and depression as a result. She couldn't understand why, but she felt better being in a different situation—even if her first day hadn't exactly run to plan. A small smile quirked on one side of her sandstorm lips. "Time to go get 'em," she said to her image in the mirror.

She washed her hands before she drew herself up to her full five feet five inches and, feeling refreshed, turned with her ponytail swinging and headed back to where Matt was waiting for her. It might be a complex environment riven with conflict, but it felt like a fresh start.

Later, when they arrived at the military police headquarters, Matt showed Kit to the sparsely furnished internal meeting room where the police held their interviews. "I suggest you take a seat here," he said. "You might want to take notes." He and Owen prepared where they were going to sit and placed notepads and pens on the table. Kit took the indicated seat and searched in her bag for her pad and pen.

"I think she speaks quite good English, sir," Owen said. "So I didn't think it was necessary to bring an interpreter." He glanced toward Kit and gave her a friendly smile.

"Okay," Matt said. "We'll ask her if she needs translation into Albanian for the written statement. I'll get her from the waiting room."

He disappeared and, after a short time, returned with a woman who Kit judged was in her early thirties. Long, light-brown hair curled below her shoulders. Her intense hazel eyes took in the room from beneath her perfectly shaped brows. She wore a dark jacket and a black dress, black heels, with a silver chain around her neck. She conveyed refined femininity with the determined set of her shoulders and jawline.

Matt introduced them briefly and indicated that Vasha should sit opposite them. "Would you like something to drink before we begin?" he asked. "Tea, coffee, water?"

"Coffee, thank you. Two sugars," Blaku replied in a deep, accented voice.

Matt nodded to Owen, who disappeared to fetch coffee from the machine.

"Ms. Blaku, thank you for being willing to speak to us. Let's start now. For the record, we're at the EUFOR Police building in Pristina. It's sixteen hundred hours. I'm Major Matt Hackman, Special Investigations Branch of the British Military Police. We investigate criminal allegations to army incidents and problems with unrest. I specifically deal with criminal investigations into serious crimes. This is Sergeant Owen Reese, who will take a note of your statement. Caitlin Chase is from the Office of the Chief Prosecutor. Her office is assisting us with our inquiries. Do you have any questions?"

"Thank you and good to see Ms. Chase here," Vasha replied, nodding toward Kit.

Kit felt pleased that she, as another woman in the room, could help Vasha feel a little more comfortable in what was likely to be a difficult interview. She wondered if there were many local women police officers or investigators in Pristina.

"How long is this going to take?" Blaku asked.

"This is a preliminary statement. It shouldn't take longer than an hour. We might need to talk to you again later. It depends on what you can tell us. Can you confirm your name for the record, please."

"Vasha Blaku."

"Please confirm your date of birth and place of residence."

"Fifteen August, nineteen sixty-seven, in Pristina, Kosovo." She gave her address and phone number.

"Are you working?"

"Yes, I'm a translator working on contract for the municipality because I speak Albanian, Serbian, and English."

"Thank you. Before we go any further, I'd like to run over a few things that are standard procedure. I suppose you already know that we're here today because you filed a formal complaint some days ago, but you haven't spoken to the military police investigations yet. I understand that you made a statement shortly after all this happened, am I right?"

"Yes, as soon as I could after my release."

"So it was quite soon after but not immediately after. Why did you delay that long and not go to the police immediately?"

"I was confused and disoriented. I wanted to go home and take a long shower. It was only after that, when I spoke to my cousin, that I decided I should make a complaint."

"Did you feel that the police officer treated you fairly at the time?"

"He was fair, but I didn't get the sense he was taking it seriously."

"What gave you that idea?"

"He didn't give me enough time to tell my story, and he seemed to be uncomfortable with the fact that sexual assault was involved."

"When I was told about your statement, I thought we should speak to you. It's important that you know we're working closely with the prosecution office. No decision has been made about what'll happen on this case, or how it'll go. But if it goes to court, it's likely you'll be called as a witness. So, as in any trial, we need to know what you witnessed." Matt looked at Blaku carefully to judge her reaction. When she nodded, he continued.

"I'd like you to describe what happened. We'll ask questions for clarification. If you agree, I'd like you to sign an official written statement for police records that Sergeant Reese will prepare based on what you say."

"Do you mind if I smoke?" she asked.

Kit was about to say, "Yes, I do mind," but Matt took an ashtray from a side table and pushed it toward her.

"I've been to hell, major, and I've come back to tell about it." She pulled down her jacket and revealed her upper arm, which was mottled with dark bruises.

"Did you go to the medical centre?" Matt asked.

She shook her head. "It was too late for that."

"I'd like you to see a doctor after this interview. There could be important evidence relating to the offenses."

"No, Major Hackman, I prefer not to be examined by a doctor."

"I can see if we can arrange for you to be seen by a female doctor," Kit said as she reached for her mobile phone. She texted Angel for the contact details of a female doctor whose report would be recognized in court. Kit knew they had to get onto it as soon as possible because evidence, if it was there, would only be detectable for seven days after the rape. Once thirty-six hours or more has elapsed, the evidence becomes weaker until it eventually disappears.

Matt picked up his pen and wrote a date on the witness interview sheet. "Alright, let's come back to that question after the interview, and we'll see what Ms.

Chase can come up with. Is there anyone you would like to be present for this interview or to pick you up afterwards, Ms. Blaku?"

"No, I'm alright for now; I've asked my cousin to pick me up when we've finished."

"Okay, fine," Matt said. "Can you tell me what happened, please? Take your time."

Vasha took a packet of cigarettes out of her pocket, opened it, took one out, and lit it with a shaking hand. She was fidgeting with her lighter as she began to speak. "I feel that it's important to tell my story. This man is so horrible—I can hardly say his name. I think it's quite likely he'll do it again to someone else—or even to me, if he got the chance." She inhaled on her cigarette and looked at Matt across the table. He nodded. Owen had a pen poised over a witness statement form.

"I really want this kept super confidential. It could have a terrible effect on my reputation."

"Of course," Matt said. "Subject to the possible court proceedings that I mentioned."

"Well ..." Vasha said. "There was nothing I could have done to stop this happening. Raco, his nephew, and a couple of his men broke into my apartment when I was alone and took me by force to a large house in the suburbs. They kept me locked in a room for the first month. Raco and his nephew took turns at coming in and abusing me. It was horrible, but in an awful way I started to get used to it. When it was happening, I thought about something else, about how much I wanted to get away and how one day I would leave Kosovo?" She paused. No one spoke; they waited for her to continue.

"There was an ensuite bathroom next to the bedroom, so I could take care of my hygiene needs. They brought me food once or twice a day. I think they started to believe that I was going along with it and wouldn't be trouble, so they decided to let me into the main house. The doors and windows were locked, and there were always at least two men who kept watch over me. The abuse continued for two more weeks." Blaku's voice shook, and when she started to tremble, ash from her cigarette flicked onto the table. Tears rolled down her cheeks, and she wiped them with the back of her hand as she struggled to calm her breathing.

Matt put a packet of tissues in front of her. She dabbed at her eyes and wiped away the smeared mascara. "Take all the time you need," he said.

"Sometimes people came to visit the brothers—criminals like them. I was sent to the room, but after a while they forgot to close the door properly and I saw who was there and listened in on their conversations."

Matt leaned forward and exchanged a glance with Owen, who got the message to pay special attention with his note-taking.

Kit was sitting quietly on a chair by the wall. She knew from experience that it was important to let a witness tell their entire story in their own words, without interruption. However, she was betting that Matt would circle back to ask for a lot more detail regarding these conversations among the suspect's criminal associates.

"I was afraid for my life. But I was also afraid for my family. I thought if I made too many problems they might go after my parents, my sisters, or my cousins. Raco said on a few occasions that I was being punished because I had a Serbian boyfriend. After all the abuse from them, he said my boyfriend wouldn't be interested in me anymore. From that comment, I started to hope they might release me alive. A woman's reputation is so important. After it became known that I had been raped and abused by two men, I was going to be a social reject—damaged goods." Her body was wracked by a sob, but with a struggle, she retained control. "I come from a family of fighters, so I'm not going to give up. Dasham needs to be called to account. But I'm going to need you to promise me and my family protection before I make an official complaint or provide more information about his criminal activities."

Kit's mobile chimed. It was a message from Angel with contact details for a suitable doctor. Angel said she could come and pick them up in an OIDC jeep with fifteen minutes' notice. When Kit had tucked her phone away, Blaku was answering questions about the particulars of the sexual assaults and providing more background information. How had she first met the perpetrator? Was she alone at the time of the abduction or could someone else be a potential witness? What did she do during the assaults?

"I made it very clear that he should stop, and I struggled, for the little good it did me. The more I resisted, the more bruises and beatings I was given. No, I hadn't been drinking alcohol," Blaku said.

She explained that they lived in a relatively small community and everyone knew everyone else, but she did not socialize with Raco or his associates. Apparently the news that Blaku was seeing a Serbian politician had become known without her being aware of it. She had been alone in her apartment when she was abducted by Raco and his associates. She tried to resist but stood no chance against four men.

THE MISSING DIARY

Matt asked about the location of her apartment and neighbors who could be approached in case they could provide further information. He then came back to Blaku's account of overhearing the conversations between Raco and his visitors. She said they were mainly men visiting, but two or three times a woman had been with them—Merita Shala, a former Kosovo policewoman. During the conflict, she fought with the Kosovo Liberation Army, or KLA, against Serbian forces. Sometimes, as the group was making plans, Blaku peered through the crack in the door. She had seen Merita writing in a brown notebook—details of where the group would meet. One person would arrange for weapons, another would find vehicles, another would get the money they needed for a job. They seemed to be trafficking in weapons and perhaps other things, such as explosives. And having confrontations with other criminal groups that involved extortion and blackmail.

Merita was a petite woman in her twenties, with black eyes and short, dark hair. Sometimes she wore khaki trousers, a T-shirt, and combat boots, but at other times she looked feminine in a skirt and blouse. She joined in the discussions as if she was one of the men, although from time to time she would touch the arm of a particular man and bring him coffee or a drink from the kitchen. Occasionally, when there was a disagreement on what had been planned, she would check in her brown book and tell them what their orders were and what had been agreed, as if she was a secretary.

"Do you know who was giving the orders?" Matt asked.

"I'm not sure. I think I heard someone called the Inspector referred to more than once. Maybe others. They all have nicknames: the Inspector, Razor, Machine Gun."

Blaku took a deep pull on her cigarette, stubbed it out in the ashtray, sat back in the chair, and drank her coffee. Kit noticed she was looking paler than when they started the interview, but at the same time her shoulders looked more relaxed, as if she had released a burden.

"Is there anything else you can tell us?" Matt asked.

Blaku paused and looked at Owen, who had been transcribing her statement by hand as she spoke. "I feel tired, Major. I should leave soon. There might be more I can tell you, but I would like some assurances about my safety and that of my family."

"I realize this must be tiring for you," Matt said, "but it's important that we make a note of as many details as possible while your memory is fresh. I'd like you to look at photos of some of the individuals who might have been involved. Do you think you could recognize them?"

"Yes. I hope and pray that I will be able to forget them one day, but right now their faces are very clear in my memory."

"Have you seen any of them since you were released?"

"No. I've been staying with my cousin out of town."

"You mentioned that you thought one of their motivations for the kidnapping and assault might be your relationship with Miloš Mandić. When did you see him last?" Matt asked.

"I saw him briefly a couple of days ago. He was supportive, but we decided in the circumstances, it would be better not to see each other for a while."

"What do you mean *in the circumstances*?"

"Well, I think the attack was to punish me for seeing him and to make him look bad, as if he couldn't protect me. The whole thing is a stain on my honor and therefore his. Even though I'm the victim, I've been blamed for it, or treated as if I am guilty. If we're seen together again, it might trigger another attack, possibly worse. Also, he's married, so it's better to keep a low profile for a while. It's possible that he won't want to see me again," she added flatly.

Owen slid a folder of photographs toward Blaku.

Kit craned her neck to see and came to sit at the table. She chose a seat beside Owen so as not to cramp the witness.

"That's him," Blaku said as she pointed to a photograph of a bald-headed man in early-middle age with thickset features and a cruel mouth. "That's Dasham Raco," she repeated and shivered with disgust. Then she pointed to another man. "That's the one they call Razor, the one Merita Shala treated as special." She went on to identify others from the group.

Matt nodded and turned the page to a selection of females with short, dark hair.

Blaku pointed to the photo of a woman with her hair cut in a short, feathery style, with dark eyes and gamine features. "That's Merita Shala."

"Thanks very much for your cooperation, Ms. Blaku. It's important that you're examined by a doctor as soon as possible for any treatment you might need and for evidence of the assaults. Ms. Chase will accompany you to the doctor, if you agree. I'd like to ask you to come back in a day or two to make another statement, this time on video. We'll go into a bit more detail on what happened at the house and confirm some facts."

"I will help you," Blaku said, "if you can promise protection. I've seen these men up close. They're brutal and very dangerous. I'm serious when I say I need help for me and my family. I believe my life will be at risk if Raco finds out I've spoken to you. He threatened me in graphic terms if I complained to the police."

Matt nodded. "Alright," he said. "I'll talk to our witness protection unit. Your evidence could be very important, not only for your complaint, but for a number of other serious criminal conspiracy charges against Raco and his gang."

"With his network of criminals, I won't be safe anywhere in Kosovo. You'll have to move me and my immediate family out of Kosovo. If you can promise to do that, in writing, then I will help you further."

"I'll see what I can do. Please give Sergeant Reese a list of people who you think need protection. But I have to warn you our resources are very limited unfortunately. We'll have to make a case that the evidence you can provide is important enough and likely to lead to convictions in order to warrant the expense."

"I can help you. I believe I have inside information that no one else can provide. I need revenge, but not at the expense of my family."

Matt stood up, signaling the interview was at an end. "I'll be in touch, Ms. Blaku. Ms. Chase will see you to the doctor."

After Kit had escorted Blaku out of the room, Matt spoke to Owen. "We need to search Raco's apartment as soon as possible. I have to get my hands on that diary."

"Merita Shala's brown book?" Owen asked.

"Yes. Put Shala and Raco under surveillance; also get wire taps. I want to know who they are calling. Kit and her office can help us apply to a judge to get the court orders we need. We must choose a time to hit both apartments when the suspects are likely to be at home so they don't get a chance to warn each other and destroy evidence."

Chapter Four

Life is like a kaleidoscope. Whatever happens daily is fractured and broken but it's part of a larger pattern that can be felt but not seen. I can only keep breathing and continue. My path is set now. It can't be changed.

Merita's diary, 22 July 2000

Merita Shala sat at the table outside on the patio, under the plum tree. Comfortably dressed in jeans and a floral, kimono-style blue top with her feet in soft leather slippers, she set her small coffee cup and saucer on the table and placed a brown, hardbound notebook next to it with a pen. Dappled light filtered between the branches of the tree and created the shadows on the table. The rustic-style garden was surrounded by a brick wall, crumbling in parts, but it still provided her with privacy. She poured a cup of hot, black Turkish-style coffee. Her profile was delicate yet athletic, and the refined line of her neck was set against a strong jawline. She sighed and let her shoulders relax.

She picked up the pen and wrote on an empty page of the diary. Every few minutes she stopped and watched a crow hop along the top of the wall and a feral cat that sprinted across the grass. She jotted down notes. Names, times, places ... the cafés where she met her lovers, in the north for the Serb, and the south for the Kosovo–Albanian. Words of love she had shared with Wolf, the plans she had made with Razor.

After some minutes, she closed the notebook and put down her pen. She picked up the coffee cup, swirled the dregs around in the bottom, and tipped them out upside down in one smooth movement onto the saucer. This was a traditional method of fortune telling that was used in the region, which she had learned from her grandmother, a Roma woman from the north. She let the cup drip its dark, grainy liquid onto the saucer, then picked it up. As she gazed into the chaos of the coffee dregs, she strove to let her mind relax and watch them take shape into recognizable forms that might show her something about her future. All she could make out was the rough form of a sword or knife. This was not the reassuring message she was seeking. Perhaps it related to the end of the armed conflict between Kosovo and Serbia now that EUFOR was keeping the peace.

She was proud that she had been able to contribute to the work of the Kosovo Liberation Army, running intel operations. But at the same time, she knew the future belonged to reconciliation between an independent Kosovo and a Serbia that fully recognized the State of Kosovo. She had cultivated links to criminal groups that were also connected to both the Serbian Army and militias, as well as to the KLA itself. This way she could gather useful information, which she could share as necessary, primarily with her Kosovar brothers-in-arms, but perhaps a few crumbs of intel to Wolf as well, since he was personally involved in a conflict. That way she could keep the flow of useful information going—which benefited everyone. Didn't it? She didn't consider herself a double agent. She knew where her ultimate loyalties lay, but for the sake of the future, she could allow herself to compromise with Wolf, whom she found an attractive man.

As her mind refocussed on the coffee dregs, she placed the saucer over the cup to cover it so she didn't have to see it until she washed it later. The sun disappeared behind a cloud, and she shivered. Autumn was on its way, and the nights were growing longer.

Visar Dreshaj, Pristina politician and former regional commander in the Kosovo Liberation Army, put down his cigarette and picked up his violin. Standing in the study of his traditional Albanian-style house in the rural outskirts of Pristina, he had a view over the city. Pristina had sprung up as many Eastern European cities had and continued to grow in the post-Soviet era without obvious planning. The city was set beneath the surrounding hills, which caught the fog and fumes from the dirty fuel burned by its inhabitants. A toxic layer hung over the city at all times and was thickest in winter. Previously run by decree from Belgrade, Pristina was now the capital of the proud new state of Kosovo, or the upstart renegade Serbian province, depending on who you spoke to and which side of the dividing line you were on.

Visar glanced around his study; his sanctuary was lined with books of Albanian literature and poetry collected during the time when he studied literature at Pristina University. Those were the years before he had left his comfortable life in the former Yugoslavia, joined the KLA to fight for independence against Serbia, and gone on the run as a fugitive from the law. Now he was back in the heart of Pristina society, and his slight yet athletic figure and disheveled hair could often be seen in the halls of the new government buildings, discussing the latest developments and seeking compromises with rival factions. Compromises that seemed ever more elusive.

He struck a mellow tone on his violin as he allowed his fingers to coax a plaintive folk melody from its strings. As he looked over the green trees and fields surrounding Pristina and toward its smog-bound rooftops, he imagined a coming time when the whole world would recognize the rightful independence of Kosovo. His people would be free forever from the impositions of a malevolent Serbia and the indifferent, oppressive international community currently occupying Kosovo under the pretext of bringing peace. Until then, he would continue his righteous fight, whether on the killing fields of Kosovo or in the debating chambers of parliament.

A soft knock came on the door and interrupted his reverie. Smiling indulgently because he knew that light knock, he put down his violin and went to the door. His small daughter with tousled black ringlets and dark eyes looked up at him. "What is it, Besa?" he asked.

Besa was his pet name for his daughter Besnika, who was named after the promise of an Albanian Kosovar who was always honored—for better or for worse.

"Mama says there are men here to see you and you should come," she said as she held her doll in one hand.

"Alright, my dear. Tell Mama I will see them in the living room." He bent and kissed her softly on the forehead. The girl turned and ran down the dark hall toward the kitchen door, from where the sounds of dishes and rich cooking smells emanated.

Visar lay his violin back in its case, pocketed his box of cigarettes and lighter, and walked through the door, closing it behind him.

Two heavyset men waited for him the formal living room with its ornate lounge suite and shiny wooden table. He greeted them and shook hands.

"*Mirëdita,* inspector," one of the men said. Visar had been the informal inspector general of the KLA, his role being to check that the troops were in a semblance of order and disciplined during the conflict. He had kept part of the title as a nickname. Most of the men had a *nom de guerre* by which they were known among fellow combatants.

"Good afternoon to you. What news do you have?" he asked.

"As you said, sir, we should avoid using our mobiles for such messages. We came to tell you that arrangements for the next delivery are in place. A van will be bringing the consignment of Kalashnikovs and ammunition from Albania in the morning the day after tomorrow."

"Good," Visar said. "I trust that arrangements for payment went smoothly."

"Yes," Razor replied. "We paid in cash in Tirana, as you said."

"And the contractors?"

"Four of them are also coming."

"Good. We can't be too careful. Even though the war with Serbia is supposedly over following the NATO bombing, we can't afford to let our weapons stores run down. Or our cash reserves."

"We know," Razor said. "As long as the Black Hands are a threat, our Eagle's Claw brigade must be ready. We'll take revenge for the killing of innocent people when we can."

Visar clapped the two men on their backs with his arms around them both. "Won't you stay for a meal?" he asked. "Please be our guests."

"No thanks, Inspector. We need to make sure that everything is organized for the operation."

"Go with God's blessing," Visar said.

High summer in Kosovo had scorched the fields to a crisp. Acrid smoke from farm burn offs and smoldering rubbish piles hung in the stifling air. A small group of men wearing black tactical uniforms were a pool of darkness in the bitter, late-afternoon sun that slid through the broken barn windows. A dead bird lay desiccated under the window where it had tried and failed to escape. The men armed themselves. One picked up a semiautomatic rifle; another fixed the clip into his pistol and holstered it. The other two checked their Kalashnikovs. Their breathing was labored in the heat. One by one, they slipped balaclavas over their heads and obliterated their identities. An old barn containing rusty agricultural machinery, implements, and assorted discarded boxes screened them from witnesses. An ancient harvester, scythes, and axes hung on the wall.

Their leader, Dasham Raco, had a thickset, robust build and handled his firearms with an easy, crisp confidence. He looked at each man, interrogating them with his piercing glance. An icy resolution frosted his eyes and as he looked at them, each responded with a curt nod as they clutched their firearms. He glanced at his wristwatch. The men waited until a phone ringing shattered the silence. It stopped after two rings. The signal to begin their bloody mission came again. Raco shifted, nodded, and led his men into the field where a red VW Golf was concealed from view behind a stand of trees. One of the men lit a cigarette and clamped it in the side of his mouth before clambering into the rear of the car. Whatever the news media had reported about the end of the conflict, a war still raged on the land and in the hearts of the people.

CHAPTER FIVE

To my Beloved—
Love is like a spilled perfume. Fragrant and sweet, but already dying as it seeps out of the bottle. Like the gateway to the highest heaven of the Sufi, it is at the same time lightness, darkness, and shattering.

Merita's diary, 23 July 2000

Angel arrived about thirty minutes later at police headquarters to collect Kit and Vasha Blaku. She drove Blaku to the doctor's surgery. Vasha's cousin had met them there, and after the examination, Kit had delivered Blaku into the care of her cousin.

Matt and Owen had traveled behind them and then taken the lead, escorting them to EUFOR headquarters where a celebration was underway. Matt suggested that it would be a good chance for Kit to meet more of the military team in the interests of closer coordination with the civilians.

Matt lead them into a makeshift, white building. They climbed rough, wooden steps up to the restaurant, where trestle tables had been set up with finger food. At the rear of the room was an improvised bar, with alcohol and soft drinks.

"What's your poison?" Owen asked the group.

"Just Coke for me," Angel said. "I'm the designated driver."

"A white wine," Kit said.

"Scotch, straight," Matt said.

Owen came back holding a tray of drinks, including a bottle of imported German beer for himself.

"Cheers!" Matt said as he lifted his glass. He explained that the restaurant had been commandeered by the UK contingent to celebrate the promotion of a colleague from sergeant to major. The officer, now a major, was an officer with the British contingent, a petite but fit-looking woman dressed in army fatigues, who wore her shoulder-length hair tied in a ponytail.

"Bet she never thought she'd be promoted in Kosovo," Matt said as he took a sip of *rakia*. He smacked is lips in satisfaction. "Not bad, this stuff. Made from local fruit, I understand."

"Yes, sir," Owen said. "I understand it's something of a cottage industry in these parts. It's supposed to be good for everything, from the common cold to stomach upsets to whatever else ails you."

"Perhaps Kosovo has its charms after all," he said dryly, looking around the rudimentary container building that they were in.

"I wouldn't know, sir," Owen said. "Good of the commander to give us the night off, though."

"It's not really a night off," Matt said. "We're supposed to have our ears to the ground in case there's trouble among the locals. Apparently there were rumblings in some of the villages that something is going to happen soon."

"What sort of *something*?" Owen asked.

Strains of Santana's "Smooth" began playing in the background. A couple of the female, noncommissioned officers started dancing. Owen grabbed a handful of peanuts, tossed them back, and washed them down with the beer.

"Probably nothing. The locals are still on edge. But since we stopped the bombing campaign, the fighting has pretty well stopped and things have calmed down."

"Serbian forces are withdrawing, sir. Things are relatively quiet," Owen added.

"What about the Kosovo Albanian refugees?" Angel asked. "Aren't some of them still being picked off as they flee toward Albania?"

"There've been some reports that we'll need to look into, but nothing proven as yet," Owen said.

Kit looked around the room, which was starting to become more animated. "How can they be so relaxed in a war zone?" she said to Angel as she sipped her wine.

"Well, there's no fighting going on right now," Angel said drily. "Some of the best parties in Dublin were during the Troubles. Something about the need to affirm life in the face of death, I suppose."

"I hadn't thought of it like that," Kit said.

The music changed to Santana's "Evil Ways" and a couple more people started dancing. At that moment, the old, black telephone on the counter in the corner of the room rang.

"Isn't someone going to answer that?" Kit asked.

It stopped ringing but started again five minutes later.

Matt tossed back his shot of *rakia* and put his glass on the bar. He sighed as he made his way past the groups of uniformed personnel toward the telephone. As he reached for it, it stopped ringing again.

"Just a moment," Owen said to Kit. "Excuse me. I'd better go and see if the major needs help. He should realize that we're off duty now and forget about the phone, in my view," he added.

"Sure, no problem," Kit said.

The phone rang again, and this time Matt was close enough to answer it right away. He listened intently for a moment before he started barking questions. He motioned to Owen to get his notebook and gave him an address.

"Party's over," he said. "There's been a killing. More than one."

Matt and Owen returned to where Kit and Angel were standing chatting.

"There's an emergency," Matt said. "There've been several calls for help from a small Serb farming community, but no one picked them up. Our emergency operators are here having a quick one. Now it's a crime scene we need to investigate."

Kit's stomach lurched. "Should we leave it to the military police?" she asked Angel.

Angel was finishing her glass of Coke. "Dunno," she said. "On one hand, I'd just like to head home to rest. On the other hand, maybe Eva would want me follow this. Perhaps they'll need my help with evidence collection."

"For Blaku's case, yes. I'm not sure about others. We don't know what's involved here." Kit thought for a moment. "I should see if I can go with Matt. It's up to you whether you want to come or not," she added.

THE MISSING DIARY

"I need to get back to the office now," Angel said. "Why don't you give me a call and I'll come and collect you when you're ready. I'll also brief Eva and let you know what she says."

"Okay," Kit said. "Let's find out where I'm going."

Kit and Angel made their way over to where Matt and Owen were deep in conversation. Matt was giving Owen instructions as to who to notify. He pulled out a map from his pocket and pointed to a location outside Pristina.

"Remind me to ask Matt later if he used to be a Boy Scout when he was young," Kit said quietly to Angel. "It looks as if he's prepared for everything."

"Yeah, looks like."

"Umm," Kit said when Matt looked up. "I'd like to come with you to the site. If it's okay, that is."

"No," Matt said. "I don't think it's appropriate. There are casualties."

"I can help with the evidence."

"Sitting in on a kidnapping case interview is one thing. Going to a fresh crime scene is another. You might contaminate the evidence. When was the last time you saw a dead body?"

"I won't get in the way. I went to the morgue once. It was a while ago, I must admit."

"Sometimes Mary used to come with us," Owen said as he tried to be helpful. "Mary was a prosecutor with your office before you arrived."

Matt bristled. "Listen, I don't have time to argue about this. We need to get to the scene as quickly as possible. I've requested the assistance of one unit to secure the scene and another two to patrol the area to make sure there's no secondary attack. There've already been delays with the request for help because of all this," he said, indicating the party, which was now more subdued and reduced in size. "No one thought about ensuring that the emergency phones were properly manned. Incredible," he added. "We're going to Lipljan, thirty minutes' drive from here."

"Angel is going back to HQ and will pick me up later," Kit said.

"Alright, you can sit in the back of the jeep. But at the crime scene, just observe please. Don't touch anything, and don't talk to anyone. For now, just try to keep up."

"Looks like I'll need to jog to keep up with these guys," Kit said to Angel. "I'll call you maybe in an hour or two to come and pick me up."

"No problem. Just text me with your location once you get there and keep in touch. I'll notify OIDC Security Service so they know what's happening."

"The place is near the crossroads coming from Staro Dorbi, close to the harvest field," Owen said.

"I'm not going to be able to finish this," Kit said as she put her glass of wine on the table. Once she'd grabbed her black trench coat, she hurried after Matt and Owen, who had already left the restaurant.

Kit sat quietly in the back of the jeep as it sped toward the crime scene. Owen drove while Matt spoke on the radio telephone and tried to coordinate backup from the different EUFOR contingents. "Just tell them to bloody get there as soon as possible," he barked. "Over," he grunted as he switched off the radio telephone and replaced the handset.

"British EUFOR heard shots and contacted a rapid-reaction force, who're there now. Apparently, the villagers have been calling HQ for help for over an hour and were unable to raise anyone. We're going to a small village of about three hundred people, one of the few in the area with mainly Serbs," Matt said.

Kit found herself feeling increasingly anxious, and with that came a sense of detachment and dissociation. She had volunteered to come with them on impulse, and she was going to confront a horrific scene like nothing she had witnessed before. She had tried to show bravado in her enthusiasm to throw herself into her job. But the fact was that she had never seen a dead body at a crime scene before. She'd only paid her respects to her grandfather in his casket at the funeral home. The body had looked like a mannequin in a department store, with no connection to her beloved Grandpa.

The suspension on the jeep was hard, and she felt every bump on the gravel road with its potholes. It was late afternoon, and windows that were halfway down offered little relief from the heat as the hot air circulated around the cabin of the vehicle. Beads of sweat broke out on her forehead and rolled down the back of her neck. The movement of the vehicle made Kit feel nauseous. Matt had seemed so relaxed and in control, but now the set of his shoulders and the tone of his voice told her that he was worried. Owen was quiet as he kept his eyes fixed on the road ahead.

When Kit felt her mobile vibrate in her pocket, she pulled it out with a clammy hand and opened the message. *Eva says okay. Keep out of Matt's way. Take notes,* Angel said.

Roger that, Kit sent in reply on the old Nokia they had given her.

Good luck see u soon, Angel replied. Kit slipped the phone back into her pocket. Although she felt as though she wanted to go home, she felt that she still had something to prove to herself and to everyone else. She could face whatever was waiting out there for them, she told herself. Reading and replying to Angel's texts while the jeep was in motion had made her nausea worse.

Take notes, the message from Eva said. She rummaged in her bag and put her notebook and pen in her jacket pocket. She wondered if she should take photos or leave that to the police. Take photos, she decided as she checked the battery on her mobile. It was low because she had forgotten to charge it. Organizing her things gave her a sense of order and purpose; she was feeling increasingly anxious as they neared the scene.

Owen pulled up to a farm gate. There were already EUFOR vehicles there; a uniformed officer nodded to them and opened the gate. Matt motioned for Owen to stop the vehicle while he exchanged words with the soldier who looked into the back and saw Kit. "Identification," he said with a Scandinavian accent.

Kit recognized the Finnish flag patch on his sleeve. She reached into her bag and produced her ID card from the inside pocket as Matt and Owen did likewise. She wondered if he would notice that it was brand new, dated the day before, but the soldier didn't react other than to wave them through.

The jeep pulled up outside a two-story brick farmhouse. It looked unfinished with its rough brickwork still showing. Behind it was a large farm shed and, in the distance, a small harvester that had stopped partway through harvesting a wheat field. There were several military vehicles, a police van, and—out of place—a black limousine with tinted windows and diplomatic number plates.

"Right," Matt said as he opened the door and swung his long legs out and onto the gravel drive. "If you don't mind, please keep your distance from the crime scene. We'll let you know when we're ready for you to take a look," he said with a quick glance at Kit.

Owen looked at her and smiled as he shrugged apologetically. "Will you be okay?" he asked.

"Yes, fine. You go. I'll just wait here."

When her mobile vibrated again, she pulled it out. This time it was a message from Xander.

Skype? R u busy? his message said.

Kit was relieved to get out the vehicle, but she still felt nauseous and uncomfortable in the heat. She stabbed at the keyboard. *Busy. Sad face. Later? XOX.* The message seemed to come from another world, far removed from this one, which at this moment felt more real and compelling than the comfortable if bland existence back in New Zealand. She looked at the ground for a moment where a small group of black ants was carrying a desiccated cicada husk. When she caught a waft of something harsh and putrid on the hot breeze, Kit staggered and braced against the jeep.

"Ms. Chase, isn't it?" an Eastern European voice said and brought her out the spiral that had been taking her in an unknown direction, which nevertheless felt as if it was downward. She looked up to see the smiling, well-groomed figure of Sergei Sokolov approaching her from the direction of the black limousine. He looked out of place among the uniformed personnel who were at the site; he was wearing a dark suit and white shirt with his jacket casually draped over his shoulder.

"Y-yes," Kit said. She brightened when she saw him and stood up.

"What a pleasant surprise to see you here," he said and smiled as he extended his hand.

"Likewise," Kit said as she shook his hand. She thought her palm must feel clammy in his as she withdrew it. She could smell the fresh scent of his cologne, which provided a welcome relief to the other smells at the edge of her awareness on the hot breeze.

"I didn't know the prosecutor's office was among the first responders at crime scenes."

"I didn't know that Russian Liaison was either," she said as she looked up at him.

"It seems that we are both in a rather special situation. Our office is sometimes called directly when there are issues among the Serb community that need to be taken care of urgently. Often we get the attention of the authorities faster than local Serbs can."

"Is that an issue?" she asked.

"It can be. We like to keep an eye on what's happening in the field and provide assistance where needed. How about you?"

"I'm new on the job. I think my boss thought she'd throw me in at the deep end to sink or swim. I'm supposed to be taking notes and keeping out the way."

"Well, this certainly is the deep end," he said as he looked up for a moment and squinted at the sun. "I was just about to speak to the person who called our office.

The Missing Diary

Apparently they were told something was going to happen over a week ago and had been calling EUFOR for protection, but no one showed up."

"Do you know what happened? Has someone been killed? They said something about a body."

Sergei looked at her and nodded gravely. "More than one, I'm afraid."

At that instant, a woman came up to them and started talking to Sergei in a language Kit didn't understand. She was a solidly built, middle-aged woman with blonde hair and blue eyes; she was wearing flat shoes and a floral-print dress. Her eyes were puffy, and makeup was smeared under her eyes. Kit guessed that perhaps she had called the Russian office for support. She left him talking to the woman and walked slowly past the house and toward the field.

The twilight was starting to deepen as Kit's footsteps crunched loudly on the gravel driveway. Everything else was preternaturally quiet. Military figures and police officers moved quietly around the field as they surrounded a combine harvester, apparently taking notes, conversing, and occasionally bending down to pick up objects off the ground or to examine something. Matt and Owen were together about thirty or forty meters away. About a dozen mounds of what appeared to be piles of clothing lay on the wheat stubble and formed a semicircle around the harvester.

A light breeze picked up and reached her from the direction of the combine harvester. She caught an acrid odor on the wind, which seemed to lodge like a bitter penny at the back of her throat. A fresh wave of nausea swept over her. It was as if her brain was trying to make sense of what she was seeing, but it took some moments for her to realize that the mounds on the ground were bodies. She swayed and reflexively reached for her notepad and pen to steady herself by doing a routine task. Eva had said to take notes. She wrote the date and time, 23 July 2000, 20:30, Staro Dorbi. Crime scene. Her underlining was wonky.

Out the corner of her eye she saw two smaller mounds, which lay away from the harvester, around which the investigators were clustered. It was much darker now. Her feet were moving slowly toward them. She had to see what they were. She was close to the clothesline, hoping they were nothing more than mounds of clothing—small piles of clothes ready to be hung on the line.

Kit gasped and bit her knuckles when she saw the girl—a child of eleven or twelve. Her clothes were in disarray and stained by dark patches of blood that had seeped into the dry, dusty ground around her. The girl's blonde hair was haloed around her head, while her still beautiful face had the pallor of death with bruising around her eyes. The other figure was a more mature woman who had died while trying to reach the girl—perhaps her daughter. Her slight body was ravaged by gunshots and contorted. The hem of her skirt was lifted above her hips, perhaps because of the way she fell, perhaps because of something else.

Was it possible that the girl was still alive? Kit knelt down beside her and reached out to try to find a pulse. She pulled back her silky, blonde hair and gently searched her neck for a pulse. The skin felt soft and doughy, already cool under her touch. Nothing. When shouting intruded on her senses, she heard or rather felt footsteps vibrating through the ground and pounding toward her.

"Stop!" It was Matt's exasperated voice, yelling the order. It was then that she remembered the strict instructions. *Do not touch anything. Do not contaminate the evidence.* She tried to scramble to her feet and step away from the bodies, but in the dark she stumbled on the uneven ground. Then she lost her balance and fell as if in slow motion; her consciousness ebbed into darkness like the remnants of the day into the deeper twilight. *I think I'm fainting.* That was her last thought before she hit the ground hard and struck the back of her head on a rock.

Chapter Six

On the day that things changed forever, my beloved warned me that something was going to happen. He said that I shouldn't worry if he went into hiding for a while. I told him that the best place to hide is in plain sight, according to my experience. He laughed and said if I needed to reach him after that, I should leave a message in Gërmia Park under the third seat from the entrance. He would find it and get in touch.

Merita's diary, 25 July 2000

Kit pushed the buzzer on the gate leading to Sergei's house, which was ringed with a high fence of metal bars. She assumed the house was provided by the Russian office. Many of the diplomatic premises in Pristina were well protected. While this was not the Russian Liaison Office, it made sense that its diplomatic staff were safeguarded. Although she found it puzzling that someone as young as Sergei had been assigned such an impressive house. The large, modern, two-story house rose above her. It was set in the hillside of Dragodan, where many diplomats and politicians lived; the area also included the former residences of dictators who had fled the area some time ago or been indicted for war crimes in the Hague. The garden was better tended than many. Kit wondered why people didn't have more pressing concerns than cultivating gardens.

It had taken her a good week to recover from passing out at the crime scene in Staro Dorbi. The incident had shaken her self-confidence. If she had come to Kosovo to prove that she could hold her own in the gritty and exciting world of international peacekeeping, she felt she had failed badly. Not only had she disturbed the crime scene and possibly contaminated the evidence by touching one of the bodies, but she had been so sickened and shocked by the scene that she had passed out and knocked her head on the ground. She was lucky not to have sustained a serious concussion. When she had come to, it was in the back of Angel's jeep, and Angel was attempting to administer hot tea to her from a thermos while Sergei and Matt watched on with concern. She learned later that Sergei had carried her unconscious body back to the driveway, where Angel had fortuitously appeared ready to ply Kit with hot tea. She wasn't sure whether she had been more mortified with embarrassment at being carried by Sergei or at having messed up the evidence and fainted in front of Matt, whom she had wanted to impress with her professional *savoir faire*. Or when Eva found out about the incident and discovered that she had disobeyed Eva's direct orders for the second time in as many days. Fortunately, Eva, who according to Angel was known as a bit of a renegade, had chalked it up to experience. She had just suggested that Kit take a couple of days off and see a doctor or the Office counsellor. Kit was to submit her report about the incident at Staro Dorbi as soon as possible.

Instead of inviting her for coffee as he had suggested on the first day they met, Sergei had invited her to supper at his residence.

There was a buzz as the gate clicked open and she entered. Steps led to the house. The path was lined with shrubs, while toward the fence, trees provided privacy. Small lights on either side of the steps lit her way in the dusk. When the door opened at the top of the steps, Sergei emerged, smiling with his hands open in welcome. He was relaxed in jeans and a cotton shirt with soft blue and white checks.

"Welcome, Katerina," he said, giving her name a Russian inflection.

"Hi, Sergei."

"I'm glad you managed to find the house. The streets are not well signposted or numbered."

"I noticed that," she said and laughed. "But the taxi driver knew the way."

"You were lucky then." Sergei smiled. "May I take your jacket? And offer you a drink? I have an excellent *rakia* from my colleague in Belgrade. He knows a guy, who knows a guy. Is that the saying?"

"You mean it's home brew?" Kit asked.

"Yes, this is one of the best fruit spirits, made out of summer plums from the mountains and distilled into something special."

From the bright hallway, Kit surveyed the interior of the house. It was a combination of contemporary design with its clean, white lines and Scandinavian furniture and a few items that looked as if they might have come from Russia. In a glass cabinet there were a number of fine ceramic ornaments, including what looked like a replica of a jewelled Faberge egg and a large piece of amber. Next to the freestanding fireplace was a pile of wood and a rustic box reminiscent of rural Russia. A handwoven throw provided an accent to the mocha-colored, upholstered leather couch. In front of this was a low, wooden table, on which an antique chess set was set up. On one wall, a large mirror in an ornate, distressed, gilded frame caught the angles of the room and made it appear even larger in the reflection. A slimline bookshelf carried volumes with both Russian and English titles, including Tolstoy's *War and Peace* and Dostoyevsky's *Crime and Punishment*. It was an eclectic decor, composing different elements that worked perfectly together.

"I see you're taking in my poorly coordinated home decoration," Sergei said as he poured Kit a shot glass of colorless liquid from a decanter.

"I was just admiring it. The combination of old and new, Russian and Western European is unusual, but it works for me."

"Thank you. There's a story attached to most of them. I like to be reminded of home by a few of my favorite things. My mother shipped them from Moscow."

Kit paused to look into the glass display cabinet and leaned closer to examine a jeweled, ridged, golden-yellow egg on a small tripod It was encircled by gold garlands suspended from cabochon-blue sapphires topped with a rise of diamond-set bows.

"What a wonderful replica," Kit said.

"Replica?" Sergei smiled as he produced a key from his pocket. He picked up the egg gently, drew it out, and held it up. It sparkled under the light from the chandeliers. "This was discovered in a private estate and found its way to my family via the Dorotheum auction house in Vienna."

Kit looked up at him, her blue eyes sparkling with intrigue. "You don't think it could be real?"

"No, I don't think so. I know so. This …" he said as he watched her reaction, "is Faberge's lost third Imperial Easter Egg."

He smiled at her intake of breath as she reached out to touch the glistening egg. "It must be worth a fortune," she murmured. "But how could you risk bringing it here? Shouldn't it be in a safe somewhere in Moscow?"

He took in a deep breath and looked directly into Kit's eyes. "I'm confident that it's safe. I'd like to talk to you more about this later, after dinner, if that's okay."

"Sure," Kit said. Her eyebrows rose at the remark, but she was still staring in fascination at the gems on the egg.

"Would you like to hold it?"

"Yes, please." She turned her hand to receive the egg. He placed it in the centre of her palm. It was cool to the touch, weightier than she had expected.

"This is perhaps one of the most beautiful things I've ever seen. Let alone touched."

He opened the egg. Inside was a ladies' watch with a white-enamel, openwork face and diamond-set gold hands.

"Oh my goodness," she gasped.

"The symbolism is as remarkable as the masterpiece. Time, the completion of all things, is held within each new beginning as the clock is held within the egg." He took the egg and gently placed it back the display case before locking it with a decisive click.

"Come. Let's see what my cook has prepared." He led her into the dining room, where a formal dinner table was set. "We begin with caviar."

Over the meal, they had a wide-ranging conversation about New Zealand and Russia and the ties between the two countries, which Kit hadn't known about before, as well as vacation plans and cultural events in Pristina, such as film festivals. Sergei talked about the importance of the Christian Orthodox faith to the Serbian communities in Kosovo and their links to the Orthodox church in Serbia and Russia, in contrast to the largely Muslim Albanian-Kosovo population. The conversation took a darker turn when he mentioned how several famous Orthodox churches has been vandalized and graveyards desecrated during and even after the conflict had supposedly finished. "The people in Serbian villages feel surrounded and afraid," he explained. Kit noticed that neither of them had directly referred to the events at Staro Dorbi, where she had fainted at the sight of a murdered mother and child.

The meal was composed of many small courses and served by Sergei's cook. However, Sergei himself served the dessert, *Ptichye Moloko*, flown in that morning from Moscow on Russian military and diplomatic air transport. The delicious and deceptively simple dessert was prepared from chocolate-glazed marshmallow.

"This is incredible," Kit said as she dabbed her lips with the white linen napkin. "I didn't imagine I'd be sampling such treats in Kosovo."

"My pleasure," Sergei purred. "My mother knows the chef at the Prague Restaurant in Moscow where the dessert was first made. She likes to arrange little treats for me, which can be sent through the diplomatic pouch."

"Please thank your mother for me."

"I will indeed."

"Do you have family in Moscow?" Kit asked. "Other than your mother?"

"I have a brother and a sister. In fact, I have a young son, Mikhail, who lives with my mother. My wife passed away in a tragic accident when he was still a young child." Sergei paused and looked into the candle flame. A sad, haunted look passed over his eyes until he seemed to shake himself out of it. "My father is also no longer with us," he said.

"I'm so sorry," Kit said. On impulse, she reached out and placed her hand over his. "I see that you understand personal tragedy."

"Yes, thank you," he said gravely, then paused for a moment. "And what about your family?"

Kit explained that her mother lived in Auckland and her estranged father lived in Australia, and that her fiancé also lived in Auckland.

"Interesting. What does Xander do?"

"He works part-time as an accountant while he is studying for his MBA."

"What kind of car does he drive?"

"He rides a bicycle. Why do you ask?"

"The type of car a man drives tells us something about him."

"He's very environmentally aware."

"I'm sure he is. How does he feel about you working in Kosovo?"

"He didn't want me to come here, but I think he's accepted it now."

"So, in the end, he just let you go."

"Yes. Why shouldn't he? He knows it's something I need to do."

"Well, if it were me, I would have found a way to dissuade my beautiful fiancée from going to a conflict zone, for whatever reason."

Kit looked down at her hands and clenched them together.

Sergei reached forward, lifted her left hand, and examined it before he looked at her with an unspoken question.

"We didn't feel that a traditional engagement ring was necessary. But I do have an Irish claddagh ring."

"Well then," he said as he replaced her hand and smiled at her, as if dismissing the topic. "Won't you join me in the living room where we can relax a little more. I'd like to show you my chess set."

Sergei eased out Kit's chair and ushered her into the living area.

Kit sat down on the comfortably upholstered leather couch in front of which stood the low, wooden table where the traditional wood-carved Russian chess set sat.

Sergei poured her a cup of hot, black tea from the samovar, the ornate metal urn that stood on the small table beside the seating area.

Sergei then relaxed on the sofa, crossed his legs, and angled them toward Kit as he put his arm along the back of the sofa behind her. He was still and composed as he looked into the shadows in the corner of the room as if he were trying to discern movement there.

Kit studied his strong profile. For the first time, she noticed the hint of an aquiline nose with a predatory edge.

"You asked how I could risk bringing a priceless Faberge egg to Kosovo," Sergei said.

Kit continued to stare at him as she sipped her hot tea in the small cup that matched the samovar.

Sergei settled back a little more into the couch. "I'd like to explain a very practical, metaphysical concept that we call *khash* for short. This word comes from the Russian word for chess, *shakhmaty,* which like the English word *checkmate* means that the opposing king is dead. Shakh comes from the word meaning king or shah, and mat meaning dead. When one player has won the game by threatening the king of the other player so that he cannot escape death, we say *checkmate*. We reversed the word for king to *khash*. These ideas originally come from a Russian philosopher, and we have developed them further."

"So this philosophy or idea has something to do with the game of chess, but with the normal rules reversed."

"Yes, exactly." Sergei beamed. "In brief, we can say that life is a game, which is usually played according to certain rules. In this philosophy, we make dreams come true by reversing the way we play that game. We use the unexpected. We use our imaginations actively. We use mirrors."

"That sounds fascinating, if mysterious. I can't pretend to understand."

"I can explain some of the principles. We start by becoming very clear about our goals and objectives. We imagine scenarios in sufficient detail so that they become lifelike, as if we are seeing the image in a mirror. And then, when we have the image the way we want it, we walk through the mirror. Then everything becomes possible. The rules of the game are reversed. We call the shots, not our opponent, not the usual rules of the world."

"How does that work? How can we create our own reality?"

"It's because the reality we see is not as solid as it appears. It can be molded on a quantum level by our thoughts, which are energies. If these are consistently applied in a certain direction, then reality is affected. We may, of course, meet opposing forces, and then we can use the powers of the chessboard if we wish. For example, we may imitate a knight and jump over characters on a board; a bishop sweeping across the board into enemy territory to claim what is ours, or what we want to be ours. The checkerboard symbolizes the opposing forces of life. It's our goal to dominate the board according to our wishes."

"That's interesting," Kit said as she reached for one of the small sugar cookies next to the samovar.

"I took the liberty of explaining this to you because I feel we have a connection, and I thought you would understand it. Most women, dare I say it, would not. We haven't spoken of what happened at Staro Dorbi, but I feel that you might truly benefit from learning about khash and how to reverse other people's rules of life in order to reach your goals. Would you allow me to teach you?"

"Uh … I don't know. This is a surprise. Although it does sound fascinating. How does it relate to the Faberge egg you mentioned earlier?"

"The Faberge Egg … it's all about being confident about outcomes happening the way we know they will. I know that it won't be lost or stolen. I have envisaged that outcome, and I have complete confidence in my vision. I have *seen* it."

He put an inflection on *seen,* which told Kit that it was not a normal kind of seeing that he was talking about.

"The way I know it will happen, not the way I think or expect it will happen. I have something here of great value to me as a kind of exercise and challenge to myself. Do I really have confidence in myself?"

"So, are you suggesting that I couldn't cope at the crime scene because I didn't have confidence in myself?" Kit asked as she shuffled her position on the sofa.

"I don't mean this as a judgement. It's just something that happened, neither good nor bad. But you could have considered more deeply before you went there. What did you want out the situation? What was your best outcome? Then actively imagined how you would go about creating that."

"So I could have seen myself as more at ease in the situation and more in control of myself. Making notes regarding the evidence, coordinating with EUFOR and my office and so on?"

"Yes, exactly."

"But I didn't know what to expect. I expected perhaps one or two killings, not a massacre, and not one involving children or innocent civilians."

"This is one of the challenges that we face. How do we prepare for the unexpected? One of the ways is to prepare in advance, so we go into a situation with a feeling of confidence, and then we experience the feeling of success when we come out. It preprogrammes the situation in accordance with our wishes without our knowing the details of what exactly will happen."

"That sounds great, but often I don't know exactly what I want when I go into a situation."

"True," he said. "We need to have great self-awareness to develop this ability. In fact, there are several different levels to khash. The first is to become aware of our goals and objectives in each situation and start to envisage them. Then later, we start to develop more subtle tools—how to respond to people in ways that can deflect or deter them from reaching their goals while we pursue our own. The element of surprise. We start to feel more comfortable navigating on chaotic seas and even bring our own creative chaos to a situation."

"Creative chaos!" Kit said and laughed. "I like the sound of that." She paused. "I don't know how my fiancé would feel if I started to bring chaos into our relationship."

"My dear Katerina, you've already done so by coming to Pristina. Kosovo is a place on the edge with a volatility that can bring sudden reversals and sudden success. Perhaps that's what you're unconsciously looking for."

Kit looked into the shadows that suddenly seemed to be deepening in the house. The large, ornate mirror reflected shapes in the room behind her that made her sense something was happening beneath the surface that she couldn't see clearly. She glanced at her watch and remarked on the time.

"Well, my dear Katerina, perhaps that's enough philosophy for the evening. I'll call you a taxi, if you wish. They're usually here in five minutes."

"Yes," Kit said as she stood up. "It's later than I thought. I should be going."

"Let me walk you to the gate. Please think about what we've discussed. If you're interested in going further with what I described, let me know. Meanwhile, perhaps we could meet in downtown Pristina for a coffee sometime soon."

"I'd like that. Maybe you're right; perhaps I need to start thinking more strategically about my life."

As Sergei escorted Kit to the gate where the taxi waited, the troubling images in the mirror dissolved into the oncoming night.

"I know what I want," she said when she reached the bottom of the steps. "I'd like to learn more about khash. By the way, who is the Russian philosopher who developed it?"

"Good question," Sergei said and then kissed her goodbye on both cheeks. "A rather misunderstood person from Russia's past set down some of the principles in his diary. It was rediscovered several decades after his death, and then a scientist developed the ideas into a system, keeping in mind the ideas of new age thought and modern quantum physics."

"Another diary," Kit mumbled.

"What?"

"Nothing. Something came up today about a diary."

"We'll discuss these things again soon. I'd like to hear all about it and how things are going with your work."

"And the philosopher's name?" Kit asked.

Sergey looked up and paused. He seemed to be inhaling the evening air, a night flowering plant nearby with a heavy, sweet scent. "He's known as Rasputin," he said as he helped her into the taxi.

CHAPTER SEVEN

Love is amazing. Literally, it's like a maze. I'm lost but I don't want to find my way out.

Merita's diary, 27 July 2000

Kit curled up on her couch with a cup of coffee and a notebook. Her laptop lay open in front of her on the coffee table. Her apartment was up three flights of stairs in a block in central Pristina. It was a simple, one-bedroom apartment with a lounge and kitchenette, which overlooked a street with restaurants, cafes, and a few shops. The trees lining the street provided some respite from the hot summer days that were yet to come. She had taken over the apartment from a former OIDC legal officer who had left Kosovo. In her experience, good apartments were often passed from one staff member to another through word of mouth. The Kosovo Albanian landlord was easy to get along with and left her alone to enjoy the apartment in peace. Angel told her that not all landlords were so considerate. There were other staff members living nearby, which would make it easier in case the conflict flared up again and it was necessary to evacuate. Proximity to other internationals also gave her a sense of security during the numerous power cuts. People could meet for coffee where there was a generator, or no electric power if it was during the day. The apartment was simple and serviceable, and the rent was low.

Things can change so quickly, which was difficult to believe at first, but now she realized there were so many new opportunities. Kit chewed the end of her pen thoughtfully and looked at the blank page of her journal. Sergei had given her a lot to think about last night. He had made her reassess about her current goals. She had come to Kosovo for a combination of reasons. When things hadn't worked out at the law firm back home, she had wanted to take her career in a different direction, but it hadn't been easy to find another position. If she was honest, she had to admit to being bored with her life in Auckland. She needed a break from the life she had known to explore the world and herself. Yet she felt affronted by Sergei's implication that Xander was not a strong enough masculine influence in her life. Xander had tried to stop her leaving for Kosovo, but when she had made her mind up, he had not pushed his point of view. That was what she wanted—wasn't it? A partner who respected her wishes.

Kit picked up the pencil. Using careful, looping calligraphy she wrote the words *My goals: August 2000*. Then she made one heading: *Partner*. Her first bullet point said *respects my wishes*.

She smiled when she remembered Sergei's comment that her fiancé didn't drive a car but rode a bicycle. Xander considered himself an eco-warrior. In his view, riding a bike or walking in the city was striking a blow against the industrial complex. He said that if everyone rode bicycles instead of driving, the world would be a better place. Kit sketched Xander's bicycle leaning against the wall of a house as her mind drifted back to New Zealand.

She wrote: *drives a new-model jeep* and sketched a jeep with the door open. Kit had nearly gone to art school but had opted for law school instead because a lawyer's income was higher than an artist's. Her thoughts and feelings took shape in the journal through her drawings. She would have appreciated it if Xander had occasionally taken her on outings to enjoy the great outdoors in New Zealand. As it was, she'd had to rely on her hatchback to transport them. He said he couldn't afford a car until after he graduated. Until then, she'd covered the majority of their household expenses. She jotted down *financially independent,* frowned, and picked up the coffee cup.

This analysis was taking her in a direction that she was not so comfortable with, so she switched back to her career goals. She wrote down *international law*. What attracted her to that? Was it the excitement of participating professionally in the international arena with the travel and jet-set lifestyle that often went with it? The generous salary was certainly worthwhile.

When she thought of that young girl who had lost her life in the massacre, she thought of her sister, whom she had lost at an early age to a rare bone cancer. How outrageous it was to intentionally rob that child of her life. The brutality and utter senselessness of war made her sick to her stomach. She remembered the lifeless child lying on the field before her mother could reach her. Kit felt dizzy and nauseous again, as she had at the scene of the massacre. As she leaned back on the couch and closed her eyes, she drew a ragged breath. Wasn't it about justice? She wrote down the word in large, wide-spaced letters and filled them in. Justice for victims. She felt a jolt of electricity through her. That's what she wanted to stand for. That was what she stood for.

As she worked on a new page, Kit's graphite pencil outlined in smudged gray lines the body of the young girl. Her eyes swam as she filled in the contours of the fragile, doll-like figure on the ground. She filled in the surrounding area: the dry tufts of grass, the stones, and the large rock she had hit her head on. Kits stomach churned as she remembered the moment when she lost her balance and fell. As she envisaged that scene, she remembered seeing a cigarette butt close to the bodies.

She froze for a moment and caught her breath. Perhaps that cigarette butt could be important. She grabbed her phone, pulled up her contact's list, and selected Matt's name and tapped a message. *Hi Matt, did you check beside where I fell—the cigarette butt could be evidence—Kit.* She pressed send and took a deep breath.

A few minutes later the phone announced a message. *Thanks. Please come to my office tomorrow a.m. to discuss—Matt.*

Kit's thoughts were interrupted by a call coming through on her computer. She sat forward to accept the call when she recognized Xander's number.

"Hi, hon," she said.

Xander's face appeared on the screen. He wore a green T-shirt, and his hair was longer and more unkempt than she remembered. She could see her aunt's garden behind him.

"Hi, foxy lady. How's it going?"

"Good, it's going good. What's up?"

"Not much. Working on my thesis proposal."

"I'm in my new apartment. Want to see?" Kit walked the computer around the apartment before she aimed the camera out the window.

"Looks okay. How's work going?"

"Pretty intense, actually. I was just texting a police inspector I've been working with."

"Getting chummy?" Xander sat back and crossed his arms in front of him.

"Nothing like that. I'm working with him on a couple of cases."

"Spill."

"I thought that the conflict had finished with the NATO bombing, but it hasn't. They're still fighting."

"I hope you're not caught in the crossfire."

"No, although I did see something that disturbed me. When innocent civilians get hurt, it really breaks my heart."

"What did you see?"

"A child and her mother had been killed. I didn't see the other victims before …" Kit couldn't complete the sentence. "I don't know if I should talk about it. Ongoing investigation and all that."

"It sounds awful. Maybe you should come home."

"I have to give it a proper go here. Besides, I want to see the case through … the cases, that is. I've realized that what matters most to me most is getting justice for the victims."

"Do you think that's really possible?"

"Not sure. I'd like to think that's what the law is about. I didn't realize that before coming here."

"And all in the first few days. I wonder what revelations will be next?"

"Why are you taking that tone?"

"What tone?"

"Sarcasm." Kit sniffed. " I'm serious."

"Are you sure you don't just enjoy driving around in jeeps with these police and military types?"

"You're jealous."

"Yeah, maybe a little."

"I like it when you get jealous." Kit smiled.

"I miss you, that's all. But I'm keeping busy. How's your social life, your colleagues?"

"I haven't had time to enjoy much of a social life. My boss Eva seems nice, if a little eccentric with her high heels and rescue dogs. The admin assistant, Angel, has been really helpful, and I've met a local Russian liaison officer."

"Come on, really?"

"He suggested I need to clarify my personal goals—and get a new car. Or at least you should."

"This guy's not making sense. You know your personal goals, and we don't need a new car. My bicycle is going very well, and I'm getting fitter by the day. Don't spend too much time with him."

"I have to for work, you know. I miss you, hon. If you were here we could maybe see some countries in the region—Montenegro or Bulgaria."

"Maybe I can come over later. But I have to finish the bibliography for my thesis at the moment; it's on profit and loss in environmental protection companies."

"How's Mum?"

"She sends her love. She dropped by the other day. She said she was thinking about working part-time in a private investigator's office."

Kit rolled her eyes and laughed. "Mum is always coming up with new schemes. What about her shop?"

"She's getting some help in. And apparently she's started seeing some guy from the senior's dating site—just meeting for coffee, she said."

"Sounds like I'm missing all the fun. I'd better give her a call later and check how she's doing."

Kit stifled a yawn. "It's getting late, hon, sorry."

Pristina's city centre was damp the next morning. Kit held her red umbrella against the rain under dense, gray clouds as she walked from her apartment to the police building where Matt had an office. Taxis and cars blocked the streets. The drains were struggling to cope with the downpour, and the gutters were overflowing with gray stormwater. Kit stopped to text Angel: *Going to see Matt—K.*

Ur supposed to be on leave—A, said the reply.

Took the time I needed. Now need to work on case, Kit replied and slipped the phone into her bag.

She showed her OIDC pass to the officers guarding the building and made her way through the makeshift container office and security check, through the heavy doors, and into the building. She caught the elevator to the third floor. As she entered the room where Matt's assistant sat, she craned her head around his door. Matt was balanced against his desk with his long legs stretched out in front of him and crossed at the ankles. He had already removed his jacket and was in working mode. Owen stood with a marker pen in front of a whiteboard with lists of names and connecting arrows.

"Hi, good morning," Kit said.

"Good morning. Come in," Matt said. "We're reviewing what we know about these cases. It's possible, just possible, that there might be a connection between them. We know from Blaku that Raco's group is involved in gunrunning and could potentially have been implicated in the massacre at Staro Dorbi."

"Would you like a coffee?" Owen asked. "We start our days here with a double macchiato or big macchiato as they call them here."

"Love one," Kit replied as she edged toward the whiteboard. "Just black though. No sugar."

"An Americano?" he asked.

Kit nodded.

"Thanks for your text. We went back to check the crime scene and picked up a cigarette butt close to the house that was missed on the first sweep of the area. Probably because officers were focused on the main group of victims where we collected some shell casings," Matt said.

Kit looked down and felt her face heat up. "Good, I hope it helps. But I feel bad about what happened the other evening at the crime scene. I can't believe I acted so unprofessionally." She shook her head. "I wanted so much to prove myself, and I completely messed up."

Matt's eyes softened. "It's happened to most of us. I remember throwing up after my first murder scene. Didn't quite make it out the door. Contaminated the evidence." He smiled wryly.

"At least I didn't do that. I'm not sure whether I fainted or tripped on the uneven ground before I hit my head." She rubbed the bump on the back of her head gingerly.

"I hope you had that knock on your head seen to."

Just then Owen reappeared with a small tray of coffees in plastic containers.

"Super, thanks," Kit said as she reached for her coffee.

With Owen's return, Matt was all business again. "I'm sending the casings to forensics for examination and requesting a DNA analysis from the cigarette butt. We can see if there's a match. Our colleagues in London will assist with analysis because we don't have the facilities here. I'll get the paperwork for that done today—or we will," Matt said with a nod toward Owen and Kit. "Also, I need your help with an application for search warrants for Raco's house and Merita Shala's apartment. I want to bring them both in for questioning."

"Sure," Kit said as she took out her legal pad and pen. "On suspicion of what charges?"

"Abduction, sexual assault, and organized criminal activities in co-perpetration. Also that other guy that Blaku identified—Merita's boyfriend. We don't have evidence linking him to Staro Dorbi, but we can base the warrants on Blaku's evidence. She's witness A, by the way. I'm going to try to get her into the witness protection programme."

Owen rolled his eyes. "All this is a lot of paperwork. I'll get you the particulars of the suspects which you'll need for the court application."

"This is a top priority, a public interest case. Are you sure you're ready for it?" Matt asked Kit.

Kit took a moment and looked down as she chewed her lower lip. When she looked up there was a light of certainty her eyes. "Absolutely."

"I'm setting up Task Force Capture for this case. You're on it."

CHAPTER EIGHT

Kosovo means field of blackbirds. There are too many crows here swooping and crying, shadowing our skies and bringing messages of death. I wish these accused birds would leave Kosovo forever. They've come to feast on human flesh. There have been too many killings here.

Merita's diary, 1 August 2000

Raco was hunting today mainly because he enjoyed killing and inflicting pain. Hunting was socially acceptable for men in Kosovo as a way to augment their meagre food supply in a number of rural areas. He excelled in several forms of martial arts, having even won two international karate competitions. As well as being a sadist, he was also a perfectionist. Hunting served double duty as a relaxing pastime and target practice. His businesses often extended to providing security for high-level officials. However, his most lucrative assignments were murder for hire, not an uncommon occurrence in the gangland subculture in parts of Kosovo. He had done five successful hits, mainly against competing crime bosses or rivals in the high-stakes Kosovo political scene.

A swarm of hundreds of black crows swept overhead, cawing noisily, wings beating as they came to roost at the edge of the forest. Kosovo means *field of blackbird*. The name came about after the Battle of Kosovo was fought between Serbia and Turkey in 1389, on a field of blackbirds. Some speculated that after that battle and other similar hostilities, the birds had developed a taste for human flesh and kept coming back for more. As if they are winged black wolves, then they are everywhere in Kosovo, particularly from autumn onward. Numerous and aggressive, they crowd the territories of many other birds, and often occupy trees in the inner city and bring shadows to the sky and foul Pristina's pavements.

For a big man, Raco moved remarkably stealthily in the underbrush beneath the cover of pine, spruce, and beech trees. He wore camo pants, boots, and a vest and carried extra ammunition. With hunting rifle slung over his back, he was searching for larger game than were endemic in the area in the foothills to the north of Pristina. With a bit of luck he might also come across some hapless Serbs, either refugees or hunters. The shadows were growing longer among the surrounding pine forest, and while theoretically he should not be hunting at night without special permission, he enjoyed the additional challenge that stalking game in the twilight or early evening gave him. A traditional hunter, he preferred to hunt with his rifle and hunting knife rather than using explosives, pits or snares, artificial lights, or other means that might make the hunt too easy. It was a way to hone his skills.

He had first learned to hunt with his father and brother when he was a young boy. They had enjoyed an easy camaraderie and the satisfaction of bringing home game that could feed the family for several days. His father had taught him to handle a gun at an early age, a skill that still held him in good stead. Unfortunately, Raco's family had been decimated when a group of Serbs came to their house. Raco had been in the mountains hunting at the time they took his father and brother away while his family was having lunch. They were never seen again. A mass grave was later found in the vicinity, and it transpired that members of other families had witnessed the executions. The bodies were not even given a decent burial. A group of irregular Serb Police and paramilitary had been mistreating and killing Albanians in the north of Kosovo as part of a semiofficial, ethnic-cleansing policy to force them out the area one way or another. Because of this, Raco felt no regret about killing any Serb, even civilians. And he believed that any bitches who consorted with them, whether Serb or Albanian, deserved what was coming to them. However, his murder for hire business also extended to Albanians who were on the wrong side of his political and criminal alliances.

Raco stopped and stood still. He'd heard a rustling in the undergrowth a few meters to his left. He thought it was an animal, maybe not as large as a stag, but not as small as a rabbit or a fox. It had been a fine, hot day, but heavy clouds had gathered over the mountain, and raindrops had begun to fall and were landing on the dry undergrowth. He glanced up at the sky. He had not calculated on a storm setting in during his hunting excursion, but if he could, he would make the kill before returning home. Lightning flickered, and he saw the profile of the female deer standing not far away. He raised his rifle slowly and took aim. Raco noted the doe's long, elegant neck and alert eyes. She was slender, probably not more than eighteen months old. Raco calmed his breathing and, between heartbeats, gently squeezed the trigger.

The deer jumped and tried to run, but the wound was too grave, and she staggered. More carelessly this time, Raco fired another shot to finish her off before she took flight and disappeared into the night to die. He walked over to the fallen deer and nudged her with his foot. There was no reaction. He hefted the limp body on to his back, unmindful of the blood still flowing from the gunshot wound and the lolling head bumping on his back. Carrying the lifeless deer back to the pickup truck would complete his evening with strength training. These preparations were important, because next time his target would not be a deer.

Chapter Nine

I'm meant for more than this. I used to be a Police officer, now I'm an irregular fighter of sorts. I try to know my future by reading the coffee grounds. But all I can see is conflict ahead. And divided loyalties.

Merita's diary, 5 August 2000

A group of police and military sat around the table while Matt displayed a series of maps on the table. Kit slipped in the door and joined the group toward the back; her auburn ponytail and high heels were out of place in the room of men in uniforms. She wore a fitted, black business jacket and skirt with a simple, white, linen blouse. Matt nodded to her and continued.

"Good morning, gentlemen. I asked Caitlin Chase from the chief prosecutor's office to join us to make sure we get the evidence we need to put these guys away for a long time. We might only get a chance to take down a crime boss like Raco once if we're lucky, so let's make this count. We want to hit two locations at once: Raco's house and Merita Shala's apartment. Each of you leads a team essential to this operation. The sites need three groups: one to secure the area, one to enter the premises and arrest the suspect, and one to conduct the search and collection of evidence. Raco is the prime suspect in several serious offences, from sexual assault to gunrunning and extortion. Probably other crimes. He is likely to be armed and highly dangerous. Shala is a hardened KLA operative and should not be underestimated either."

"Why don't we put them under surveillance for a while and see what other evidence can be collected?" a blond man with an Eastern European accent asked.

"We need to move quickly because Raco could be preparing to commit other serious offences right now. We need to check for arms, ammunition, and explosives as a priority and also seize the cell phones and any computers on site. In Shala's case, we understand that she keeps a detailed diary of the criminal activities of the group. This is the top priority when searching her apartment. In both cases, check for any photographs, letters, documents, or other records showing their associations with other people. Other suspected gang members will be put under surveillance. The prosecutor's office has that in hand. Kit?"

"We're preparing the court applications as we speak. These will allow police to monitor the cell phone messaging between all suspects as well as intercepting their telephone calls."

Matt pointed to a map showing the street where Raco lived. "Alpha team, I suggest you do a recce around this zone as soon as possible before the operation. Check around his house and the nearby streets for exits and entries; also for any high-risk vulnerabilities in case he starts shooting or explodes an IED."

"Do you think that's really necessary?" the Eastern European man asked.

"Yes, it is."

Gregor Petri, the blond man with an Eastern European accent, crossed his arms. "That's not the way we do things in Romania. The target should be put under surveillance for longer. Let us see what he's up to and who he's talking to."

"I know we have an international team here, but I'm in charge of this task force. Sorry to pull rank, but things are going to be done as I direct," Matt said.

Petri shrugged and leaned back in his chair. "As you say, Major. Just don't blame me if things go wrong."

"Things won't go wrong if we all follow procedure."

"Which procedure?"

Matt ignored the last comment and continued. "Sergeant, I want Team Alpha to check the perimeter of the operation, get an overview of the premises, and report back. Team Bravo will enter and secure the apartment, arrest Raco, and provide security to Team Charley, who will conduct the search for evidence."

"Which team do you want me on?" Kit asked.

Heads swiveled toward her, the only woman present. Some of the men smirked; others looked on with curiosity.

"Team Charley. You're to observe the collection of evidence and coordinate with the Chief Prosecutor's Office. We need to make sure our case is watertight. The search should be from the outside in, from bottom to top, one room at a time. Team Charley, if you find something, tell the forensic officer, who will take photos, bag, and tag. Don't forget to search Raco's vehicles and garage. Before entering the house, make a note of the layout of the entire place, the yard, and every room before the search starts."

"And the woman suspect?" Petri asked.

"Same procedure, although in her case, a smaller team is needed. I want her brought in for questioning. By the way, make sure there is at least one female officer in that group."

"Why?" Petri asked.

"Because I don't want any claims that she's been mishandled messing up our case. At this stage, there aren't sufficient grounds to arrest her, but we need to persuade her to come into the office for an informative chat. I'm mainly interested in the results of the search of her apartment. Make sure your teams keep alert for a diary or a journal containing handwritten notes. She's a KLA fighter, so I don't exclude the possibility that she could also have been a shooter at Staro Dorbi."

"Sir, what evidence do we have that they were involved in Staro Dorbi?" Owen asked.

"Nothing definite, but our confidential witness said that she heard them discussing an operation involving firearms shortly before the killings. The timing could be coincidental, but it might not be. Pay special attention to any guns or ammunition that you find on either sites."

"And cigarette butts," Kit interjected.

"And cigarette butts." Matt nodded in Kit's direction. "We found one close to two of the victims—a brand that was not recognized by the surviving occupants of the farmhouse. We've sent it for testing. In any case, we should take DNA samples from both suspects."

Kit made a note.

"What's being done to search the farmhouses around the actual crime scene?" Petri asked, looking dubious.

"That's in hand. We'll organize that search just as soon as the crime scene is secured and we make sure we collect whatever evidence is there and interview witnesses close to the field. I'm still waiting for the results of the postmortem examinations too. Then we'll have a clearer idea what we're looking for."

"It seems to me," Petri continued, unswayed by Matt's effort to round up the discussion, "that we're going too slow where we should be going faster and too fast where we should be going slower. You know that the Serbian farmers requested protection from EUFOR but they didn't have time for it."

"Thanks for those observations, Captain Petri. I'll keep that in mind."

"Major," Petri corrected him. "I'm a major in the Romanian Army."

Matt nodded curtly to him. "That's all for now. Thank you, gentlemen and Kit. Let's meet here tomorrow morning eight a.m. sharp. I want to hear from each team leader about how preparations are proceeding. I also need at least one canine unit."

Whatever the tensions between Matt and Petri, the investigation was moving into high gear. Kit hoped that soon they would have the evidence they needed to put Raco away.

Kit slid into the back of Matt's jeep, and Owen drove them to the hospital. She had agreed to accompany them to the city morgue where the bodies of the massacre victims had been taken for a postmortem, confirmation of cause of death, and formal identification by family members. Kit was interested to meet the pathologist, an Indian woman, who had been working to confirm cause of death.

Kit was wearing tailored, navy slacks and jacket with flats, which she found more convenient for sliding in and out the military jeep rather than a pencil skirt and high heels. Her hair was in a ponytail, and her black legal briefcase was tucked under her arm.

Dr. Jyoti Prabhu came to meet them at the entrance to the morgue. She was in her late thirties. A small diamond stud gleamed on one nostril beneath her kohl-rimmed eyes. Dr. Prabhu wore her hair drawn back in a chignon, and she had a white coat over her black trousers and colorful tunic.

"Hello," Dr. Prabhu said with a smile as she extended her hand to Kit. "You must be Ms. Chase." The two women shook hands. "Major," she said to Matt. "Sergeant," she said and nodded to Owen.

"Good morning, doctor," Matt said. "I brought Ms. Chase with us to introduce her to you and your facility."

"Please come inside."

The four of them entered the large glass doors and went into the lobby.

"This is my office." Dr. Prabhu indicated a small functional room to the left. "I usually have a colleague and an assistant here as well. Would you like to sign in and we can then view the bodies from Staro Dorbi."

Kit stopped and blanched. "I didn't think we would actually view any bodies."

Dr. Prabhu stopped and studied Kit's face briefly. "It's okay," she said. "If you prefer, you can wait here. I'll ask my assistant to prepare you some tea."

Kit got out her mobile and started checking it absent-mindedly for messages.

Matt and Owen looked at her. "Up to you, Kit," Matt said.

The evening at the crime scene came back to her; the swimming blackness as the ground rose up and she struck her head on the rock. The flash of white from the cigarette butt made her feel nauseous yet again. Kit took a deep breath and gripped her mobile and her bag. "It's okay," she said at length. "I need to do this." She looked at Dr. Prabhu. "Sorry, I had a bad experience the other night at a crime scene … but I need to get over it."

Dr. Prabhu didn't comment; she merely stood there waiting.

"Alright," Matt said at last. "Lead the way, doctor." With a glance at Kit, Dr. Prabhu nodded briefly and turned toward the double doors leading deeper into the building.

Dr. Prabhu lead them into the morgue where there were several drawers set into refrigeration units. Three stainless steel tables occupied the antiseptic room. "As you know, Major, EUFOR brought us fourteen bodies. We have examined all of them, but there was not room to store all the bodies here, so we sent some to other facilities. Four bodies are awaiting formal identification by their families before they arrange burial."

"When are you expecting them to come in?" Matt asked.

"Later this morning."

"Can you summarize your findings?"

Owen took out his notebook and started writing.

"They've all been shot, probably by automatic weapons. In some cases the bullets were still in the bodies. I've removed them and will have them sent for forensic examination."

"Thanks. What about time of death?" Matt asked.

"Probably not long before your arrival at the crime scene. Two, three hours at most."

Kit had also taken out her notebook and started writing in it. Under her notes about the cause and time of death, she wrote in capital letters: *KHASH. GOAL: Justice for victims.* She took a deep breath and studied the page. To be effective at her work and help bring the perpetrators to justice, she needed to toughen up fast. She had to be ready to enter the killing field and hunt the hunters—not collapse in shock at the first glimpse of what she found there. That was her goal, and if she had to step over her shadow, her naïve, sensitive self, she would do it. Sergei was right.

While Kit was lost in her thoughts and looking at her page, Dr. Prabhu continued talking as she pulled open one of the drawers. It was a man who had suffered bruising and lacerations to his torso and face, as well as three bullet holes: one in his head, one close to his heart, and one lower down on his torso. "Several of the victims were disfigured with blunt instruments," she said. "But the cause of death was the gunshot wounds. The mutilations were probably inflicted after death."

"What blunt instruments did the killers use?" Matt asked.

"It seems likely, as you say, Major, that there was more than one killer. Quite possibly rifle butts or farm implements that were close at hand. And I recovered bullets from at least three different guns."

Kit looked at the bruised and battered body of a middle-aged man on the metal surface. She felt solid on her feet, and the room wasn't tilting. That was a good sign. There was a pungent odor mixed with a sweet tinge, although a high-capacity air exchange unit took care of most of it. She rubbed the back of her neck, swallowed, and took a step forward.

"Has he been positively identified?" Matt asked.

"Based on the ID card he was carrying, he's probably Jovan Simić. Immediate family members are coming in this afternoon to make a positive identification and take the body for burial."

"Thanks, Dr. Prabhu. Sergeant Reese will come to collect the evidence and your report as soon as it's ready. We need to do ballistics tests on the bullets as soon as possible."

"We've been working around the clock at three locations to get you this information. Based on our preliminary assessment of the bullets we've recovered, the killers used five assault rifles, 7.62 mm, and two pistols."

"Much appreciated. Could have been Kalashnikovs," Matt muttered.

"Some of the victims were shot in the head at close range. The pistols were probably 7.62 mm."

Matt looked down and took a deep breath, then let it out slowly. "There's an amnesty to encourage KLA fighters to hand in their weapons. But the returned firearms are just the tip of the iceberg. For everyone who's handed one in, there will be two or more hidden at home."

"They're still bristling with weapons. In case the Serbs come back," Owen said.

Kit was preoccupied with her notebook. "Are the bodies of the woman and child here?" Kit asked.

"No, they were sent to the other facility. However, I can say that it's possible that they were both killed by the same bullet, which passed through the mother and hit the child," Dr. Prabhu replied.

Kit bit her lip and scribbled in her notebook. She felt better believing that the death of the child was a terrible accident and that the mother and child were united at the moment of death, although the circumstances at the scene of the massacre made this cold comfort.

"We're about to search the suspects' houses. If we find weapons, we might be able to find a match to the bullets or the casings from the crime scene," Matt said. "Please provide Sergeant Reese with a list of the names of family members who come to identify the bodies. We might need to talk to them as well."

Chapter Ten

I go about my daily life, busy with inconsequential tasks. Sometimes, it seems as if nothing matters, not even life. I feel like a speck of dust blown about by a merciless wind—until I'm in my beloved's arms. Then I know I'm home and things start to matter again. My warrior brothers live on the edge between heroism and betrayal. Living so close to a deep ravine is exhausting.

Merita's diary, 5 August 2000

Unmarked police cars sped toward their destinations—Raco's house and Shala's apartment. Lights fixed to the roofs of cars flashed. The tense task force team members, wearing masks and tactical gear, including bulletproof vests and black clothes, were already on alert inside their vehicles. Matt, Owen, and Kit followed the cars heading to Raco's house in a military jeep. According to their latest intelligence, Raco was at his house with one of his associates.

Kit wore her hair tied back in a club over her bulletproof vest. The thunderous, dark clouds that had been brooding on the horizon for several days had given way to rain. Fat raindrops splattered on the roof and released the stench of hot asphalt from the road. The men seemed more apprehensive and focused than usual. Matt was on his radio phone coordinating both teams and confirming the route.

Kit felt her pulse beating quickly in her throat; her mouth was dry. She wished she'd brought a bottle of water. Regardless, it felt good to be taking active steps toward catching the perpetrators, although at the same time she couldn't see any definitive link between Raco's group and the Staro Dorbi massacre. Matt thought that they might find evidence connecting the two. But based on Blaku's evidence alone, Kit was looking forward to seeing Raco taken into custody, along with that horrible Shala woman, who had written so much in her diary but apparently had not done anything to stop Blaku's abduction and assault.

Kit felt clear enough about her role during the search of Raco's house. She was to ensure that the evidence was collected properly, the chain of custody was established, and there was no contamination of the evidence. She had contacted the office the evening before to inform Eva that she was joining Task Force Capture this morning. Eva had seemed preoccupied on the phone, but she told Kit to go along with Matt and to report back to her as soon as possible. "Try not to get into trouble" was her final comment before she disconnected the call.

By the time they turned left up the hill to the Dragodan district, everyone on the team knew what they were supposed to do—or at least, they thought they did. The first car peeled off to keep watch on the lower street in case Raco fled in that direction. The other two, followed by the jeep, continued straight along the street toward his home.

The three vehicles pulled up outside a large, crouching gray house. It was modern in its way with a rounded-steel roof and had been architecturally designed for a politician who had fled Pristina. When Kit saw how huge and fortified the house was, she felt uneasy. The house seemed sinister and far from normal. The officers piled out the vehicles. Some checked their equipment while others looked toward Matt for guidance. Matt went to the front of the group and issued instructions in a harsh, low voice.

Kit stayed back, preferring to watch the men who were preparing to do the search. When movement caught her eye, she glanced up. A drape twitched. If that was Raco, they had lost the element of surprise. She looked at the row of cars parked on the street. Intelligence had indicated that there could be at least one other suspect with him. Would they submit quietly?

"Your first EUPOL search?" a voice behind her asked.

She turned and saw a tall man with a weather-beaten face and a friendly smile. His vest had K-9 unit written on it. Beside him sat the canine part of the unit, a large dog with pointed ears. The dog panted and watched with interest.

"May I?" Kit asked as she looked at the dog.

"Sure," he said with a nod. "He doesn't bite. Unless you happen to be a criminal."

She smiled and bent over to pet the dog's head and scruffle his velvety ears. He had a beautiful, rich mahogany-colored coat, with a black overlay.

"What's his name?"

"Max. He likes that," the officer said as Kit petted the dog.

"Is he a German shepherd?"

"No. Belgium Tervuren."

"Matt said that there could be dogs." Kit inclined her head toward the house.

"People often have them for security, so it's possible. Max is trained to find explosives, among other things. I do double-time as canine-unit leader and general dog handler. My name's Don, by the way. Don Edgson."

"I'm Kit," she said as she extended her hand. "That sounds like a Southern accent."

"You got that right. Dallas, Texas."

"I thought this was a European team."

"I'm on secondment from the US Military Police to help set up the canine units."

"Cool. I like dogs …" she said. "By the way, I think I saw movement at one of the windows. If we had the element of surprise, I think we've lost it."

"Let's see," Don said. "They're starting to move."

Matt nodded to Bravo Team, who fanned out around the house to secure the perimeter. They moved briskly in a semi-crouch. Then he nodded to the leader of Alpha Team, who walked up to the main door and knocked. "This is EUPOL. Dasham Raco, we have a warrant to search your house. Open the door."

Kit held her breath. It seemed that the world held its breath with her. There was an eerie silence, and even the raucous cries of the crows had stopped. Whether Matt had felt the shockwave, Kit wasn't sure.

"Down! Incoming!" he shouted. From the upstairs window where she had seen movement, a small object hurtled towards them. The officers scattered and moved back for cover. Was it a grenade? Kit braced for an explosion. It was a tear gas canister, which emitted acrid smoke that roiled poisonously and moved toward them.

"Tear gas!" Matt shouted.

Owen turned and ran back to the jeep to fetch gas masks for her and Matt. Kit took the mask and fumbled with it as she tried to put it on. She had never handled a gas mask before. She was surprised at the team's preparedness for such an attack. Don helped her fit it before he put on his own, then indicated that he was taking the dog away from the gas as he went back to the vehicle. Other officers scrambled for their own masks as another projectile spun from the window. They scattered as a third one flew through the air. This time they were smoke grenades, and a layer of dense smoke mixed with the tear gas and formed a toxic blend.

"We need to go in now before he escapes," Matt yelled.

Alpha Team sprang into action. The door burst open when one of the men smashed it with a heavy, black battering ram. Kit caught a glimpse of the lobby and a long hallway. Then another projectile was lobbed toward them. The Alpha Team scattered. This time it was a stun grenade. Kit felt a detonation, and a flash disoriented her. Don interposed himself between her and the house and walked her toward the vehicles. Her ears were ringing, although the gas mask had provided limited protection against the effects of the detonation.

"Go! Go! Go!" Matt yelled. She saw a blur of movement as black-clad figures stormed into the house. Mere moments later, she heard sporadic gunfire. As minutes passed, the smoke began to clear. The intermittent gunfire seemed to come from the depths of the house.

"That's our cue," Don said. "Max and I are going in." He opened the car door, and the Tervuren jumped out.

Kit followed and kept to the left of line of sight from the house. She felt she was moving in slow motion. Her feet in their tactical boots registered the uneven path leading to the house. Heavier raindrops were falling and combining with the toxic blend of tear gas, smoke, and gunpowder. She was uncomfortable in the restrictive gas mask and, encumbered by the Kevlar vest, she felt insulated, removed from the surreal scene. Sporadic gunfire continued in the rear of the house.

Kit eased through the door and peered down the dark passageway into the living room. EUFOR men were crouched low and exchanging gunfire with the two targets. Matt was giving instructions. They had not been expecting trouble but had come prepared for it. Seconds after Albanian voices started shouting, a stun grenade landed in the hallway. The chaos of light and deafening sound was followed by voices bellowing. It was then that a heavyset man in camouflage fatigues hurled himself at the large window with his forearm raised to protect his face. Glass shattered and gunfire spluttered from the remaining gunman's weapon. When Owen tackled him, the gunman fired. Owen cried out in pain and slumped forward onto his opponent. Matt and two of his men ran to assist Owen. As they lifted Owen off his assailant and laid him on the ground, other officers pinned the shooter to the ground and secured his hands in cuffs behind his back. A bullet had got under Owen's bulletproof vest. Blood was soaking into the carpet. Owen's face had turned gray, and sweat beads had broken out on his forehead.

Matt cursed under his breath as he punched in the code for emergency services. "Officer felled by gunshot. Send an emergency medical team immediately," he bellowed as he motioned to the remaining officers to pursue Raco.

Kit leapt forward. "I've got him until the medics arrive. You go." She stuffed a towel one of the men had found down the vest to staunch the blood flow spurting from Owen's chest while another man ran to the car to retrieve the first-aid kit.

"I've done emergency first aid for the field," Kit said when she saw the questioning look on Matt's face.

"I've got to get that bastard before he gets away," Matt said as sirens sounded in the distance. Matt sprinted toward the back door, heading for the section behind the house. Three officers went with him.

Raco braced for the impact as he burst through the pane of glass and landed on the grass below. Using his martial arts expertise, he rolled as smoothly as his bulky frame would allow. As soon as he was on his feet, he took an overgrown, slippery path to the left. The rain was even heavier now. He had planned this escape route weeks ago in case the law came to his front door. Although he hadn't planned his dramatic exit through the window, that had gained him valuable time but cost him a bloody gash on his right forearm. He couldn't feel pain yet; even so, he knew it would need stitches. As he swerved down the path, he opened his mobile and speed-dialed a number, sent a single digit, pocketed the phone, and continued down toward the next street. Raco spotted the unmarked police vehicle on the road below his house straightaway. *At least they had planned that far ahead.* He smiled grimly. *But not well enough.* Bent over double, he skirted across several properties to his right until he was out of sight.

The Dragodan Steps, the concrete staircase from the centre of Pristina, were at the top of the hill. He sent another code to the same phone number with a change of plans. The steps were broken and crumbling in parts, but he knew them well. He bounded down, three at a time. In his peripheral vision, four figures were gaining on him from the left. It had not taken them long to find him. One of the officers slipped and stumbled on the wet, uneven ground and hit it hard as Raco increased his pace. The heavy rain stung his face. Through the downpour, he could make out his nephew on a motorbike speeding along the main road at the bottom of the steps. The young man had obeyed his uncle's prearranged coded message about where to pick him up in an emergency. Sirens wailed in the distance as they came closer; the breaths of his pursuers were loud, or perhaps it was his own.

The motorcyclist skidded to a halt and revved his engine as Raco leapt onto the back. "Go!" he snarled. The motorbike took off and left Matt, who was soaked in rain and sweat, at the bottom of the steps. "Damn," he muttered. The motorbike had no number plate.

"The bastard got away." Matt was weary. Kit was standing next to Owen as the medics worked on him. They had taken off his vest and cut open his clothing. One was endeavouring to staunch the flow of blood from the wound while another had set up a mobile intravenous drip. "How is he?" Matt asked.

Kit shrugged and looked at Owen, her face creased with concern. "He doesn't look great, but he's in good hands."

Matt thumped the wooden doorframe hard, his face taut with anger. "If Team Charlie had done their job properly, we would have arrested Raco. I can't believe they let him slip through. I'm going to lodge an official complaint about Major Petri's incompetence."

The medics transferred Owen to a stretcher. "Let me give you something for the pain," one said to Owen, who grimaced, then nodded. The medic rolled up what was left of Owen's long-sleeved jersey and injected him using a syringe. Owen relaxed as the drug took effect.

"We stabilized him for now, but we need to get him to hospital right away," the young, male medic said as he looked at Matt.

"Where are you taking him?" Matt asked.

"To the nearest military clinic in Pristina. After the doctors have checked him out, we might need to take him to Camp Prizren for surgery. They're better equipped with a German-owned clinic and doctors. The bullet might have torn an artery."

Matt looked at Owen with worry. "Don't let me hold you up then. Reese, I want you back on the job as soon as possible. Do you understand, Sergeant?"

"Roger that, sir," Owen said weakly before he coughed. The medics exchanged glances. "One, two, three, lift," one said. They picked up the stretcher and headed to the military ambulance.

"At least we managed to arrest one suspect," Kit said. "Thanks to Owen."

"True," Matt said with a sigh. "It's a nightmare though. Owen is a good man, and he's taken a bad hit.

THE MISSING DIARY

Raco is out there armed and dangerous. I'm going to issue a lookout call for him."

"How did he escape?" Kit asked.

"He dodged Petri and his team. Someone on a motorcycle without a number plate picked him up. I'm sure he has places to hide until things cool down. To top it off, with the firefight outside, it's just a matter of time before the press show up." Matt ran a hand through his hair.

Kit heard the dog barking and whining nearby. Max was pawing and barking at the edge of a Turkish rug. "He's signaling," Don said.

"Alright," Matt, who was back in control again, said. "Alpha Team, secure the perimeter and put up crime-scene tape. Beta Team, let's search this place. Photograph the outside and the inside of the property before you search everywhere— outside and inside, including upstairs. Right, let's see what the canine unit's found. I hope Charlie Team hasn't lost the other suspect on their way back to the station."

Matt looked around the room for a moment. Ordinarily, he would have given instructions to Owen to follow up with Charlie Team and report to the base that Raco was on the run. He issued instructions to one of the other officers while Don pulled back the edge of the carpet and uncovered a trap door. Matt helped Don move the table and chairs away and pull the carpet back further. When the door was opened, it revealed a ladder leading into a dark cellar.

Don showed his approval by patting the dog on the back. Max barked. "Max thinks there's something of interest down there."

"Let's see what it is," Matt said as he pulled a small torch from his tactical vest. He clicked it on and cast a powerful beam of light into the darkness, flicking it as far as possible in all directions. "It seems clear. I'm going down." Matt scrambled to the floor, and once he'd gained a foothold on the ladder, he entered the cellar. At the bottom of the ladder, it took a moment for his eyes adjust to the darkness. Don came next. Max whined with excitement when he was lowered through the door. Kit and two men from Bravo Team followed. They peeled off their balaclavas in order to see better. The air was cool and damp as they stood on the beaten-earth floor and looked around. Kit smelt the musty odor of damp earth and mildew. On one side, light showed under a doorway which provided an external exit and emphasized the gloom that surrounded them. Max continued to whine. He was attracted to a particularly dark corner of the cellar.

Kit shivered and hoped that Max hadn't smelt a rat. The basement would be the perfect breeding ground for rats, although she was reminded that not even rats survived long on the streets of Pristina with its marauding packs of feral dogs and wild cats.

"I'm guessing explosives and weapons," Don said as he penetrated the darkness with his torch. A moment later, he found cases of ammunition and a rack of guns. "AK-47s, a couple of different machine guns, a grenade launcher, and probably boxes of anti-tank mines. I'm sure there are more arms and explosives under that tarp. Raco isn't known as Machine Gun for nothing."

"We'd better call in the EUFOR explosives experts straightaway. Take care. The place could be booby-trapped," Matt said.

Kit gasped.

"Don't worry," Don reassured her. "Just walk slowly backwards, exactly the way you came in." His Southern drawl sounded almost relaxing. She edged toward the ladder.

But Max continued to bark and whine, reluctant to join the team in its careful retreat. Don stopped and swept his torch beam into the far corner of the basement.

Kit heard a muffled sound as the torch beam focused on a figure huddled under a thin blanket.

"Someone's there," Don said.

Matt ignored his own instructions to be careful and approached the cowering figure.

Kit stood still. In spite of the chill of fear she felt in the pit of her stomach, a thread of sweat trickled down the middle of her back. "Who is it?" she whispered.

Matt dropped to one knee in front of the person. "We're EUFOR Police. Don't be afraid. We're going to get you out of here. I'm going to remove this blanket," he said. "Can one of you translate into Albanian?" he said as he turned toward the team.

While a local officer translated in Albanian, Matt slowly removed the blanket. The torch beam illuminated the huddled figure. It was a woman; her light-brown, curly hair was pressed against her head by the masking tape that gagged her mouth. Her eyes were bruised black and blue, and she had a jagged cut above one eyebrow. She had been badly beaten.

"I'm going to remove the gag," Matt said as he reached forward and removed the tape from her mouth.

Kit gasped with shock. Forgetting her own fear of tripping a booby trap, Kit rushed forward. Out the side pocket of her bag, she produced a small knife that she carried to meet whatever the day might bring, whether it was cutting fruit or opening or severing bindings. She cut through the duct tape that held the captive's hands behind her back.

"Help!" Vasha Blaku said in a shaky voice. "He's going to kill me."

Chapter Eleven

I loved my job as a police officer, but during the war, law & order broke down. Police work became useless. If I had to fight for justice at all costs, even at the expense of the law, it didn't matter to me. Maybe I made some mistakes, but I've got no regrets.

Merita's diary, 10 August 2000

Kit poured herself a generous glass of robust Stone Castle red wine from a winery in Rahovec, in Western Kosovo. What a day it had been. She sat down on the couch and put her wine glass and small bowl of almonds on the table in front of her. She exhaled a long breath. Right now she would love to be home in New Zealand; she began to reminisce about happy times in Auckland, meeting friends for coffee at fashionable cafes on the downtown pier where she gazed at high-tech yachts and their crews who had been attracted by the America's Cup. She had enjoyed the fresh, warm ocean breeze and jogging with Xander along the waterfront in the late afternoon before relishing a glass of chardonnay with him on the terrace at home. She missed the easy intimacy they enjoyed—a shared joke, super-fresh gourmet food, and falling into each other's arms after a busy day. Or shopping with her mother in quaint, upmarket Parnell Road with its cobbled alleyways, well-tended cottage gardens, and trendy restaurants situated in the beautifully restored colonial villas. Were those memories rose-tinted because of the warm Pacific sun that seemed more real than the gritty and dangerous world of crime fighting in Kosovo?

At that moment, as if on cue, her laptop notified her of a call on Skype. The patchy internet had just enough connectivity to have a conversation with New Zealand, even if it was prone to interruptions.

"Mum! Hi!" Kit said. Just the person she wanted to speak to. "How's it going?"

The video image of her mother appeared. Her salt-and-pepper hair with pink highlights looked freshly coiffured and framed her face. Rosalyn's hazel eyes sparkled and matched her diamond earrings. "Fine, dear. How are you? What's the time there?"

"Nine p.m. What time is it there?"

"Nine a.m."

Kit laughed. "What's up?" Kit took a sip of wine and noticed with amusement a similar gesture as her mother sipped her cappuccino.

"Nothing much," Rosalyn said. "I've hired a new assistant at the shop. She's Chinese and working out well. Linn is her name. She's helping me out a couple of mornings a week before her university lectures. She's giving me more *me time*."

"I see." Kit smiled. "I heard you've been going out for coffee dates."

"Who let the cat out the bag?" Rosalyn said with mock anger. "Xander told you, didn't he? Well, at my stage of life, dear, I'm entitled to have some fun, aren't I?"

"You are indeed. I want to hear more about this guy. I hope he's appropriate."

Rosalyn rolled her eyes. "The less appropriate, the more fun."

"Mother!" Kit raised her voice. "Mind you, I could do with a bit more fun here. You wouldn't believe what happened today."

"Tell me."

"I went with the EUFOR Police to search the home of a crim. What a disaster. It turned into a firefight. They had a cache of weapons, guns, grenades, tear gas …"

"Oh my God," Rosalyn gasped. "Are you alright? What about the police?"

"I'm fine, if a little shocked. Owen, one of the EUFOR guys, was wounded. He's a really nice guy from Wales. He's in intensive care. We arrested one of the suspects, but the main one got away. He was unstoppable. Rained hell down on us with all kinds of weapons before he jumped through a plateglass window and escaped. That's why I need a glass of wine."

"Oh my God" Rosalyn repeated in a louder voice. "That's terrible, darling! How's the wounded man?"

"He's not out of danger. I don't know the details though. I think he might end up at a good military hospital in a nearby town."

"You must be exhausted. I wish I could come to your place and cook you something nice. A good stew with some wine."

"I've got the wine in hand." Kit raised her glass.

"Listen, maybe you should come home. It sounds too dangerous there."

"I was never in danger," she said. On this occasion.

"Was that the end of it?"

"No, we found a trapdoor into the basement where there was an arsenal of weapons." She paused and took a deep breath.

"Go on," Rosalyn said.

"There was a hostage in the basement. A confidential informant. I'd been there when she was interviewed a couple of days ago."

"Was she okay?"

"Yeah, but she'd been roughed up quite badly. She's pretty scared. The suspect had been trying to find out how much she had told us."

"Why would she know anything?"

"I can't talk because of confidentiality, but she had overheard stuff."

"Did the suspect know her?"

"Yes, she'd been victimized by him."

"Do you think the police will catch him?"

"I don't know. It's a wild frontier out here. He's gone into hiding."

"Oh my goodness. It sounds terrible. I hope they find him and put him away for a long time."

"Me too. I'm concerned about the victim though. She's really afraid. She'd already asked for protection, but it wasn't forthcoming. Something similar happened last week too. Some farmers asked for protection and then …" Kit's words trailed away as she swallowed the lump in her throat. "Never mind. Anyway, the guy came after her, and it was lucky we got there when we did. If Max hadn't found that trapdoor, she would have been left down there, and I shudder to think what might have happened to her."

"Max? Who's Max?" Rosalyn asked. "A nice policeman?"

Kit smiled. "Max is a wonderful officer. He comes from Belgium."

"Belgium sounds exotic."

"He's a Belgian Tervuren."

"What's that?"

"A dog breed similar to a German shepherd."

Rosalyn chuckled. "You had me going for a moment there. Nothing like a man in uniform. Or, in this case, a dog in uniform."

They both laughed, which felt good until Kit became serious again. "Our witness really is at risk. Matt, the major who's heading the investigation, checked and the OIDC witness protection programme has run out of funds. Partly because the entire immediate family has to be relocated, not just one person. A threat to one family member can extend to others. I don't know what we can do. She's at a safe house at the moment, but she can't stay there."

"What's she like?"

"A lovely, spirited young woman who's very smart. She's a translator. But maybe she made some bad choices with men."

"What woman hasn't?" Rosalyn said before she took a sip of her cappuccino. "You know, my friend Charles used to support the witness protection programme in his last job."

"EUPOL has relocated several confidential witnesses to other countries in Europe, even as far afield as Canada. The problem is when they have to relocate whole families, there just isn't enough money."

"Does this woman have a large family?"

"No, she's single. She has a cousin she's close to. Not sure who else. Matt, the major, is from the UK. I'm sure he can check with London. Wouldn't it be great if they could relocate her to New Zealand?"

"That would be wonderful, darling. I think you should also relocate back to New Zealand, sooner rather than later. You must be careful!"

"I'm always careful, Mum." At least most of the time, she thought.

"Well," Rosalyn said. "I've got to go to my line dancing class now. I'm meeting Josh there, and after, we'll go for coffee."

"Is this your new beau? Did you meet him online?"

"Yes, with the Silver Service Dating Agency. They say we should be a good match."

"I want to hear more about him later, but I'd better let you go to your class."

"Thanks, dear. See you later. Take care." Rosalyn blew her a kiss and clicked off.

Kit sat back and smiled as she took another mouthful of wine. It seemed her mother had a more active social life than she did. She wished Xander would come over so they could explore the Balkans together. Kit sighed and opened the contact's list on her phone. Her eyes alighted on Sergei's details. Their conversation had been interesting the other night. His ideas about goal setting were fascinating and had really helped her. On impulse, she sent him a text. *Hi, Kit here. How are you?* Then she flushed with embarrassment and put the phone down as if it was too hot to handle. Why had she texted him? He might think she wanted more than coffee. After all, she had Xander back in New Zealand. But another part of her felt reckless. She was miles and miles from home; no one would know about Sergei unless she told them. Besides, they were just friends.

He replied three minutes later. *Good evening Katarina, I'm fine. How are you? Can I call you now?*

Sure, she replied. Why did he insist on calling her Katarina? It almost felt as if he wanted to Russianize her. Or perhaps her New Zealand name sounded strange to him. Anyway, it made a welcome change from the annoying *foxy lady* as Xander insisted on calling her.

Thirty seconds later, her phone rang. "Good evening, Katarina. Sergei here. I was just thinking about you when I got your message."

"Me too … obviously." Kit felt awkward but relieved that he couldn't see her scarlet face.

He laughed softly. "Remember that coffee we were talking about the other night?"

"What about it?"

"Let's make a time."

"Okay. Do you know Prizren?"

"Prizren? Yes. What are you thinking?"

"Well, I'd like to visit a colleague who's in hospital there in a couple of days. I'd love to see the town as well."

"Is he or she in the EUFOR military clinic there?"

"Yes, he is."

"Alright. Here's what I suggest. Why don't I pick you up on Saturday morning. I'll drop you off at the clinic and then we can meet say … an hour later and spend some time looking around the town."

"You don't want to come in?"

"No, I think it's better if you see your colleague alone so it's not too tiring for him. Anyway, I don't think they'd let me in. The camp only admits people from EU member states or OIDC employees like you."

"Alright, let's do it." She gave him her address, and they agreed to meet on Saturday morning at the base of her apartment.

Kit noticed that a message had just arrived from Eva, so she let Sergei go. She took a deep breath to clear her head before she opened the message.

Please come to the office 9 a.m. tomorrow. Meeting with mission head and VIPs. Don't be late. EVA.

Thanks, I'll be there CC, Kit replied. She didn't like the implication of *don't be late,* although she had to admit she had been out the office more than in it since she had arrived.

She leaned back and drew up her feet onto the couch to reflect on her evening so far. Owen had been stabilized and would be transferred to the medical clinic in Prizren for further assessment and treatment tomorrow, Thursday. She should be able to visit him on the weekend and then spend time with Sergei exploring Prizren.

On the table lay one of the few guidebooks she had been able to find in her mother's airport shop on southeastern Europe and the Balkans. It said that picturesque Prizren used to be the center of Turkish Ottoman rule in Kosovo, and it was graced with picturesque mosques and churches and overlooked by an eleventh-century fortress. Prizren sounded fascinating and exotic. She was also looking forward to continuing her conversation with Sergei about the Russian goal-setting system he called khash. She had always thought of Rasputin, its creator, as a sinister historical figure. He was a monk of sorts, who through his powers of persuasion, had gained undue influence over the Tzar's royal family in Russia. She hadn't read much more about him except that he had been difficult to kill. Apparently, he had succeeded at what he had put his mind to, but history had cast him as a dark shadow.

Once again a message interrupted Kit's thoughts; this time it was from Matt. *Interviewing suspect MS tomorrow p.m. Please join. Matt.* MS must mean Merita Shala. After all the drama at Raco's house, she had forgotten that the police had searched Shala's apartment for her diary and brought her in for questioning. Kit had a lot of questions for Matt, but they would have to wait until after the high-level discussions at OIDC headquarters tomorrow—and that raised even more questions.

Chapter Twelve

It's important for me to keep a record of our plans. It helps me to feel more grounded, and puts things in order. People depend on me for my notes.

Merita's diary, 13 August 2000

The next morning, Kit arrived at OIDC headquarters at eight forty-five a.m. Eva was in her office smoking a cigarette by the open window, while Bambino was having his breakfast beside her desk.

"Hi. How are you?" Angel was sitting at her desk behind a stack of papers that had grown ever higher since Kit had last seen it.

"Fine, thanks," Kit replied.

"What's new?"

Before Kit could answer, Eva stepped into the middle of the room and took another drag on her cigarette. "That's what I'd like to know," she said. "And so would the head of mission."

"Sure," Kit said.

"This is your chance to tell us both," Eva said. "Mueller has asked for a briefing at nine a.m., followed by a discussion about the recent massacre near Pristina with some of the key diplomatic players."

"What would you like me to tell him?"

"Well," Eva said as she blew cigarette smoke out the side of her mouth. Bambino sat down beside her, apparently satisfied after his breakfast. She reached down to pet the dog. "I suggest you make it as brief as possible. We need an overview of what happened. We've been getting enquiries from local news agencies about the massacre, as well as a disturbance yesterday involving international police in a firefight with a suspect."

"I can brief you," Kit said.

"Good," Eva said. "Let's go. Angel, would you mind taking Bambino out for a five-minute walk? He's finished his breakfast."

Angel got up and turned to pick up the small dog's leash. Bambino whined with excitement and pawed at Angel's leg.

Kit suppressed a smile. "I met a Belgian police dog yesterday called Max," she said.

"Perhaps we could set up a playdate for Bambino and Max," Eva said. "Bambino would benefit from socializing with other dogs."

Kit wasn't sure whether Eva was joking or not. "If I get a chance to talk to his handler again, I'll mention it." Talking about the dogs relieved some of the tension Kit felt.

The two lawyers climbed the wide, marble steps to the top level of the building where the head of mission had his office. Eva led the way to the room occupied by Brendan, Mueller's personal assistant.

"We have an appointment to see the boss," Eva said.

The young man at the desk looked up. "Right. Let me check if he's ready."

Moments later, he ushered them into the spacious office with windows overlooking Pristina. There were two large rubber plants on either side of the desk, while behind the desk was a dark-blue OIDC flag with the symbol of the organization on it—a large map of the world supported by two hands on either side. Arranged in a U-shape in front of the windows was a black leather sofa and three chairs. In the middle was a low table.

Mueller glanced up at them from behind his desk. He signed a document from a large pile of papers on his right and moved it to a smaller pile on his left. Without greeting them, he signed more documents. Kit shifted her weight from foot to foot, wondering if she should say something or sit down. But Eva had not moved, so she decided to follow her example. Eva caught her eye for a second and then went back to looking out the window. Kit felt as if she was standing in front of the headmaster at school and about to be punished for skipping classes. She guessed that was his intention and decided not to buy into it.

Finally, Mueller eased back his chair, stood up, and looked directly at the two women. "Please sit down," he said.

Kit and Eva took a seat on the couch, while Mueller sat opposite them in a high-backed leather chair.

"What can you tell me about the massacre at Staro Dorbi and the law enforcement at yesterday's incident?" he said without preamble as he looked directly at Kit.

Kit looked at his pinched face and watery, blue eyes. She could not shake the feeling that she was talking to her former headmaster.

"Er, well, sir," she said. "As Eva no doubt has already told you, I accompanied the military police inspector to the crime scene at Staro Dorbi." She paused and looked at her white-knuckled hands clasped in her lap. Suddenly the events of that night came back to her, and she felt embarrassed yet again by her lack of professionalism. She chewed her bottom lip.

"Ms. Chase was at the crime scene at my request to represent the Office of the Chief Prosecutor. She was instrumental in identifying potentially crucial evidence that could link one of the suspects to the atrocity. It's too soon to be sure, but it could be that the organized crime boss Dasham Raco was the ringleader at that multiple-murder scene. The DNA on a cigarette butt is being tested and compared to DNA lifted from Raco's house yesterday. Caitlin, could you please explain what we know about Raco," Eva said.

"Yes, ma'am," Kit said, relieved that Eva had glossed over the precise details of what had happened that night. "A confidential witness has identified Raco as a likely suspect involved in an organized crime group which is involved in gunrunning and murder for hire, among other crimes. When the police went to search Raco's home yesterday, they were met with armed resistance. One police officer was seriously wounded, and Raco escaped. He jumped through a plateglass window and escaped on the back of a motorbike. The confidential witness was being held hostage in the basement of Raco's house. At the same time, the house of another suspect was searched—a young woman by the name of Merita Shala. We understand from the confidential witness that Shala kept a personal diary detailing many of the criminal activities of the group." Kit paused and took a breath as she looked first at Eva and then at the head of mission.

"Did they find the diary?" Mueller asked.

"I'm not sure. I'll find out this afternoon. The head of investigation, Major Hackman, has invited me to attend the questioning of Shala."

"Let me know as soon as you find out more."

"Certainly, sir."

"Are there any further leads?"

"Not to my knowledge. Ballistics is examining the bullets and shells found at the crime scene, and investigators are examining the autopsy reports and interviewing possible witnesses in the area."

"What makes Major Hackman think there is a connection between the massacre and Raco?"

"Something that the confidential witness said. It's not been confirmed that Raco was involved but he's certainly guilty of serious crimes, including sexual assault."

Mueller stared at Kit for a moment. She felt sure that he remembered her from her ill-timed interruption at the conference, but he didn't mention it. At that moment, she was grateful for his Germanic reserve.

"What would you like us to do at the next meeting, sir?"

"I've invited several important representatives to meet with me this morning. I'd like to discuss cooperation and coordination on the investigation into this serious crime—the massacre at Staro Dorbi. The Serbian community has major security concerns. They blame EUFOR and this organization for not providing sufficient protection. We need to show that the matter is being taken seriously and is being properly addressed by the authorities. There could be liability issues for the organization as well as repetitional issues."

THE MISSING DIARY

"I understand," Eva said.

"At the meeting, don't speak unless you're spoken to," Mueller said. "I would like you there to answer questions, if that's necessary. Ms. Chase should take notes." Maybe he wanted to make it clear that she should keep quiet after her inappropriate remarks at that conference.

"Yes, sir. May I ask who's coming?"

"US Ambassador Frank Stanton, Serbian representative Miloš Mandić, Kosovar Albanian member of parliament Visar Dreshaj, and I have also asked a representative of the Pristina Russian office, Sergei Sokolov, to be present."

"That should be interesting," Eva said.

"If this organization and EUFOR cannot be seen to keep the peace, it undermines our whole position in Kosovo and the future of the mission."

Kit unzipped her bag and took out her notebook to jot down names and details of the meeting. She let her hair fall around her face, hoping that no one could see that she was blushing at the mention of Sergei Sokolov. She hoped that he would not say anything which might compromise her professional profile by suggesting they had a personal relationship. She decided it was time to cultivate a poker face. There had been an intimacy in their encounters that she did not feel ready to share with her superiors, or anyone else for that matter.

Just then there was a discrete knock on the door. Brendan pushed open the door. "Sir, your guests are here if you're ready."

"All of them?"

"Yes, sir. We have the US ambassador, a gentleman from the Russian office, the Serbian representative, and the Kosovar-Albanian representative."

Mueller got up and walked through the door. Kit and Eva glanced at each other and followed.

"They're in conference room one, sir," Brandon said.

The group made their way toward a well-appointed meeting room with chairs arranged around a large, rectangular table. The men around it were wearing dark business suits, shirts, and ties. The OIDC flag was displayed prominently on the wall behind the head of the table. When Mueller entered the room, they stood up, and one by one, he shook their hands. Eva and Kit waited until Mueller had taken his seat at the head of the table. Eva sat down on his left, and Kit positioned herself behind Eva on the second row of chairs around the room's perimeter.

From this position, Kit could study the men around the table. She recognized them from the conference on her first day, but could see them better at close quarters now. Solid, tending toward overweight, Ambassador Frank Stanton was a tall man in his late fifties, with salt-and-pepper hair falling to one side of his face. Sporting a trimmed beard and a bow tie, he exuded informality and bonhomie that would help him to get along with people of different nationalities and persuasions. Serbian representative Miloš Mandić was well-groomed and smooth-shaven, his graying hair was neat, and he wore a well-cut business suit. His open, appealing face took on a more solemn look when he glanced at his Kosovo counterpart across the table. Known as one of the more moderate Serbs who was not averse to occasionally coming to Pristina from Northern Mitrovica, Mandić took the opportunity to lobby players in the international community when he got the chance. Local sources had linked him with war crimes against the Kosovo civilian population shortly after the war officially ended, but nothing had been proven. Visar Dreshaj was a younger man with short, disheveled, dark-brown hair. His alert face had an almost impish look, Kit thought, or would have had if it had not been cast into a look of distain at the sight of the Serbian representative across the table. He was shorter than the other two but appeared fitter, or at least he carried less weight. A former academic and KLA commander, he had returned to politics in Pristina, as had many former KLA leaders.

Then there was Sergei. Kit's breath caught short when she turned to him. He was jotting notes on a Kremlin writing pad with a fountain pen, and he looked younger and more at ease than the other men. He seemed comfortable with himself and the situation and lounged in his chair with his legs stretched out. When his amber eyes met hers, she looked away, pretending she was preoccupied with her own notes. A memory of the delicious chocolate-glazed marshmallow dessert that they had shared at his residence returned to her unbidden.

Mueller welcomed the guests and thanked them for coming to what he hoped would be a constructive exchange of views. Kit noted that Mueller, who had been so superior and taciturn in his office a moment ago, was now beaming at the visitors as if cajoling them into a fascinating discussion of the greatest interest. He spoke excellent English with only a slight Germanic accent. She could see how he had made such rapid progress in diplomatic circles, where courteous niceties often counted more than substance.

An attractive, young Kosovar woman who couldn't have been much older than twenty-one, with long, braided, chestnut hair and large, brown eyes appeared at the door and asked who would like coffee. Eva ordered her usual single espresso; Mueller ordered a black tea with lemon. Kit was very aware of Sergei's presence in the room but did not look at him. While the assistant took the coffee orders, Mueller informed the men that Eva and Kit were lawyers from the Cef Prosecutor's Office, in case there were any questions about the ongoing investigations.

"I thought it would be useful if interested representatives could join us to discuss the dreadful events at Staro Dorbi. Whatever our positions may be on other matters, we can unite in condemning this atrocity unequivocally," Mueller said.

The US Ambassador nodded, while the others seemed to be waiting for Mueller to come to the point. "I think it would be appropriate if we could agree a statement to that effect should be issued under this mission. It should condemn the attack, emphasize the importance of the rule of law, and assure the public that authorities from all communities will cooperate fully in finding the perpetrators."

Frank Stanton spoke first; his American accent was sonorous. "Thank you, Jacob, for this initiative. My government considers it to be of the highest importance that the perpetrators are found as soon as possible, and both the Kosovo and Serbian sides need to show their commitment to effective law-enforcement action. Anything we can do to help—my government's resources stand ready, including the FBI and the CIA if appropriate to assist."

Mueller nodded toward Eva. "We will certainly take a note of that and pass on the offer to the experts in EURPOL," Mueller replied.

Visar Dreshaj picked up a cigarette box from the table. "May I?" he asked and lit up. Kit noticed that Eva was restless and thought that she would also like to enjoy a cigarette with her coffee. "At this stage we do not have any suspects, but be assured that we are taking all steps possible to further the investigation in cooperation with our EUFOR colleagues," Dreshaj said.

"Belgrade is very concerned that so little has been done and that there are no significant leads. We are not at all persuaded that the Kosovar authorities are willing or able to investigate the killing of these defenseless Serb farmers. I would strongly suggest that the investigation be turned over to Serbian Police authorities. They should be given the powers to properly investigate and prosecute the matter in Kosovo. This crime scene is dangerously close to one of our most precious Orthodox monasteries, Serbia's cultural heritage in Kosovo. We cannot let this threat go unanswered," Mandić said.

Dreshaj took another drag on his cigarette and leaned back in the chair as he looked at Mandić with obvious loathing. "I need hardly dignify that statement with an answer, but that is never going to happen. Serbia does not exercise law-enforcement jurisdiction in Kosovo anymore. These sites are Kosovo's cultural heritage now."

Mueller turned to Sergei and interrupted the growing confrontation. "You are quiet, Mr. Sokolov. Do you have anything to add from the Russian side?"

Sergei glanced around the table. "Gentlemen and ladies," he said and nodded toward Eva and Kit. "As you are aware, Russia fully supports Serbia's position in this regard. If, as seems likely, Kosovo cannot or will not bring these criminals to justice, Moscow is ready to provide forensic and other support to Serbian investigators and law-enforcement agents should the need arise."

"Will information be exchanged between Serbian and Kosovo authorities about the investigation?" Mueller said. "The fullest information possible to benefit to both parties."

Dreshaj shrugged as he tapped ash into the ashtray.

Kit interpreted the gesture as a grudging acceptance, or at least acquiescence to the proposal. What would happen in reality would be a different matter.

"I think we have a situation here that harms both sides," Mueller said. "Surely it's in the interest of Kosovo to show that it can conduct an effective investigation into this heinous crime. It's certainly in the interests of the Serbian community to have normality restored as soon as possible and to know that the perpetrators are safely behind bars."

When no one commented further, Mueller turned to Eva and asked her if she had anything to report about the investigation.

"I have been informed the EUFOR Military Police Investigation Unit has active enquiries underway. It's only a matter of time before they find the perpetrators," Eva said.

"We saw on the news that there was a firefight yesterday and a suspect escaped," Mandić said. "Was that related to the investigation? How was it that one man was able to elude several police units? It almost leads one to question the commitment to catch these terrorists."

Eva did not answer immediately, and Kit shuffled in her seat. She leaned forward and touched Eva on the arm as she looked at her with a silent question. Eva nodded. "While it's true that one suspect escaped, another was arrested and is being questioned. In addition, the home of yet another suspect was successfully searched and she will also be questioned. There's little doubt that these lines of enquiry will bear fruit, whether about this particular crime or others," Kit said.

"What other crimes?" Mandić asked in an aggressive tone.

Kit took a breath and was about to reply when Eva jumped in. "That's not clear yet. The police are assessing the evidence, and the results will be shared in due course."

Kit sat back. She had the feeling that Eva did not want her to explain too much, and at least on this occasion, she was pleased to let her chief take the lead.

Visar Dreshaj checked his watch. "If that's all, Jacob, I have to be on my way," he said. "I have a meeting with the prime minister in twenty minutes."

"I must insist that Kosovo and EUFOR Police share any information that they find with Serbian authorities," Mandić said.

Mueller nodded, his thin face taut with resolution. "We need to issue a joint statement—something along these lines. Keep everyone happy, including headquarters in Berlin."

Kit knew that OIDC European headquarters were in Berlin.

"I have no objection," Dreshaj said, "if it means I get to my appointment with the prime minister on time." He pointedly stubbed out his cigarette in the ashtray.

"Good," Mueller said. "I'll have my people prepare something and send it to your office if that's acceptable to everyone."

"It's a step in the right direction as long as there's proper follow-up," Mandić said.

"I'll run it past my people," Stanton said. He had jotted down a few notes in his leather bound note book, which he now snapped shut decisively.

"It seems we agree," Mueller said. "If there are no objections, we'll proceed on this basis." He glanced at Sergei, who continued to make notes. "I take it that there are no objections from the Russian side."

"We reserve our position at this stage," Sergei said.

"That sounds like no objections to me." Stanton hit his palms on the table in a mock indication that the meeting was coming to a conclusion.

"Thank you very much for coming, gentlemen. I appreciate the spirit of cooperation in which we have met today. Our legal team will prepare the draft press release and send a copy to you all as soon as possible," Mueller said.

They stood up, and Mueller shook each man's hand. Eva let all of them go before she left the conference room with Kit trailing behind her.

"This is the first time I've ever been asked to draft a press release," Kit muttered under her breath. "I don't think this is appropriate use of the resources of the Chief Prosecutor's Office. And he was rude to us before the meeting started."

"You and me both," Eva said, "but we need to keep in his good books, and at least that way we're in the loop. We can control the spin on the story better if we write it ourselves. Let him think that he's lording it over us."

"There is that," Kit said, smiling. If Mueller had her drafting memos that should be prepared by someone with half her qualifications and experience, then he wasn't planning to fire her for any of her recent slipups—yet.

"What do you think of Sergei Sokolov?" Kit said casually.

"The boy seems to be more or less okay—FSB, of course, a successor to the KGB. It's more his handlers that I'm concerned about."

"What do you mean?"

"Well, the Russians are the chess masters, and one never quite knows what their long game is. Did you notice how he spoke last and reserved his position?"

"Yes, I did. But he was clear in his support of Serbia," Kit said. She wanted to ask even more about these handlers, but she didn't want to seem unduly interested in Sergei. She would save those questions for later.

"That's nothing new. Ever since the US and its European allies pushed through the United Nations Security Council resolution, Russia insists on preserving Kosovo's status as a territory, not a state, and protecting Serbia's claims on Kosovo."

"Do you think that's going to change?

"Not any time soon, if you ask me," Eva said.

"In the meantime, we're busy drafting press releases. I would have thought the information service should do that."

"Don't worry about it," Eva said. "At least we're in the thick of things."

"Or at the cutting edge," Kit said.

CHAPTER THIRTEEN

These internationals think they can play us for fools, but it's them who are transparent with their childish schemes. They think they can control everything, but they understand nothing. Nothing about the people and what they've suffered, and what it means to be committed to a cause.

Merita's diary, 15 August 2000

Kit was late for the team debrief at the main police building. She slipped in the door and sat toward the back of the room. She arrived just in time to witness a bitter argument between Major Gregor Petri and Matt Hackman. Recriminations were exchanged regarding the escape of Raco.

"I told you not to blame me if things went wrong," said Petri, who was stretched out insolently on his chair, with his arms and legs crossed.

"Things went wrong because of your incompetence," Matt said. "You were instructed to detain Raco if he fled. Somehow he managed to elude your whole team."

"If your teams had managed the entry to the premises properly, you could have successfully detained both suspects and avoided the exchange of fire and explosions that attracted so much local media," Petri said with a sneer.

"It strains credibility that you were unable to intercept a single man running from his own house. A man who jumped onto a motorcycle and drove away. Did you make any effort at all to stop him?"

"My team had all the exits covered. Their attention was taken by the wide range of explosions and other pyrotechnic displays taking place at the search site."

"Did you make any statements to the media?"

"In the interests of transparency with the local community, one of my liaison officers may have provided some information."

"Thanks to your indiscretion, the story has been plastered across the local newspapers and media."

"I don't think any indiscretion on my part was needed. Because of the fireworks, the locals were able to pinpoint the crime scene."

"I find your attitude completely unacceptable, Major Petri. I intend to submit my full report to central command. I am sure that EUFOR Command will take a very dim view of your lack of coordination and insubordination."

Petri shrugged and smirked, then turned to look at his Romanian colleague sitting behind him. "Do what you need to, Major Hackman. I've already submitted my report."

"As of now, you are off Task Force Capture," Matt said.

"I don't think so. This task force was put together at a higher level up the chain of command, and you don't have the authority to remove the Romanian contingent."

"We'll see about that."

There was a stony silence for a few moments.

Matt picked up one of the files and started leafing through reports on evidence and photographs from the crime scene. "I'm not continuing with the briefing until you leave, Major Petri," Matt said at length.

"I don't want to delay you any further," Petri said as he gathered up his documents and placed them in a folder with exaggerated slowness. "We'll see what the commander has to say about all this. I doubt whether he'll be very impressed. He might even make changes to the command of Task Force Capture." He tapped the documents noisily on the table before putting them away. He nodded to his two lieutenants sitting behind him and wandered to the door. "Enjoy the rest of your day, Major," Petri said and was gone.

Matt took a moment to arrange his own documents. He was clearly flushed and angry from the exchange.

Kit wondered if she should say something to try to get the meeting back on track. After hesitating for a moment, she tentatively lifted her hand. "I have a question, Major, if I may," she said. She was, after all, a full member of the task force and was as entitled to speak as anyone else, although at the same time she felt it was something of a boy's club.

Matt looked up at her, anger and vexation stamped across his face. "Yes, Ms. Chase."

"Sorry I'm late," she said. "I've just come from a meeting with the head of mission. There was a briefing for the political side of things, and this operation was discussed briefly. Anyway, my question is, what happened during the search of the other suspect's apartment? And also, have you had any news about Sergeant Reese's condition?"

The Missing Diary

"To answer your second question first, Sergeant Reese is comfortable and doing as well as expected in the circumstances. He has a serious injury, but he is stable. As to your first question, I was about to ask the team leader who searched Shala's residence for his report."

A Finnish officer put up his hand and pointed to a report sitting on the table. He was clean-shaven with his fair hair cut in a short crew cut. "Yes, sir," he said in his clipped Finnish accent. "We searched Shala's residence, and we found a brown, hardcover notebook containing diary entries written in Albanian. We have taken it as evidence, and we're currently obtaining a translation."

"Get that done as quickly as possible. And for goodness' sake, keep that notebook away from Petri," Matt said.

"Yes, sir. We'll do our best, er . . ." The officer seemed embarrassed by the reference to keeping information from Major Petri. "We should have a translation ready in a couple of days. We also seized Shala's cell phone and personal records. We found two pistols, ammunition, and a knife."

"I assume you took the weapons as evidence," Matt said.

"Yes, sir, and the ammunition and one or two other items. I'll provide you with a full list of the schedule of evidence."

"Good. We can take DNA swabs for future reference and compare the ammunition with the ballistics reports from the crime scene. I can tell you that we found a considerable number of items of interest at Raco's residence. He had a medium-sized arsenal there. In addition, we freed a hostage, who was our confidential informant."

"Where is she now?" Kit asked.

"She's in witness protection at a safe location," Matt replied.

Kit had more to say about this, but she sensed that this was not the time or the place to discuss the matter in any detail with Matt. He was standing there alone without Owen to back him up and upset by the confrontation with Petri. She had to admit that the search had not gone well with the escape of their prime suspect. Fortunately, the news media had not yet learned all the details, such as the fact that Blaku had been held hostage. She would tell him later about the offers of assistance from both the American and Russian sides. Something told her that he would not be particularly pleased about the offers, which suggested they thought the investigation was not being handled well. If national police forces were difficult places to work, then international ones would be even more so with so many different nationalities and practises. In addition, the political dimensions of the post-conflict environment added even more complications.

"Well, gentlemen," Matt said. "Please continue with your interviews and enquiries including door-to-door visits to neighbors at Staro Dorbi. See whether anyone can provide information about who was seen at the farm that night, or anything else of relevance. If necessary, we can obtain search warrants to search premises if they seem to be hiding something or there could be a weapon's cache."

"They all have weapons," an officer with a Scot's accent said.

Matt sighed. "True," he said. "Use your discretion. That's all. I want us to meet every morning at eight a.m.

to report any progress or new information. All leave is cancelled for the next two weeks."

The men looked at each other. There was some rolling of eyes, but they all got up and left. Kit got to her feet and waited for Matt by the door.

"You didn't mention that we have Shala in custody," she said.

"I told them earlier, but you didn't hear because you were late," Matt said.

"As I said, I was at OIDC headquarters with our head of mission, the American ambassador, the Kosovo and Serbian representatives, as well as the guy from the Russian office. I couldn't get away any sooner."

"I want to hear about that later. I've been to see Owen. They've made him comfortable, but he'll probably be out of action for at least a couple of weeks."

"Thank goodness he's okay," Kit said. "Do you think it's all right if I visit him?"

"New Zealand isn't a member of the EU, so I'm not sure whether they'll give you access to the base. Do you have any other nationalities?"

"Yes, Irish."

"Good. Take your Irish passport and your OIDC ID. I'll send a message to let them know when you're coming. I think Owen's going to get bored. I'll give you some reports for him to read. If he's up to it."

"Sure. Why should he need rest? He's only got a life-threatening injury," Kit said with irony.

Matt smiled. "Come on. Let's see what Shala has to say for herself."

Kit and Matt left the meeting room and made their way down the corridor to the elevator. Matt pressed the call button. The elevator was an old, cage-like structure. They took the lift down to the floor where Shala was being held.

"Do you think there'll be anything useful in the diary?" Kit asked.

"I have no idea," Matt said. "I'm hoping the preliminary translation will be available tomorrow afternoon."

"Blaku seemed convinced that it documented Raco's criminal activities."

"It might not prove anything by itself, but it could provide useful lines of enquiry."

"I agree," Kit said as the elevator shuddered to a stop on the second floor. "Have you had a chance to talk to Shala yet?"

"Not yet. It's times like this I miss Owen. I'll have to get one of the other sergeants to take down the statement. Before we go in, what happened at the meeting at OIDC today? What did they say about the investigation?"

"No one seemed happy. Although everyone offered help with the investigation, especially the Americans and the Russians. I had the feeling that Visar Dreshaj wished that they would all go to hell and let you and the Kosovo Police get on with the job."

Matt had his hand on the door handle but still didn't open it. "And what did Mueller say?"

"He wants to issue a media release saying that both sides agreed to exchange information regarding the investigation and how important cooperation in the rule of law is in Kosovo. You know, the usual thing."

"And what about Raco's escape?"

"The Serbian representative said that was a sign of incompetence and that their help is necessary and, in fact, they should do the investigation themselves. He was hinting that the Kosovo Albanians have no interest in finding the killers."

"I hope you reassured him that we were doing our best," Matt said.

"Yeah, I did, and I reminded them that we have two suspects in custody and a lot of evidence to sort through."

"No news on Raco, though," Matt said.

"That guy is scary. I wouldn't want to meet him alone in the dark alley," Kit said.

"I'm sure many would agree with you."

Matt entered the room first and sat down at the table facing the young, dark-haired woman. One of the police sergeants was already there with his notebook out. Kit sat down beside Matt.

Shala's lips were full, almost too full for her face, while her eyes were large, dark-hazel pools that spoke of fear and defiance in equal parts. She sat sullenly with her arms crossed.

Matt introduced them all and explained that Shala had been linked to Raco and his gang. He said that he wanted to talk to her about what happened on the day of the massacre, as well as about events at Raco's house a couple of weeks before that.

"Thanks for coming in," Matt said.

Shala sat impassively. "You didn't give me much choice," she said. Her English was good, if heavily accented.

"I understand that you can you give us information about Raco and his group."

"Who said that?" Shala asked.

"Doesn't matter. We have it on good authority that you've been frequenting Dasham Raco's house."

"What if I have? That's not a crime as far as I know."

Matt raised his eyebrows. "That remains to be determined," Matt replied. "You've been seen there on several occasions when Raco was discussing criminal activities."

Shala shrugged. "Why did you search my apartment? Who gave you the authority to do that? Am I being charged with a crime?"

"I'll ask the questions."

"And I don't have to answer them," she said. "I know police procedures well. I was in the police myself until recently."

"Where was that?" Matt asked. He was keen to keep her talking since she had offered some information, even though he already knew the answer.

"I was with the police in Ferezaj before the war. After that it was impossible to continue."

"What did you do when you couldn't continue to serve as a police officer?"

"I was a liaison officer with the Kosovo Liberation Army."

"And what did that work entail?"

"Just coordinating with different people," she said and shrugged.

"Was Raco one of those people?"

Shala maintained eye contact with Matt before replying that he might've been.

"When was the last time you saw him?"

"I can't remember," she said.

"Was it within the last week, the last month, or the last year?"

The Missing Diary

"I guess it could have been within the last year," she said.

"It's come to my attention that you keep a diary or a journal. Is that correct?"

For the first time, Shala showed surprise; her eye brows lifted momentarily until she quickly recovered her poker face. "Maybe," she said.

"What do you write in the diary?"

"Not much. Just random thoughts and fantasies. I want to write a book someday, so I record my imaginings."

"What sort of imaginings?"

"You tell me," Shala said.

Matt looked exasperated and tapped his pen on the table. He sat back and took a deep breath. "Maybe we should leave you in the cells for a while and see if you're more talkative after that."

"If you're not going to charge me, Major Hackman, I think I'd like to leave now," she said by way of interruption.

Matt's day had been difficult, and it wasn't getting any easier. "Ms. Chase, are there any questions you would like to ask Ms. Shala?"

Kit started with surprise. Matt had not asked her to actively participate in interviews before. Perhaps it was because Owen was missing. So far, the interrogation was a failure. She decided to go in hard and try to break Shala's composure, to force admissions out of her.

"Certainly, Major," Kit said. "We have reason to believe that you have been engaged in a criminal conspiracy with Raco and his associates. What do you have to say to that?"

"Who are you?" Shala said.

"As I have already said, this is Ms. Chase from the prosecution office. She's assisting us. Ms. Chase, please proceed," Matt said.

Kit and Shala locked glances. "That's for you to prove if you think that is the case. I deny any wrongdoing," Shala said and shrugged.

"I put it to you that you have conspired with Raco on a number of crimes and you have recorded the details of these in your diary. That's correct, isn't it?"

"As I said, I have literary ambitions and I merely record my fantasies."

"We'll see what fantasies you've recorded," Kit said.

"That was an illegal search without proper cause," Shala said. "Nothing that you have taken illegally can be used as evidence in a court of law." She glared at Kit.

"We'll see what the diary says. It's being translated as we speak," Kit said.

"You do as you wish," Shala said with a sneer. "You don't have anything on me or anyone else. I'll deal with any threats."

"What does that mean?" Matt asked.

Shala shrugged. "We'll see." She turned to Kit. "You're with Eva Refazo's office, aren't you?"

Kit refrained from answering.

"That's on Agani Street. I saw you going in there. Your apartment is close by so you can walk to work."

Kit felt cold in the pit of her stomach. It seemed that Shala had been observing her, or one of their confederates.

"You must let me go, Major, unless you're charging me with more than just hearsay and accusations." Shala grimaced and exposed her pointed teeth. "Listen to me. You don't have anything on me or you would've already arrested me."

When Shala stood up, Kit took in her slim, athletic build. The fact that she was short was of no consequence. She wore a black sweater over khaki pants, which gave her a semi-military appearance.

"You're wasting your time, both of you," Shala said. "I've done nothing wrong. We've done nothing wrong. Stop meddling in things that you don't understand." She walked toward the door and opened it. "I hope you enjoy my literary efforts. Show me the transcripts of my so-called diary when they are available. Meanwhile, you'll be hearing from my lawyer. I'll get back everything of mine that you've confiscated and bring a claim for false arrest. The local news media will be interested to hear about the nonsense that EUFOR and the prosecutors are up to these days." With that, she marched out the room and slammed the door behind her.

Kit and Matt sat in stunned silence for a moment. "Make sure she leaves through the proper exit," Matt said to the young officer.

"Our good-cop-bad-cop routine didn't get us far," Kit said.

"It doesn't matter," Matt said. "We'll return her mobile and get an interception warrant to see who she talks to and what she does next. I want her under surveillance. I see the game she's playing about the diary, but it could contain information to point us in the right direction."

"I can't wait to see what's in that diary."

CHAPTER FOURTEEN

My motto is fight fire with fire. If the Serbs are bad, we must be even worse in self-defense. We need to keep our guns until the homeland is safe. Both men and women need to be ready to fight. Bring on the blaze.

Merita's diary, 20 August 2000

On Saturday morning, Sergei collected Kit from outside her apartment. It was a gorgeous day with a hint of autumn in the air. Sergei was driving the office Audi. Kit wore white capri jeans and a white linen top with a camisole underneath. She carried a woven tote that she had picked up in Bangkok on the way to Europe. Her concession to fashion was a sparkly clip on one side of her hair. She wore white lace-up sneakers with a raised sole. On impulse, she had decided to wear the greenstone pendant that her mother had given her on the day she left New Zealand.

Before she went to meet Sergei, she looked at herself in the mirror and placed her hand over her heart. The claddagh ring glinted dull gold on her right hand. She took it off and reversed the direction so that the heart faced outward, rather than inward, to indicate her emotional availability. She sighed. She wished that her heart only belonged to Xander. She didn't want to fall in love with anyone else and knew that it was unwise to continue to see Sergei alone. He was clearly playing a deceptive game with her and had his own agenda, which she didn't—couldn't—understand. But at the same time, she had never felt the way she did when she was with him, as if she was on the edge of something big. An edge that made her dizzy and too excited not to take the next step closer to the brink. She hadn't told anyone from the office about her plans to see Sergei. When Angel had asked what she was doing for the weekend, she was vague and said she was thinking about shopping for stuff for her new apartment. His company was a guilty pleasure—one she couldn't resist—but she didn't want to admit that to anyone.

Sergei was wearing blue jeans with a freshly laundered white cotton shirt. He grinned as he opened the car door for her.

"How are you today, Katarina?" he asked.

"Very well, thank you," she said. "Perhaps I should call you Steve, the New Zealand version of Sergei, since you insist on calling me Katarina when my name is Caitlin." She spoke in an argumentative tone, but her voice was pitched too high to be relaxed and she felt jittery.

"Don't you like it?" he asked.

"I do actually," she replied. "That's why it disturbs me."

He chuckled as he pulled into the traffic, and he drove them toward the main road leading from Pristina to Prizren.

"It's a good thing. To feel disturbed, I mean. It shows that your habitual perspectives are being challenged," he said. "If you like, we could continue our discussion about khash. As I'll explain, it can be a good thing to keep people off center, or as you put it, disturbed."

"I've thought quite a bit about what we discussed last time we met. I find it fascinating—and yes, a little disturbing." She laughed. It felt good to indulge in lighthearted banter and intellectual discussions with Sergei; a welcome relief from crime-scene investigations. Although it was more the proximity to him that made her feel agitated rather than his offbeat philosophical ideas.

"I suppose you're referring to our discussion over dinner the other night, not our discussion at your mission headquarters," he said.

"Yes, although those work-related discussions were also interesting, don't you think?"

Sergei indicated and pulled out smoothly into the outside lane to overtake a slower moving vehicle. "I'd like to hear what you think," he said. "Are you finding your work in Kosovo interesting?"

Kit looked at the passing scenery. A number of the ramshackle buildings were in the process of being rebuilt, while others were still in ruins or disrepair. Even so, the fine day made her feel optimistic.

"Yes, Kosovo is a fascinating place to work. Sometimes too fascinating."

He looked at her quizzically. "How can something be too fascinating?"

Kit shrugged. "Let's not talk about work. What can you tell me about Prizren?"

"I think you'll like it; it's more picturesque than Pristina. Prizren is the second biggest city in Kosovo, and it's more historic than Pristina. It used to be the center of the Ottoman ruled region of Kosovo. There's a beautiful Orthodox church and monastery which we can visit. There are more mosques per square kilometer there than in most places. The Serbian Orthodox Church was converted into a mosque during the Ottoman Empire and then back into a church again. Maybe we can visit one of my friends there, Father Peter, if he has time."

"I'd love to, although I know very little about the Orthodox church. In New Zealand, we have mainly Catholics and Protestants."

"I think you'll like it. We have beautiful icons and stained glass windows. Cultural heritage is very important to Serbia and Russia, plus in Prizren they make beautiful silver-filigree jewelry. A small river runs through the town, which adds to the atmosphere. Overlooking Prizren is an old Ottoman fortress we could walk to."

"That sounds wonderful. I haven't had a break from work since coming to Pristina."

"If you're working too hard, then I can find a way to distract you."

Kit laughed. She stretched out and enjoyed the drive as she watched the scenery unfold around her. As they approached the mountains, clouds were gathering around their summits. Sunlight shone through the layers of clouds and struck the mountain crags and forests below.

Sergei slowed down as they entered the town and drove slowly along the cobbled street which lined the river flowing through the centre before he pulled into a parking space below a steep cliff. He suggested that they walk to the top of the old Ottoman Castle, which overlooked Prizren, to get a good view of the place, and then once they'd worked up an appetite, they could have coffee or an early lunch. Kit readily agreed, and they set off along the rocky path leading up the hill. Kit was pleased she had worn practical shoes. She hadn't kept up with her fitness as she did in Auckland, where she trained and jogged regularly along the waterfront. As she gazed out over the impressive view, she was out of breath.

"The fort was built to guard the approaches to Prizren by the Ottomans," Sergei said as he took her arm to steady her when she momentarily lost her balance. "The climb is a little steep, but worth it."

"Can you take some photos of me so I can send them back to New Zealand?" Kit asked.

"Sure," Sergei said as he put out his hand to take her mobile.

She took a moment to catch her breath and then posed with the impressive view behind her. When they reached the top, the remains of stone battlements and colonnades caught her attention. The air was much fresher as she looked down upon the river sliding slickly like a ribbon through the town. Toward the other direction were untamed, green hills, which led to a mountain pass.

"It occurs to me that Prizren is a place of vision. I always feel that I get a new perspective when I'm here. Perhaps the ancient Ottomans chose it for that reason," Sergei said.

"Were they the ones who built the mosques?" Kit asked.

"Yes. The brand of Islam in Kosovo is similar to that found in Turkey ... relatively secular, although the Saudis have started to take an interest in the place. Potentially, it could become a recruiting ground for Jihadi foreign fighters."

The Missing Diary

"I've never understood why great world powers take such an interest in the small territory of Kosovo," Kit said.

Sergei looked out into the distance and squinted. "It's a small but strategic territory. My government feels that it's important because of its interest in the Balkans as a whole, and I think my American colleagues have the same impression. But you don't really want to talk about work, do you?"

"It's probably better not to, but I don't really get much of a chance to discuss philosophy with my colleagues during the week."

"It's always good to get fresh perspectives."

They walked around the perimeter of the hilltop. Kit enjoyed the fresh air and the crunch of dry gravel under her feet. When she began to feel hungry and lightheaded, she thought it seemed like time for lunch. She was about to suggest they return to town when Sergei pointed to a path off to the side of the main viewing area.

"Let's have a look down there. I came up here once with a local guide who showed me there's a better lookout spot down there. More private."

Kit agreed and followed him down the uneven stony path, which led through bracken to a narrow ledge on the side of the hill. It felt as if she was hovering in the air, perhaps on a magic carpet, overlooking the mosaic of buildings below.

"It's magical," she said and took a deep breath. The air was still, and the sound of birdsong came from behind them. "Did I mention I get vertigo sometimes?" she added and moved back toward a piece of rock large enough to the sit on, which protruded from the hillside.

"No, you didn't," he said. "It's quite safe here as long as you keep away from the edge."

She perched on the edge of the rock and hung on to it for safety. It was then that she became aware of his closeness.

"Do you mind if I sit on that rock beside you?" he asked.

She tried to make room for him, but there was only space for one person. She felt as if she was suspended in the scented warm air when he wrapped his arm around her shoulders. She was holding her breath when he leaned into the side of her neck. The proximity of his lips made her moan softly. She exhaled the breath she had been holding and turned toward him.

He tilted her chin and brought her face closer to his. His amber eyes were glowing like a predatory animal's. He paused and searched her eyes. The time for talking was over, and he was waiting to see whether she would come toward him or pull away. Instead, he felt her tremble and saw surrender in her eyes.

He kissed her, tentatively at first, savoring her full, soft lips. When she moved closer, he pressed more firmly, and she opened her mouth to admit his tongue. Her mouth tasted of honey, and the vanilla and violet fragrance of her perfume mingled with his senses.

She was the first to break the kiss as she came up for air and looked over the precipice again. A voice at the back of her mind was saying *What are you doing? This isn't supposed to happen.* But her body was soft and receptive; she wanted more. The vertigo she felt mixed with her excitement that was caused by being close to Sergei. She enjoyed the muscular strength of his arms and couldn't help comparing it to Xander's more wiry build. In a flash, she thought of a scene she recalled from Bible class: the temptation of Christ where the devil took Jesus to a high place and offered him all the kingdoms of the world if he would give himself over to temptation.

"Are you going to offer me the world now?" she said.

"What?" Sergei mumbled as if he was emerging from a deep dream. "What are you talking about?"

"You know, 'He took Jesus to a high place and offered ultimate power if Jesus would worship him.' It feels a bit like that story from the Bible up here; or flying on Aladdin's magic carpet."

"I prefer the magic carpet," Sergei said. He pulled back. People were approaching. "I think people are coming."

Kit got up, straightened her clothes, and checked that her hair was in place with her hands. Her lips tingled from Sergei's kiss. Without saying more, Sergei started up the path and offered her his hand to help her climb back up to the main viewing area on top of the hill.

As they wended their way back down the rocky slope, Sergei was attentive when she slipped on a loose patch of gravel. She wasn't sure that she liked this more vulnerable side of herself. He was different to Xander. Kit had a pang of guilt; she hadn't thought about her fiancé at all today.

It was close to one p.m. when the call to prayer began in one minaret and soon became a synchronized cloud of sound with a haunting and otherworldly soundscape. Kit stopped for a moment to listen. It was times like this that she felt the reality of being away from home. She felt vertiginous as she came to an outlook that jutted over Prizren.

"We could go the back way if you prefer," Sergei said. "It's a bit longer but less steep."

"Can we get there easily from here?"

Sergei pointed to a narrow path leading around to the back of the hill. "Why not? Maybe it would be nice to see another side of the mountain."

They diverted along a different path to the left. Kit was thirsty and regretted that she had not brought a bottle of water with her or eaten breakfast before setting out. She had thought that her customary cup of coffee would be enough. "I wish I'd bought a bottle of water," she said.

"I've got some," Sergei said as he dug into his pocket and produced a small metal flask, opened it, and took a sip of the contents. "It's not a water, but I can promise you it's very good for you."

"Vodka?"

"What else?" He offered the flask to her, but she waved it a way.

"What I'd like is a nice, tall glass of mineral water with ice and lemon."

"We'll do that very soon," he said.

Fifteen minutes later, they rounded the side of the hill, and Sergei pointed to a cafe restaurant that was situated partway up the base of the hill near the river. Kit chose a table close to the river with the best view toward the old town. She ordered a mineral water immediately. Sergei placed the stainless steel flask on the table.

"You could add some to your water," he said.

Kit was relieved to reach the safe haven of the cafe and enjoy the shade of the sun umbrella and the splashing of the small but energetic river. She looked around and enjoyed the atmosphere of the historic town.

"You've got me curious about how it tastes now," she said. "Maybe a bit later."

"One of the reasons I like this location is because the fortress reminds me of the castle in a chess game. Often when I go to an old city, I head straight for the castle."

"There are several bishops and imams here. I'm not sure about the knights and queens."

"You would be the white queen—and as for me, what else could I be but a humble pawn," Sergei said.

Kit laughed and then got up to wash her hands before lunch. She still felt dizzy from their encounter on the mountain. The visit to the bathroom and washing her hands made her feel more grounded. When she got back, she looked in her bag and, after a moment of panic, said that she couldn't find her mobile.

"Looking for this?" he said as he produced her phone from his pocket. "Sorry, I forgot to give it back after it took your photo. Would you like me to take one of you here?"

"Sure, or we could ask the waiter to take one of us together. You really had me worried there for a moment."

The waiter delivered the first course, which was freshly baked flatbread with tapenade and seasonal vegetable soup. Kit ordered red wine and Sergei ordered white. Kit asked the waiter, a young Kosovar man with a sharp haircut, to take a photograph of them. They leaned together, raised their wine glasses, and the waiter took the photo with Kit's phone.

After they completed the first course, Sergei suggested they continue their discussion about khash. Kit was feeling much more relaxed after water, wine, and something to eat. She felt a sense of well-being in Prizren, and she was enjoying the adventure with Sergei.

"Yes, I'd like that."

"Dining under the shadow of the old fortress is a good reminder of the player's piece, the castle, in chess. Chess was originally a game of kings who sought to hone their skills in warfare. In khash, we can envisage life in different locations as if it's moving between various theaters of conflict, much like the alternating black and white squares on the chessboard. These might be controlled by ourselves, our allies, or our adversaries. We should analyze each scenario that we find ourselves in. Who are the main players and what are their motivations? Who do they serve? What threats and opportunities are in each space in which we find ourselves?"

"So you'd see conflict inherent in each situation, each scenario?"

"This is a simplified view, but perhaps a useful one. There is usually a conflict in each scenario that we find ourselves in, and if so, we can become more aware and therefore be better able to control what happens. We can use chaos and reversals to our advantage."

"What do you mean?"

"Once we accept the premise of the game, which is ultimately to promote our own success, we can use any element of a situation to our advantage. Sometimes problems can be solved by reversing our approach to them. I believe the Americans sometimes call this *thinking outside the box*."

"How could I use that at work?" Kit asked.

"That's an interesting question. Having done our analysis of the potentials of each scenario, each square, we can then use visualisation to maximize our advantage. Without fixating on it, we create a clear intention of what we want to happen, which path we wish to follow, or which chess pieces to follow."

"You mean, for example, me and my allies succeed, rather than my opponents?"

"Yes, exactly. Too often we go from place to place without taking full awareness of the potentials of the situation. Dreams can give us insights into current conditions and future possibilities. Our brains and unconscious minds have registered these, but perhaps our conscious mind is not fully aware of them. We can find hints in our dreams."

"Maybe you can give me some suggestions on how I could tackle some of my work situations," Kit said.

"Sure, explain one to me."

"I can't say much because of confidentiality, you understand."

"Of course."

"You know what we were discussing at the meeting the other day." Kit picked at her salad for a few moments as she considered what to say. "And by the way, I felt slightly embarrassed. I'm not sure why. Maybe because the last time we had seen each other was over dinner and no one knew that, not even my boss," she blurted out.

Sergei reached over and touched her arm reassuringly. "Don't worry about it. Life is about developing alliances and understandings; sometimes the only way this can happen is behind the scenes. But I have no doubt that we can mutually benefit each other," he said in a low voice.

"Maybe you're right. I found our conversations very interesting. And they helped me get over what happened at the crime scene earlier. I was much better able to handle myself at the next difficult situation."

Sergei smiled. "You have no idea how happy it makes me to hear that," he said.

"What you said about clearly visualizing outcomes helped me to figure out what's really important to me."

"And what is that?"

"Well, it starts with justice for victims."

"That could be a good start, but it's not the end of the story. We can discuss a bit later what else might also be important."

"The situation that we are facing, me and Major Hackman, is that our main suspect escaped, and the other suspect, who was briefly detained, is uncooperative. We understand that she keeps a detailed diary of everything that happens to her, including her involvement with a criminal group. Matt seems to think that this might contain important clues relating to the massacre."

Sergei nodded as he cut into his chicken breast. "Go on," he said.

"How can we progress the case given that the prime suspect has disappeared and the other witness is not cooperating? Something else that disturbed me was that the suspect had captured our confidential witness. Goodness knows what would have happened if we hadn't got there in time."

"This is a complex situation. Sometimes we can find solutions by taking a step back and looking at all the elements of the situation, as on a chessboard. Look at how the different pieces can interact together and try to determine the gameplay of the opposing side."

"That sounds like an interesting idea, but I don't know how to do it."

"When you have a chance, why don't you try that as a visualization and see what connections appear, perhaps.

The Missing Diary

You need to get used to seeing the energy plays in each scenario without forgetting that you can influence these with your own thinking."

"How would you recommend I do that?"

"When you get home, choose a time when you won't be disturbed and lie down or relax and just imagine the whole situation with all the players as if they're pieces on a chessboard. Ask yourself what hidden connections are there? It could be that this diary is one of the key elements. For each square on the playing board, each scenario, think about your own wishes, articulate your intentions, and this will help you to move forward. I have the feeling that you will find the suspect quite soon, or he will find you. It's also important to recognize when it's appropriate to retreat, to back off, and let others take the lead."

"Do you think this is the case now?"

"Maybe you could step back from the situation and then decide how you'd like to play it. I think you'd be wise to let other people in your office take the lead on this case. These criminals can be dangerous even to police and prosecutors, and what happens if they get to know about you? And we can use reversals and inversions to surprise our opponents."

Kit thought with a shudder how Raco had come after Blaku again when she had decided to give evidence against him. "I hope not. But what's an example of such a reversal?"

"Doing the opposite to what people think you will do. I suspect you might have a knack for that. Even though you were embarrassed after, you stood up and gave your view about conflict-related sexual violence. You hadn't fully thought through the roles of the various people there, but at the time I thought it was a courageous move and showed your potential as a powerful khash player."

"Really? You saw that? I thought that was so embarrassing, as was fainting at the crime scene. Oh my God! I think I need another glass of wine."

Sergei laughed. "My dear, it's your ability to act unexpectedly that makes you a worthy adversary."

"Adversary?"

"Symbolically speaking, for your suspect and Merita Shala."

"How do you know her name? Did I mention it?"

"Yes, you did," he said. "In any case, I make it my business to keep informed about these things."

Kit picked at her food. She wondered how he knew so much about her work, which was supposed to be confidential. It was then that she decided to steer the conversation away from work.

"Where did you originally learn about khash?"

"From my mother. She has links to the Orthodox Church, and to some rather unorthodox parts of the Orthodox Church, if you'll excuse the turn of phrase."

"The Rasputin connection," Kit said and laughed. "I hope you'll tell me more about that."

By this stage, they had made good progress through their main courses. Kit pushed her Greek salad to one side.

"I can recommend the *tres leche*," Sergei said. "It's a specialty of the region; it's for sale in just about every restaurant and quite delicious. Not as good as the Russian desserts of course."

Kit laughed. "My favourite desert back home is apple crumble," she said.

"You must make it for me one day," Sergei said.

"If I can find the proper ice cream or whipped cream to go with it, I will. Or perhaps the pavlova that is so popular in New Zealand."

"Named after the Russian ballerina Anna Pavlova."

"I knew it was named after a ballerina, but not that she was Russian."

"You see what a cultural exchange we can have."

They laughed and then stood up. Sergei slid a bank note into the folder containing the bill. He waved away any suggestion from Kit that she could contribute to meal. "It's my pleasure. I've taken your Saturday morning, so the least you can do to allow me to pay for lunch."

They walked slowly and companionably back toward the town center, passing a historic mosque with a water tap and bowl outside for religious ablutions. Nearby was the impressive Orthodox Cathedral.

"There's also a small Jewish community here. Prizren is an example of interfaith tolerance, although they do need to post police guards outside the Orthodox church."

In the center of town there was an open, cobbled square. In the middle sat an ancient fountain that supplied drinking water from artesian wells. Most of the women were dressed fashionably in western European-style clothes, but one or two were dressed in more traditional Turkish-style clothing, with long skirts, long tunics, and some form of head covering. The Roma people had darker skin, and the scene was colorful and friendly. Sergei explained that minority communities in Kosovo included Roma, Ashkali, and Egyptian groups, who were even more vulnerable in some ways than the Kosovo Serbs or Kosovo Albanians.

When a loud group, including drummers, came across a stone bridge, it transpired that it was a bridal party. The bride and groom were walking together and surrounded by well-wishers, musicians, children, and dogs. It was a large retinue. As the party came closer and closer, the noise was almost deafening. Sergei took Kit's arm and nodded toward one of the small shops set at the perimeter of the square. It was a traditional jewelry shop containing locally made silver filigree. It seemed like a good idea to retreat to a quieter place.

They entered the shop, and as the rickety door behind them closed, the noise of the celebration diminished. It was a tiny shop. At the back behind the counter, a middle-aged man sat at a desk working with silver wire. The display cases contained rings, necklaces, earrings, and bracelets. Some items incorporated colorful stones. There were also other decorative household items, such as picture frames also made from silver filigree.

"Wow," Kit said. "My mother would love this."

"Why don't you buy her something. The jewelry is not so expensive by international standards."

Kit greeted the shop owner and asked if they could look around. A balding man in his forties with friendly, brown eyes gestured with his hand toward a display cabinet on the right. "Please, be my guests," he said.

In the cabinet Kit saw wonderfully ornate pieces.

"Have you seen filigree jewelry before in Kosovo?" the man asked.

"No. It's my first time in Prizren."

"We also have a branch in Pristina. Close to the Grand Hotel."

"Thanks, the pieces are fantastic. We don't have work like this where I come from."

The Missing Diary

"And where is that?"

"New Zealand," Kit said and smiled before she pointed at a particularly dramatic pendant with a green stone rimmed by silver filigree in a floral design and asked if she could take a closer look at it. The man opened the cabinet with a key and took out the pendant. She also asked to see a couple of rings. Sergei, who had apparently seen it all before, only took a cursory interest in the workmanship. The shopkeeper explained that the silver filigree had been traditional in Prizren since the seventeenth century. While Kosovo had plenty of metals, including silver, it was no longer extracted from the mines in Trepča, and now the artisans have to import it. Kit examined the silver pieces under a jeweler's loop, which the shopkeeper offered her along with small glasses of black, sweet tea, which she and Sergei both accepted. She also examined a decorative wall plaque which was, in fact, a curved Turkish dagger. The intricacy of the work was remarkable. The complex design of thin, silver wire woven precisely into the shape of a dagger with ornate curves and loops fascinated her.

"What do you think it says about the culture?" Kit asked Sergei.

"What do you mean?"

"Well, the designs look complicated and intricate. You almost get lost trying to follow the metal wire moving through so many shapes. I don't know how they keep track of it all."

The shop owner chuckled. "You might like to visit the workshop and see how they make their pieces. It's a process passed down from father to son through the generations. They learn when they're very young."

"I'd love to, thank you very much. Maybe I can take one of your cards and do that next time I'm here. I think we need to get back to Pristina now." She looked at Sergei.

He nodded. "I think it'll be safe to go outside now. The wedding party has gone."

"I love these pieces. I'm sure my mother would adore this pendant. And I like the amber earrings so much." She bought the pendant, a pair of earrings, and an ornate silver-filigree ring with an aquamarine stone. "My mother has a crystal shop in New Zealand. Perhaps she would like to import some items from here to sell; they would be interesting and, of course, unique."

"I'm sure we could give you some good prices if you come back to our shop," the owner said as he wrapped her purchases.

"There's one other place I'd like to show you before we leave," Sergei said once they were outside. He pointed to another shop, the window of which was filled with elaborate perfume bottles of different sizes, colors, and shapes. "They import these bottles from the Middle East, and you can buy scented oils, perfumes, and attars. They always claim that the finest ingredients are used, but I'm not so sure. Anyway, they also make nice gifts. And just for fun, the guy there has an aunt who reads coffee grounds. Maybe if we're lucky she might be available."

"Sure, I love fragrances. I've never heard of reading coffee grounds though. Is that like reading tea leaves?"

"Yes, exactly. The tradition comes from Turkey. They believe that they can read someone's fortune from the coffee grounds. Some of the readings can be quite interesting and occasionally accurate. I said that it's just for fun because I don't believe in these things. I believe we shape our destiny with our intentions and actions. What do you think?"

"I'll give it a go. Maybe the reader picks up something from the person and then it's projected in the coffee grounds, like a kind of Rorschach blot. Do you know what I mean?"

"By the Rorschach blot test, do you mean the psychological test where people say what they think the inkblot looks like, and that it shows something about their personalities?"

"Yes, that's the one."

"That might explain how readers get it right occasionally."

Kit selected three small, chiseled glass bottles, which the young man filled with her chosen scented oils: jasmine and violet and a replica of a popular *eau de toilette*. They had copies of all the major perfume brands. While he wrapped the purchases, Kit and Sergei went into the back room. A comfortably built woman wearing a traditional Muslim headdress and a long skirt was busy making coffee. The young man spoke to his mother and asked her if she could give the visitors a reading. She spoke limited English but knew enough to politely enquire how their day was going and how they were enjoying visiting Prizren. Then she nodded toward Sergei. *"Rusça?"* she asked. It sounded to Kit like *Russcha?* Kit guessed that she meant, *Are you Russian?* Sergei nodded. She shrugged and carried on making the coffee. Kit guessed that Russians were not popular among the Muslim population because they had backed the Serb offensive in Kosovo. But under the new international order, all different ethnic groups had to be respected—at least in theory.

The woman presented them each with a small cup of Turkish coffee and told them to drink. Then she offered them a plate of *baklava*. Kit took a bite and rolled her eyes with pleasure. It was possibly the sweetest, most delectable pastry she had ever tasted.

The woman chuckled at her reaction. "If you like our sweets that much, I think you will be very happy in Kosovo."

Kit laughed. "Quite possibly." She had downed the small cup of hot, sweet, strong, black coffee quickly, then stared at the sludge of black grounds in the bottom. Sergei watched on with amusement as the woman picked up the cup, swilled the grounds around in the bottom of the cup and, with a deft motion, turned it upside down on the saucer. She then righted the coffee cup and peered into it.

"I see you have no financial problems—that's good. In matters of the heart, I see changes ahead—but do not worry. Things will turn out for the best."

Kits could not help glancing at Sergei. He was listening with skeptical silence, but at the same time watching her reactions with interest.

"I see a snake on one side of the cup—this means you should be very careful. Not everyone is as they seem. I see the head of a dog in the cup—perhaps one will be coming into your life quite soon."

"You got that right," Kit said. "There are already several dogs in my life; they belong to my colleagues."

"A dog may help you with the snake," she said. "I think you will like your time in Kosovo if you steer clear of the snakes. You may end up staying longer than you expect." Then she placed the cup on the saucer. Kit thanked her and offered a couple of coins in payment, which the woman swept up and placed in a bag attached to her waistband.

"Now you, sir," she said to Sergei. "Would you like to see what lies in your future?"

"Sure, why not?" Sergei shrugged and looked at Kit. Kit smiled as the woman picked up his cup and studied it. She turned the cup this way and that, tilting it and letting the grounds settle on one side then the other.

"Sir, you are one of the few customers whose coffee grounds I have difficulty reading. I see something that resembles part of a chessboard, but little else." She squinted at the dark mass of coffee grounds. "Maybe a desk, you are passionate about your work—a master chess player perhaps. I see a woman, perhaps your mother."

"It seems that you see a lot in my coffee grounds, madam," Sergei said. "You might be right about it all. Can you tell me more about the chessboard?"

"Not really. I see white and black squares. Perhaps you have the choice of which side you wish to play for."

"Well played, ma'am," Sergei said. "That's definitely worth crossing your palm with silver." He produced two coins and slid them across the table.

"No, no—please keep your money to buy the young lady another piece of baklava. The reading is complimentary today," she said as she pushed the coins away. It seemed odd to Kit that the woman wouldn't take Sergei's money.

"As you wish," Sergei said as he retrieved the coins. "Well, Katarina, should we collect your things and go?"

Kit nodded and thanked the woman. In the main part of the shop, the young man asked how they had enjoyed the reading. "My mother's never wrong, you know. The women of my family have been doing this for generations," he added.

"She told me to beware of snakes bringing too much *baklava*," Kit said with a smile. "And she thought I would have a long stay in Kosovo."

"I hope you do," the young man said and smiled. "And come back soon."

Once they got outside, Kit asked Sergei why the woman hadn't taken his money. "I suspect that she doesn't want to do business with a Russian, although she was curious to see what the coffee grounds held for me. Unfortunately there is still distrust of our people here, however unfounded."

Kit and Sergei had spent a lovely time together, feeling closer and closer all the time. When Sergei opened the door and they stepped out into the main square, the heat had built up over the time they'd spent in the two shops. The square was filled with the smell of grilled meat, popcorn, and freshly washed laundry. The sun felt warm and humid. It made her feel sticky with perspiration.

"I've arranged for a taxi to collect you and take you back to Pristina," he explained.

"You didn't mention that before," Kit said. "I thought we'd go back together."

"I've got business to attend to," he said.

"Is it something with the Orthodox priest you had suggested we meet?" she asked.

"We took longer in the shops and restaurant than expected. I think Father Peter has already started the afternoon religious service. However, perhaps next time we could visit him."

Kit put a hand on her hip and looked at him sideways. "So, what kind of business do you have here on

Saturday afternoon?" He had seemed so charming up to this moment, and now he was bailing on her.

"Russian Liaison Office business," he relied.

"What, like spy stuff or something?" she asked.

"Or something," he said.

"Well, you could have warned me in advance. I could have arranged for a driver to collect me." She glanced at her watch. How long would it take for a driver to get there?

"No need," said Sergei. "You should go back. I'll contact you later," he said.

"Okay," she said. "It sounds like you got it all figured out. I don't want to get in the way of your business." She wasn't sure how she had imagined their excursion ending, but this wasn't it.

It was five p.m. when Kit and Sergei said their goodbyes and she got into the waiting limosine taxi. He had at least hired good quality transport for her. Sergei had suggested that she take the scenic route back to Pristina. He had called one of the local taxi companies, negotiated her fare, and slipped the driver some German mark notes. They agreed to meet later in the week. The daring part of Kit couldn't wait to pick up where they left off after the kiss on the mountain, while the sensible part of her said she needed time to cool off and think about things more clearly.

Kit relaxed into the comfortable rear seat of the limousine. Her head was still spinning after her day with Sergei. She appreciated this downtime and the hour's drive between Prizren and Pristina, during which she could get her thoughts together. When she checked her mobile, she saw with a pang of guilt that Xander had left her a message while she had been with Sergei. She decided to return his call later. Putting Xander out of her mind, she turned her attention to taking photos of the picturesque mountains that were now visible out the car window. It would be good to show the folks back home where she had been. Sergei was right about this being the picturesque route back to Pristina. He also recommended a cafe restaurant where she could stop for a coffee, and she was wondering how far away it was when she noticed that the driver kept looking in his rearview mirror. His expression was troubled, and he was driving faster even though the road through the mountains was vertiginous.

"Is there something wrong?" Kit asked.

"Not sure."

Kit swiveled in her seat. Behind them a large, black SUV with tinted windows was gaining on them. "He's following a bit too close," Kit said to the driver.

"Yes, I think so."

At that moment, the black car accelerated to pulled abreast of Kit's vehicle. She looked at the driver—he was wearing a balaclava. She gasped her shock. She could not tell whether there was anyone in the back of the car because of tinted windows. She felt a surge of fear. The car carried on beside them.

"Oh my God!" Kit shouted as she slid across the back seat.

The taxi driver shouted something unintelligible in Albanian and put his foot down despite the winding road. The limousine pulled away from the other vehicle, but the SUV accelerated. Kit turned to look at it again. The vehicle had no number plate. And it was equipped with far more horsepower than the limousine. Her hands shook with fear as she reached for her mobile and sent a text to Angel. *Call Security. Being chased by black SUV. No number plate. Thanks, K.*

Angel replied instantly. *Where are you?*
Shari Mountains near Shari Café.

At that moment, Kit's phone flew out of her hand. The SUV had bumped against them. The limousine swerved toward the edge of the road. Kit leaned across the back seat, grabbed her phone, and thrust it into her bag. She pressed herself into the corner of the car as she tried to get as far away as possible from the impact. Her driver cursed as he floored the accelerator yet again. Then he grabbed his handset and made what Kit guessed must have been an emergency call to his base.

Kit looked up again at the driver of the other car. He was heavyset and looking at her from behind the wheel. Primed with adrenaline, her brain worked fast. She recognized the build of the man from the figure who escaped the police raid. It could be Raco, although she wasn't sure. Then she remembered what a police officer had once told her. He had survived a violent carjacking by rolling out of the car while it was still in motion and gone into hiding. The other passengers had been shot.

"When you can, slow down the car," Kit said as she leaned forward to talk to the driver.

"What?"

"I need to get out. He's after me. Slow the car right down and I'm going to roll out."

The driver did not answer. Instead he braked, and the limousine slowed dramatically as it approached a bend. The SUV was taken by surprise and overshot them. As the taxi slowed almost to a halt, Kit opened the door a crack. She secured her bag across her shoulder, gripped it with whitening knuckles, and as they reached the farthest point of the bend, she rolled out. There was gravel on the shoulder of the road, which led to a ditch. Beneath that lay a steep riverbank. She hit the ground hard and rolled, bruising her ribs. Once she stopped moving, she did a quick audit of her body. It seemed that she hadn't broken anything, or at least it didn't feel as if she had. As she scrambled over the gravel shoulder of the road, she cut her hands and bruised her knees, but she was too full of adrenaline to feel it.

The cars disappeared around the bend. The right-hand passenger seat door of the limousine was open. She made it over the lip of the road and into the ditch on the other side. She stopped and dared to look toward the vehicles. They were no longer is sight. She scrambled down a steep hill, slipping and sliding as she lost her footing several times and tripped over branches and roots before she arrived at the base of the hill close to the river. Without looking back, she chose what appeared to be the safest, most shallow place to cross and picked her way over the rushing water, searching for stable, flat stones to step on. Eventually, she reached the other side, which led into a forested area at the base of the mountains. Once she reached the forest, she stopped and rested as she got her breath back.

With shaking hands, she took out her mobile. However, it had shattered with the impact of her fall. She turned it on. It was dead. Swearing softly under her breath, she put it away and decided that it would best to go deeper into the forest in case Raco, or whoever it was, came back to look for her.

She found a rough path along the side of the hill underneath the pine trees, which led around the corner and into what on another day she would have thought was a lovely clearing, surrounded by undergrowth and old trees. The mountain stream had formed a pool which trickled down to meet the river at the base of the road. She squatted by the pool and rinsed her bloodied hands before taking a sip of the fresh mountain water. Her hands stung, but the water soothed her parched throat.

Angel knew her location approximately, so help would be on its way soon, even if they didn't know exactly where she was. Then again, neither did Raco. She hoped that the taxi driver had not come to any harm. However, it seemed likely that her attacker would be able to work out where she had exited the car based on when the door was flung open. She balanced the two imperatives: how to avoid her pursuer and to be found by OIDC Security. Her dilemma was that she needed to be far from the road to hide from her pursuer, while she needed to be close to the road to be rescued. She would go back and listen for the sound of vehicles. Would she be able to tell which was the SUV and which was the OIDC security vehicle? She figured it would take security at least thirty to forty minutes to reach the area, whereas it would only take Raco about ten minutes.

She moved deeper into the forest. She'd wait there for fifteen minutes and then walk back toward the road. That way she could best avoid Raco and be close to the road when security drove past. She kept thinking it was Raco. Who else could it be? Her lawyer's mind started working, and she thought about what evidence she had of her attacker's identity. She had to admit, very little. Black masks were common in this region and were used by criminals and guerrillas as well as police. Even EUFOR officers used masks.

The question was, how had he known her location? Was it a random attack? That seemed less likely. It was more likely that the attack had been linked to one or both of the investigations. Blaku had been hunted and victimized a second time. Had he followed her from Prizren? Or from Pristina? Or had someone told him where she was? Merita Shala had hinted that Kit had been followed and observed before. Kit sat down on a rock and massaged her forehead. She needed to think. There would be time enough in the coming days to rehash all the possible scenarios and discuss them with law enforcement experts such as Matt.

The heavy rhythm of the diesel engine alerted her—the SUV perhaps. She got to her feet. Further up the hill through the trees was an indentation in a rock that was partly covered by undergrowth. She would wait it out there, by which time OIDC should have arrived. As she climbed, her feet sunk into a soft, mossy layer of leaves and twigs on the forest floor. If she kept quiet, with luck she wouldn't alert anyone to her presence. She hoped she hadn't left an obvious trail behind her. In retrospect, she should have been more careful. Maybe her wet footprints would have disappeared by now.

Using a branch for support, Kit pulled herself up to the opening in the side of the hill. It was a small cave. She bent over double and went inside cautiously. Once her eyes had adjusted to the darkness, she looked around. The cave went back several meters but was not particularly deep. She sat on a large, flat rock to one side. Concerned about someone seeing her footprints, she went back to the opening and obliterated her tracks with a fallen branch before she pulled more branches over the opening.

Sounds were muffled inside the cave. However, she could hear the sound of a powerful vehicle coming closer until it slowed down and eventually stopped, probably close to where she had rolled out the taxi. A sense of dread filled her, and her heart began to beat quickly while her mouth was dry. Her mind raced ahead to possible scenarios that included abduction, sexual assault, being taken hostage, or even worse—murder. She looked around the cave for a rudimentary weapon. There was the tree branch and a few stones, but that was all. She had seen Raco's physical strength, and she doubted her ability to fight him off, although she had achieved well in her Krav Maga classes. But Raco had escaped three teams of police officers and was armed and dangerous.

At that moment, she heard an unexpected rustling sound behind her. The cave was dark and she had no light source, so she had not been able to give the interior more than a cursory inspection. She turned to search for the source of the sound. For one terrible moment, she was afraid that she would see a man-sized shadow lurking in the back of the cave, and that somehow Raco had beaten her inside. When the movement came again, she knew whatever it was, was too small to be a man. It must have been some kind of animal. She dreaded the thought that she had disturbed a rat's nest or even a bear or a wolf. Kit didn't think there were wild bears in the area, but she wasn't sure. As the sound continued, a small, pointed canine muzzle became visible. It looked like a small, red dog. When the creature edged its way forward, she saw that it was a thin red animal, most likely a fox. Apparently she had disturbed its sleep, and now it was going to leave the confines of the cave by keeping as far away from her as possible.

At the entrance to the cave, the fox smelled the air but didn't move any further. It sat inert, its form silhouetted against the light that penetrated the leafy-green cover. Kit too sat absolutely still, hardly daring to breathe in case she disturbed the animal. It was a novelty being so close to a wild fox, which showed no sign of fear in the presence of a human being. She slid her hand into her pocket and removed a strip of beef jerky. Slowly she broke the seal and unwrapped it before tossing it toward the fox. She'd eat the other half of the jerky. All of a sudden she was hungry.

The fox looked up, and as it kept its eyes fixed on her, it crept forward and delicately picked up the dried meat with its teeth. Moments later. it swallowed the jerky in one smooth motion. Seeing the fox relaxed enough to accept food from her made Kit feel protected from the drama outside. She felt timeless in the peaceful confines of the dark cave, where she and this miraculous wild being had shared a moment of communion. The fox looked outside again and growled softly. Kit wondered whether it was male or female. It was small, so she thought it was probably female, a vixen. Why was it alone? Did it have a mate nearby? Then the fox turned toward her and sniffed. When it moved stealthily toward Kit, she was nervous because it was a wild animal and it could have rabies. Kit searched her pocket for more dried meat, but it was all gone.

Kit's mood lifted, and somehow her pursuer seemed less formidable. She felt more confident that things

THE MISSING DIARY

would turn out okay. Sergei's advice replayed in her mind. If there was ever a time to use the technique that he had begun to teach her, surely it was now. As a feeling of safety and protection grew within her, her heartbeat returned to normal. She felt calm. It was then that she heard more vehicles arrive. Doors closing were followed by the sound of voices and a dog barking—Max from the EUFOR canine unit. The EUFOR Police had arrived, probably with OIDC security. Then came the sound of heavy footsteps retreating rapidly. She hadn't been aware he had been so close. The police must have seen the SUV. Kit edged toward the opening of the cave.

Kit took her time, even though she felt certain that help was at hand. Outside the cave entrance were easily discernible boot prints that led toward to the right. She wouldn't have been surprised if they were Raco's. Instinct took over, and she followed the footprints as they wove between the trees and toward the river. Who did the footprints belong to? In that moment, she had transformed from the hunted to the hunter. However, five minutes later, her tracking was interrupted by Max, who bounded up to her and greeted her by barking. She petted the dog's velvety head and bent down to hug him around the neck.

"You found me, boy. I guess I'm safe—for now."

Chapter Fifteen

My love has gone into the mountains. My days are empty now, like the dregs in my coffee cup. Do they hide my destiny, or is my destiny as dark as the burned ash?

Merita's diary, 22 August 2000

Kit had finished her morning workout in the home gym she had set up in her apartment. It was nothing fancy, but it had all the essential elements—free weights, a stationary bike, and a yoga mat. When her mobile announced the arrival of the message, it was from Matt and typically brief. *Meet you at the White and Black Cafe 8.45 a.m. need to debrief—Matt.*

Kit took a shower, slipped into her tailored, blue linen dress and comfortable walking sandals, grabbed her briefcase, and headed downtown. She pulled her auburn hair back and knotted it into a bun. When possible, she preferred to walk to work. It was a warm, balmy day in late autumn, and there was still a shimmer of heat over the roads. Kit paid careful attention as she walked to avoid twisting her ankle on the irregular surface and potholes on the pavements. There was plenty of traffic, but when she crossed the road, the cars generally slowed or stopped for her.

The Missing Diary

She arrived to find Matt sitting away from the tables and chairs that had been set out on the pavement. He was one of the few people sitting inside the cafe, close to the window. She was surprised to see him smoking for the first time. When he saw her, he signaled to the waiter. He knew she'd want an Americano. She added to the order with a freshly baked croissant, which were excellent at the White and Black Cafe.

While Matt sometimes looked rough around the edges, today he seemed even more fraught. It looked as if he hadn't shaved, and his eyes were bleary.

"Good morning," Kit said.

"Thanks for coming. Take a seat. I wanted to brief you before we meet at the office. And I wanted to ask how you are. I didn't think Raco would come after you personally."

"Nor did I," Kit said and shuddered. "I'm okay, but I have a few bruises from jumping out the car."

"That was probably a smart move. The bastard got away yet again. He had already disappeared by the time we alerted the police. We're still trying to reconstruct his movements. The taxi driver has been helpful. Fortunately Raco didn't attack him. Until we catch him, it's probably better that you don't travel alone for a while. What were you doing in the Shari Mountains?"

Kit looked down, pulled a flake of pastry off her croissant, and spread a layer of raspberry jam on it. "I thought I'd go to Prizren for the day. I caught a taxi." She looked at him. "It seemed like a nice day for it." She hoped the taxi driver wouldn't mention that Sergei had ordered the taxi. She felt protective of people knowing about her private life; she knew they wouldn't approve of her spending time with a Russian.

"I'm probably safe in public, but I'll keep it in mind, thanks. How's Blaku?"

"She's doing okay. I got a call from MI6 yesterday. I keep in touch with my colleagues in British Security. They're offering to facilitate her relocation to New Zealand." Matt stubbed out the cigarette and reached for another one.

"That would be great," Kit said with her eyes fixed on the cigarette butt in the tray. "That's a nasty habit, you know."

"Yeah, I know," Matt replied. "I had given up, but occasionally I need a smoke."

"I know the feeling," Kit said.

"I'm concerned about the loss of confidentiality, but New Zealand could be a good option for Blaku after she gives evidence against Raco. I'd like to speak with this friend." He paused. "By the way, the ballistics tests showed that some of the guns in Raco's basement were a match to the bullets fired at Staro Dorbi."

"Great," Kit said. "That's really going to help our case. Even if we can't prove that he was directly involved in the killings—yet."

"True. That's the good news of the day. The bad news—and you won't believe this—Shala's diary has disappeared."

Kit was in the process of putting down her cup of coffee when she startled and spilled it into the saucer. "What? How could that be?"

"The Romanians had the diary when it was confiscated from Shala's apartment. They took it back to the station. Two translation teams were assigned to prioritize it. They had no special lockup area to keep evidence, and somehow the diary went missing."

"I wouldn't have thought that was possible," Kit said. "Once the diary was signed in as evidence, wasn't someone responsible for it?"

"I would have thought so," Matt said. "Apparently it was seen coming in, but after the two translations were made, it couldn't be found."

"Can we use the translations then?" Kit asked.

"What we have are two translations that seem to bear very little resemblance to each other."

Kit shook her head. "None of this makes sense. Given that the original can't be found, neither translation would have much evidential value in court. But maybe we can take a look at the translations; perhaps that might point us in the right direction."

"I can tell you that the two translations are completely different and don't make much sense. You're welcome to take a look though." Matt removed an envelope from inside his jacket pocket and slid it discreetly under the table to her. Kit put it into her briefcase without looking at the contents.

"Yes, I'd like to take a look, but I have to say that I'm surprised by all this. It would never happen in New Zealand."

"It's hard to imagine it happening in the UK either, although things have gone missing from the evidence locker room before. Usually drugs or cash."

"So, the diary was checked in as evidence and then shared with two of the translation teams, and from there it seems to have disappeared. Is that right?"

"Something like that."

"Can we talk to the translation teams and see if they kept copies of the original? Or just ask them what happened."

"You can try, but the translation work is briefed out to external companies, and it can be difficult to find out exactly who had their hands on the diary."

"It's not like you to give up so easily," Kit said.

Matt sighed with frustration. "Here's the other news. From today, I am off the case."

Kit jerked backward, putting down her coffee and the piece of pastry that she had been toying with. "Why? What happened?" she asked in an astonished voice.

"Apparently, that bastard Petri went over my head. Even though he was the one who let Raco escape, he blamed me for it and said that the operation was poorly planned and gave Raco every opportunity to escape arrest. The commander is even blaming me that Owen was shot. He says that I put him in harm's way without proper protection, and I also endangered public traffic and public welfare … the list goes on. The way they see it, it might be difficult for me to avoid doing time."

"This is outrageous." Kit's voice was loud. "So who's in charge of the operation now?"

"Who else but Petri. From what I heard informally, it seems that someone higher up contacted the commander. They need someone to blame for the public relations disaster of the firefight and the escape of the main suspect. Plus no one has been arrested for the massacre, and this is embarrassing all the authorities, both police and your organization."

"They're not setting you up to take the blame, are they?"

Matt shrugged. He waved to the waiter and ordered another espresso. "It looks like it."

"I don't think I can work with that slimy Petri."

Matt eased forward in his chair. "Here's what I think you should do. Keep working with the task force, but remember that someone is playing a political game. They don't necessarily want the guilty parties to be captured. I never said this, but I intend to continue investigating in my own time. I don't trust Petri or his team." Matt's voice was quiet.

Kit's mobile beeped. A message from Angel told her to report to OIDC as soon as possible. *What's it about?* she texted back. *We'll discuss that when you come in,* came the response.

"What was that?" Matt asked.

"I don't know, something from my office."

"Be careful, Kit. I'm not sure what's going on, but I intend to find out. I'm going to make my own enquiries and try to locate the diary. Give it another day, and then let's brief your boss Eva. If you get called to a Capture Task Force meeting, go and take notes. It looks like this morning's regular meeting has been cancelled."

"Okay. You take care. If they want to take over the case, it might mean that you're getting closer to something that someone doesn't want discovered. This is an ethnic and political powder keg."

"One other thing. Let's keep this possible relocation of Blaku to ourselves for now. I want to handle this myself through the appropriate channels."

"I'd like to see her if possible and explain the situation. I feel that she's trusted us and no one else."

Matt agreed and told her the address of the safe house on the outskirts of Pristina. "This is highly confidential," he said. "Eva and Angel both know the location. I suggest you go with one of them. And don't write down the address anywhere, please."

Kit stood up and left money on the table for the waiter.

"There is one other thing. It was always unclear whether the office would decide to press charges against Raco for sexual assault. I know how important this issue is to you, and if it was up to me, I would have pressed the issue. But now with Petri in charge, they have decided not to pursue that part of the investigation."

Kit looked at Matt with an incredulous stare. She shook her head. "No, it can't be. How can they do that?"

"The office has discretion not to investigate and proceed to prosecution."

"Why are they going to do? Just focus on the organized crime aspect or gunrunning?" The pitch of her voice rose.

"I suppose so. The story is that there isn't enough evidence to support a conviction."

"No evidence—only the testimony of the victim," Kit said in exasperation.

"Yes, I know. I thought I'd give you a heads-up. I'm still going to try to get her protected witness status and perhaps relocation, even to New Zealand if possible."

"That's something, I suppose, but it's so unjust. What's wrong with this world?" Kit picked up her briefcase and left the cafe. A row of taxis waited a few meters up the road. She elected to avoid the many unmetered ones and jumped into one of the more reliable cabs from a radio dispatch firm. She asked to be taken to OIDC headquarters.

She found Angel sitting at her desk typing beside Eva's empty office. At her feet sat Bambino with his head on his paws as he snoozed.

"Hi. How's it going?" Kit bent down to pet the dog. "Where's Eva?"

"You know; same old, same old. In court for the morning."

"So, what's happening?"

"I'm not sure," Angel said. "Last thing yesterday one of the HR assistants called and asked for your attendance records. She wouldn't say why, but this morning I got a message from the head of personnel saying that she needed to meet with you as soon as possible. Eva said that you should go and report back to her later."

"Can I take a look at my attendance records, please?"

Angel handed Kit a blue folder. "It's times like this that you realize we're working for a big bureaucracy," she said.

"I'd better get it over with," Kit said. She took the blue folder, a notebook, and a pencil, and went downstairs to the personnel section. She knocked on the door of the chief human resources officer, a solidly built Jamaican woman with short, curly, black hair held back by a hairband. Kit introduced herself. Samantha Brett indicated that she should take a seat.

"Good morning, Caitlin. I hope it's okay if we use first names. Thank you for coming in. I'm sorry we haven't had a chance to meet earlier."

"How can I help you?"

"I'm sorry that our first meeting had to start like this, but there have been questions asked about your attendance over the last month. I understand that you were put on administrative leave with pay, but you came back to work sooner than expected. In addition, according to the attendance sheets, you haven't been signing in regularly, and you've been keeping irregular hours."

Kit felt blindsided. No one had told her about the requirement to sign in, and no one had complained when she had come back to work a few days early.

"But my supervisor Eva Refazo never said anything."

"That's why I am here to ensure that the personnel rules of the organization are properly observed."

"Well, since the rules have now been brought to my attention, I'll make sure that I familiarize myself with them," Kit said in a lawyerly way.

"There's more, I'm afraid. I've also received a complaint from the office of the head of mission. Apparently you made some ill-advised, unauthorized comments at an important public forum."

"Who told you that?"

"As I said, the information came from the office of the head of mission. The highest level. This combination of factors is unfortunate. You didn't take the administrative leave when required, you have irregular attendance records, and furthermore, you have made unauthorized public statements, which apparently embarrassed the head of mission, all in the span of one month.

"I need to discuss this with my supervisor. She hasn't mentioned that it's a problem." Kit looked down and fidgeted with the papers in her folder.

"I rather think that Eva Revazo has her own problems right now."

"Quite frankly, I'm astonished by all this," Kit said. Then she paused, registering the implication. "What problems does my boss have?"

"Never mind that. I am obliged to tell you that your probation contract is now under review."

"What probation contract?"

"I assume it was explained to you that for the first two months, you must achieve satisfactory performance or your full contract will not be confirmed."

"No, this wasn't explained to me."

"I will arrange for you to be briefed by one of the human resources assistants to make sure that you are fully aware of all your obligations to the organization."

"I would appreciate that," Kit said as she took a breath and collected her thoughts. Fragments of the conversation with Sergei at Prizren came back to her. She remembered he was talking about how each scenario was like the square of the chess game, contested by opposing forces. While her first reaction had been one of surprise, her fighting spirit was returning. Her hands clenched briefly, and she stared for some time at the cold woman across the desk. She was not willing to concede this argument. "It seems that I have not been properly briefed by your department. It also seems unlikely that there is much that can be done at this stage which might challenge my probation contract. Questions could be asked about your own conduct. I've been working very hard, including extended hours at a crime scene locations assisting the police investigation into serious crimes. These include the massacre of twelve people. I hardly think your quibbling over time and attendance would go down well."

"Perhaps you should explain that to the head of mission. He described you as a loose cannon."

"I'd be delighted to discuss this with Mueller if he wants to talk to me. When he met with the US ambassador and the Russian head of liaison and several other important local interlocutors, he asked me to take notes, and he didn't mention any issues."

"I suggest you be more careful in future. You might have landed yourself some choice cases, but political fortunes can change with the wind here in Kosovo."

"Thanks for the advice. I won't forget it. I would be pleased to receive a briefing from your office when they see fit to contact me. This is the first time I've spoken to anyone in the human resources department. Any lack of awareness on my part would fall on your department, so you're responsible. If that's all, I have to rush to a case briefing."

"It's a staff obligation that they acquaint themselves with the rules of the organization."

"I'd be surprised if there are no obligations on behalf of the organization, but I will be sure to discuss it with my chief. A lot of people have learned from experience that it's difficult to win an argument with a good lawyer."

As she took the stairs to the prosecution office, Kit felt a headache coming on and stiffness in the back of her neck. She needed a quiet space in which to think about what had just happened and also about Matt's news. Was it possible that the same people that wanted him off the case also wanted her out and had somehow extended their influence into the OIDC office?

Angel looked up at when Kit arrived back in her office. "How did it go?" she asked.

"Not great. Apparently I need to pay more attention to my time and attendance, among other things." Right now she really felt a need to get out the office. "I think I need a breather," she said. "Maybe I can take the dog for a walk."

"Great idea," Angel said as she clipped his leash onto his studded collar.

The Missing Diary

Kit led the small dog out of the building. The OIDC compound was close to a small public park with roses, a few basic benches, and gravel paths. The day was wearing on, and it was not improving. She had the impulse to pull out a cigarette and light it, even though she didn't usually smoke. She felt sympathy for Matt, who had done just that. Where had the pressure come from to remove him from case? The two events could be completely unrelated, of course, her and Matt being leaned on, but what if there was a connection? It seemed clear that in his case he had found an adversary in Major Petri from Romania, who had replaced him on the task force. Perhaps she was seen as being too closely associated with Matt.

Then there had been the attempt on her life, if that's what it was. What was Raco's motivation for attacking her? The people in this territory seemed to have a knack for intimidation. When her mind returned to the personnel office, she shuddered as she relived that very unpleasant interview. Had the head of mission complained about her after having asked her to take notes at the meeting? She thought he would have said something when she and Eva were in his office. The whole situation was getting more and more untenable. She felt attacked not only by the criminal underworld, but also by her own office, who should have been more supportive. Kit was looking forward to discussing it with Eva and seeing what she thought. And what were the problems Eva had? Bambino was sniffing around the herbaceous border when her mobile rang. It was Xander.

"Hey, hon. What's up?" she said.

It was a video call. Xander was stretched out on the couch with a glass of whiskey on the rocks sitting in front of him. It was around midday in Kosovo, so it would be past midnight in New Zealand.

Xander launched into a rambling account of his day. He had been to a party and probably had too much to drink. He thought he should let her know he had found another apartment, because it didn't seem right that he should stay in her aunt's house while she wasn't there. Kit had a sense of disorientation and a cold feeling in the pit of her stomach in spite of the fact that it was a warm late-summer's day. She had imagined that Xander would still be there when she got back to Auckland.

"What brought that on?" she asked.

"There've been some changes in my life recently. I feel like it's time to move on."

Kit's body tensed and her grip on the phone tightened. She turned so that her shadow fell more onto the screen and she could see him better.

"What changes? Why don't you come over here for a while?"

"I'm too busy with my studies," Xander said defensively; his voice was slurred. "I need to tell you that I've been seeing someone else—one of my tutors from the university."

Kit got up and started pacing up and down the gravel path. Then she started to walk them around the perimeter of the small park. "Are you moving in with this person?"

Xander squirmed on the couch, then knocked back another slug of whiskey.

"I've been out on a few dates with her, that's all. I'm not proposing to move in with her or anything, not at this stage at least. I just feel that I need more support at this crucial time when I'm about to defending my PhD." He was rambling now.

"I didn't want you to leave to go to Kosovo. You insisted on it. You always put your needs in front of mine," he concluded.

"You're drunk, Xander. I think we need to talk about this later when you're sober. I hope you're not throwing away the relationship that we've worked so hard on these past three years. This assignment is just short-term, for goodness' sake. It's not open season for dating other people."

"So, I guess you haven't been dating anyone else," Xander said pointedly.

"No, as a matter of fact I haven't," Kit snapped. Did Sergei count as a date? She pushed that thought aside. Denial seemed like the best strategy. She hadn't intended that anything would challenge her relationship with Xander, which she thought was on firm ground.

"That's your story anyway," Xander said petulantly. When she heard his phone ringing, he excused himself to take the call. *It's probably her.* Kit speculated whether she was older or younger than Xander. She didn't bother to wait for Xander to return to the call. She disconnected. Life was getting worse by the minute. Maybe she did need that time off that Eva had insisted she should take. But now that her probation contract was being questioned, she couldn't afford to be seen to take the time off without any justifiable medical reason. Kit sat down on the park bench again and put her head in her hands. This felt like a bad time to be away from home.

Kit collected herself after a few minutes, called Bambino, and walked him back to the building. Suddenly she felt the need to touch his reassuring warm body. She wasn't sure whether it was to help him or comfort her. The dog had had a broken leg when Eva had found him in the rescue shelter, and he walked with a limp.

Meanwhile, Eva had arrived back from court and was toting a load of legal files up the stairway into the building. She looked so tired that Kit hesitated to burden her with her own concerns. However, it was urgent to get things off her chest, and so with Bambino's leash in one hand and legal briefs in the other, Kit accompanied Eva up the marble steps.

"Can I talk to you about something?" Kit asked.

Eva glanced at her out the corner of her eye through a lock of hair that had found its way out of her messy bun. "Can it wait until I've had a cigarette?"

Kit laughed. "I can do better than that. I can get us some coffee if you like."

"Deal," Eva said.

They went into Eva's office and deposited the files on her desk. It was difficult to find a clear space, but Kit balanced the ones she had been carrying horizontally over the documents in Eva's in tray.

"Thanks for taking Bambino out. He doesn't get enough walks these days."

Just then Angel appeared in the doorway carrying a tray with coffee and a small plate of cookies. "I thought you might appreciate these," she said.

"Thanks," Kit said. "I was just going to get us some coffee."

"Your wish is my command. It looks like you both could do with some," Angel said.

Kit and Eva sat down on the brown leather sofa. Eva lit up her cigarette, and Kit dipped a cookie into her coffee.

"I'm not sure where to start. A lot has been going on. I was called into the head of personnel's office an hour ago. They have problems about my attendance records, and apparently someone from the office at the head of mission has complained about my statement at the conference. She threatened to give me a poor grade on my probation assessment. Then there was Matt's news."

Eva raised her hand to indicate that Kit should stop. "These people are impossible. Sometimes I wonder how they get into the organization. It's a complete disaster. I told them that you are doing excellent work and not to worry about a few missing hours—or even days—on the attendance records. I don't think it's Mueller who's making the problems. It might be his assistant or maybe someone has gotten to his assistant. Or the deputy head of mission, or the senior political adviser … Who knows? Sometimes our work can be subject to political interference—and as often as not, you'll never know where it's coming from."

"Well, that's reassuring. The personnel officer was threatening. I told her that if I didn't know the correct procedures, it was her fault for not informing me."

"That's the way. It's hard for them to understand the kind of world we live in with these prosecutions to manage. Did you tell her you'd been working on the massacre case?"

"I talked about the caseload, although not about the details. She seemed to know about it and said that I was lucky to be given important cases, but I shouldn't get ideas above my station—at least that was the way I understood the message."

"I'll make sure that you get your contract confirmed. We're overwhelmed with work here at the moment. I might need to ask you later to assist with some other cases."

Kit nodded. "And about Matt …" Kit paused before she recounted her meeting with Matt and him telling her that he'd been taken off the case in favour of Major Petri.

"We were supposed to be keeping a watching brief on the cases and the evidence collection, so I suggest you continue to attend task force meetings, but try to keep a low profile—if you can manage that." Eva gave Kit a direct look and continued. "If you think it's necessary after the incident with Raco the other day, then we can assign you protection."

"I've thought about that," Kit said. "But I'm not sure it would help at this point. Maybe next time I take a trip through the Shari Mountains, I might keep that in mind. I haven't felt threatened here in Pristina. I don't think he'll come here because of the warrant for his arrest, which is outstanding."

"Yes, it'll keep him out of the city centre for a while. Let me know if you change your mind about the close protection. A couple of months back when I was working on a major organized-crime case, I had protection until we arrested the main suspects and put them in detention. It was a bit of a drag having men trailing around after me."

"Did you get the convictions you were after?"

"We got one. And we managed to find enough evidence to open another case on bribery and corruption. But it's like a Russian nesting doll; you open one and find another and another and another. Sometimes it gets bigger and bigger, in fact."

THE MISSING DIARY

Kit remembered that Samantha Brett had said something about Eva having her own problems, but she decided maybe it was better not to ask. "And one other thing. Things aren't going so well at home with my boyfriend. I don't think he's adjusting well to my absence."

Eva paused for a moment to absorb this news. "I'm sorry. That must be tough."

"I want to see what he does. Maybe it's better that this comes out before we marry rather than after. It's disappointing though."

"Sometimes it can be easier to sort things out in person. Maybe you could bring him here for a while."

"I did invite him, but I know now why he wasn't so enthusiastic about the idea."

Eva uttered an expletive when Bambino stood in his water bowl. Kit took that as her cue to leave. It was getting late, and she decided to take some documents home to read in the comfort of her apartment. She was halfway down the stairs when she realized she had not briefed Eva on the lost diary and the fact that she was carrying one of the translations. It wouldn't do any harm to keep it in her bag with the other documents. She would tell Eva about it later and put it in the office safe tomorrow.

Chapter Sixteen

I'm all for talking things out. But sometimes only the use of force can solve our problems. I'm not afraid to take action, when I have to. I fight for what I believe and I'm proud of it.

Merita's diary, 25 August 2000

Kit took the work shuttle bus into town and walked to her apartment from there. She was dragging her feet and felt very tired. She was still bruised and hurting from rolling out of the taxi. She had hit the ground hard and was black and blue on one side. Fortunately, the doctor who checked her had told her that she hadn't broken anything. But even so, she had gone from one shocking event to the next. The news from Xander had hurt her more than being rammed by Raco's car at high speed. There had to be some good points about the situation, but at the moment, she couldn't see them. She worked well with Matt and Owen, but Owen was in hospital and Matt was no longer leading the task force. Now she had a problem with the personnel department, and she didn't know why. It was true that her hours had not exactly been regular, but she had been putting in the work. Her time with Sergei had been a high point, but she felt unclear about what was going on there. Why did she feel unable to tell anyone about their meetings? It had felt awkward when they'd had the meeting at work and he was there in his official capacity. But nevertheless, she felt she had learned some useful ideas from him. For example, she asked herself what her intentions were at the present moment. It was positive that Blaku might go into a witness protection program in New Zealand. New Zealand—things would not be the same if Xander was not there waiting for her.

She thought about things from different angles as she approached her apartment block. As she trudged into the building through the main door, she about to punch the elevator button when she saw an out of order message taped over it. Kit rolled her eyes. All too often the elevator was out of order. She lived on the fifth floor, and she didn't enjoy climbing the internal staircase. Internal staircases could set the scene for crimes—she had read of several occasions when people had been robbed in them. She tried to look on having to use the staircase when the elevator was out of order as a good workout. Sighing, she started to climb the staircase. It had looked new when she moved in, but already the walls were starting to look less than clean. There were smudged dark spots in areas and already some graffiti had appeared.

Kit was on the fifth floor and was reaching for the key in her handbag when she noticed her apartment door was open. A cold tension convulsed in the pit of her stomach. Her tiredness was gone in an instant and replaced by alertness. She had definitely locked the door when she left this morning. She pushed it open and looked down the hallway. Drawers had been pulled out and their contents strewn around. She froze. Someone could still be in there. Her skin crawled at the thought of encountering Raco again. She took a deep breath. Her fight or flight impulses warred for control. Then her curiosity arose. She wanted to see for herself who might be in there.

She decided to report it and call for help immediately. She was inside when she pulled up Angel's number on speed dial, but something hit her hand that was holding her mobile and sent it flying across the hallway. It smashed into the wall and fell to the floor. When the door slammed against the wall, she turned to find Merita Shala, who had been hiding in the utility room.

Shala was wearing black stretch jeans with sports shoes, a black T-shirt, and a hooded, light jacket. Her makeup highlighted the smoky depths of her eyes, which flashed at Kit.

"What are you doing here?" Kit blurted out, even though she knew.

"Still asking questions?" Shala said with a sneer. "I'm asking the questions this time."

Kit's hand stung from the sharp blow delivered by Shala. The fingers on her left hand were still numb after having had the door handle wrenched out of it. Kit tried to assess her best escape route. But Shala was standing close to the one and only door. The windows were too high above the ground to jump, and her mobile was out of reach.

"Where's my diary?" Shala shouted aggressively.

"I … I don't know. That's the truth. It's missing. I don't have it."

"Where are the translations?"

The Missing Diary

"You've searched the place quite thoroughly and you didn't find them. What does that tell you? What's in the diary that you're so concerned about?"

"As I said at the police station, I'm a keen creative writer and I'm eager to get my work back."

"Why are you so determined to get it back when it's full of fantasy?"

"Clearly you are not a writer or you would understand."

"Don't be ridiculous. If you leave now I'll wait a few minutes before I call the police."

"What's in your briefcase?"

Kit looked down at her briefcase. She had forgotten momentarily that it contained a translation of the diary. Kit didn't reply; instead she gripped the bag more tightly. It was then that Shala made a move to snatch it.

Kit braced herself, grabbed Shala's wrist, kicked her right knee, and stomped on her foot. She moved forward quickly, struck Shala in the face, and snatched the briefcase away to a safe distance. It was Shala's turn to be surprised. She froze briefly. Her head snapped backward, but she recovered quickly and swung at Kit with an uppercut.

Kit's Krav Maga training kicked in, and she attacked Shala with as much force as she could muster. Shala had been surprised for a moment, but then her own training took over. She had been trained for combat in the field both as a police officer and a KLA soldier. Kit was taller and stronger than Shala, but Shala was faster, more vicious, and more experienced as a fighter.

"Make my day, bitch!" Shala taunted.

Kit's right cheek was stinging from the painful blow delivered by Shala, and she tasted the metallic tang of blood in her mouth.

"My pleasure. You're going away for a long time, sooner rather than later," Kit tossed back.

As Shala attacked again in a flurry of flying limbs, kicking, scratching, and poking, Kit blocked again and again as she was forced back into her living room. The briefcase served as an improvised shield to block several punches. However, Kit knew that sooner or later, Shala would wrench it away from her. She had to think more strategically and not just react to Shala's onslaught.

All she could think of was a simple plan, but one that might serve her. If she could retreat up the hallway, grab her mobile, and then run out the apartment, she had a chance to escape with the briefcase and save the translation of the diary.

Kit looked around quickly. Without her attention leaving Shala, she searched for something that she could use. There wasn't a lot at hand, but she grabbed a pot plant and threw it hard at Shala, who blocked it with her forearm and came up underneath to grab yet again at the briefcase. Kit used the second it took Shala to block the flying plant to move past her and up the hallway. She dashed toward the mobile phone, picked it up, and ran for the door. Shala growled with frustration as she sprinted after her. Shala tugged at the carpet in the hallway. Kit stumbled forward but stayed on her feet and made it out the door. Kit bolted toward the stairwell. But she was not as fast as Shala, who was wearing her running shoes as opposed to Kit's sandals.

Shala took down Kit in a flying tackle just as she started down the stairs. They landed hard in a heap on the landing where the stairs led the next floor down. Kit yelled at the top of her voice and pounded Shala's head.

The Missing Diary

She was hampered by the briefcase in one hand and her mobile in the other. She didn't want to lose either. Shala focused her attention on the briefcase and ignored Kit's blows and screaming. She rolled on top of Kit and pinned her down. With a knee on Kit's belly, Shala scrambled to her feet and stamped down hard on Kit's outstretched arm—the one holding the briefcase.

Kit tried with all her strength to move her arm out from underneath Shala's foot. She let go of her mobile and did her best to gain purchase on Shala's body to flip her over. But Kit was unable to move the arm that Shala had effectively pinned. As she strained against her leg and the full body weight of her opponent, Shala wrenched the briefcase out of Kit's trembling fingers.

"Not bad for an international," Shala said with a sneer. "I'll give you some more training someday. Thanks for the briefcase. I'll be interested to see what's inside."

"You're nothing more than a thug and a thief," Kit said from between clenched teeth. "Give my bag the hell back!"

"Pleased to oblige, ma'am, when it's empty and I've finished with it. I'm just taking back what belongs to me."

Shala kicked Kit's mobile down the stairwell. Kit heard the sickening clunk of it hitting the stairs and bouncing from one level to the next. That hurt on many levels.

"See you around," Shala said as she left Kit lying on the floor of the stairwell and raced downwards, taking two steps at a time.

Kit lay on the cold concrete without moving. She hurt all over, and she wouldn't have been surprised if she had concussion. She already had bruised ribs, and she knew that all her muscles would be sore the next day.

There were probably major bruises on her belly where Shala had pushed her down using her knee. Worse than that, Shala had stolen the translation. At least it told her that it was not Shala or her associates who had stolen the original diary.

Kit didn't want any of her neighbors to find her lying in a crumpled heap on the stairwell, so she got up gingerly. Her body was aching, but she did not seem to have broken anything. She groaned softly as she made her way back up the stairs toward her apartment. What a disaster. The door was still hanging open, and the keys were dangling out the lock. Then she remembered her mobile. She didn't want anyone finding it, so slowly and painfully she climbed down the five flights of stairs to look for it. It was at the base of the stairwell and looked very much the worse for wear; its screen was shattered. She bent down, picked it up, tucked it into her pocket, and headed back up in the elevator, which strangely enough was now working.

After returning to her apartment and locking the door, Kit reviewed the situation. Her first reaction could have been to call the police. Ordinarily she would have done that immediately. However, her mobile phone was broken, so that knee-jerk reaction couldn't happen. Then she wondered what would be achieved by reporting the incident to the police. They already knew that Shala was associated with criminals.

She went into the bathroom and peeled off her clothes. They had taken a beating as well, and her top was torn. She looked at herself in the mirror. Her ponytail was still tied in place, but strands had escaped and hung about her face in messy disarray. The bruises on her ribs from her experience in the mountains had taken on a deep-purple hue, and she had fresh bruises and grazes on her elbows, knees, and her jaw. What she needed was time to think. She took three ibuprofen tablets with a glass of water. Then she turned on the water for a bath and sat on the edge. She sprinkled a few drops of lavender oil, a gift from her mother, into the bath. The aroma was both fragrant and relaxing. Her mother had said that lavender oil helped heal bruises; today was a great opportunity to test that theory.

She took stock of what was in her briefcase. Fortunately, it was not that much. She didn't usually carry much cash on her, although she would need to request a replacement bank card. There were files in the briefcase—which she didn't want Shala to see. There was a draft conflict-related, sexual-violence policy paper that she had been working on for Eva, and a rough notebook. The breakage of her mobile phone was perhaps the worst thing, but she figured she could probably move the same SIM card to another phone and that would keep all her contacts and other calling information intact. She would have to notify the OIDC Security Service about the loss of her security card.

When the bath was drawn, she lowered her body into it carefully and allowed the hot, scented water to cover her up to her neck. The painkillers was starting to take effect. As steam rose from the water, Kit tried to think strategically. What good would be accomplished by reporting this incident? She was already exposed at work and didn't want to draw more attention to herself by being at the center of another drama when her position was precarious. Major Petri was now in charge of the investigation, and she viewed him as a hostile. Moreover, people at the mission tended to panic, and she didn't want to be followed everywhere by a minder or be investigated for losing official evidence.

She would tell Matt about it tomorrow. She wasn't sure whether she would tell Eva or not. Maybe it was better to keep things simple and keep working with Matt behind the scenes. She would keep going to the task force meetings as she had been told to but keep the rest to herself. In fact, the translation of the diary did little to help Shala. It gave her more information, namely that Kit did not have the stolen diary. Kit decided that it was time to resume her Krav Maga lessons in earnest, if she could find a good local teacher. That seemed possible, because Kosovo did well in martial arts and hand-to-hand international combat competitions. Shala had certainly illustrated that point.

Her mind drifted to Sergei. When she was with him she felt excited and safe at the same time. She loved hearing his ideas about the khash philosophy. She tried to imagine what he would say about the situation she was in now. Perhaps he would say she was like a knight who had just been taken by another knight or even a more lowly piece, perhaps a pawn. But she was still in play in spite of all that had happened. At that moment, a message came through on her mobile. She was surprised it was still working. That was one piece of good news. Sergei. Yet again he had contacted her when she was thinking about him. *Drinks at the Gallery Bar—tomorrow 7 p.m.? S,* his message said.

Sure—see you there, Kit replied. She would have to find a way to disguise her many scrapes and bruises before work the next day. She was already thinking of the high-necked blouse she could wear to hide her injuries. She would let her wavy hair fall around her face for a change, which might cover some of the bruises around her jaw and neck. Makeup would help too.

Sergei might know where she could learn self-defense. Thinking about Sergei brought to mind the last conversation she'd had with Xander. She still felt terrible about it, but maybe it was better that it happened now rather than later. That was the whole point of getting engaged, wasn't it? To see if things were going to work out. She had only been away a short time, and there he was seeing other women. She wiped the cracked surface of her mobile phone on her bathrobe and looked more carefully at the screen. She had two missed calls from Xander and two unopened messages. He had no clue what she was going through while he lolled around on the couch, drinking whiskey and dating another woman. She deleted his messages without opening them. He was the last person she wanted to talk to. Kit looked at her claddagh ring. Xander had brought it for her on their trip to Galway. It glowed golden fire on her right hand. As it faced outward, it showed that her heart had not been taken.

CHAPTER SEVENTEEN

I consider myself to be a creative person. I look for new solutions to old problems. My daily journal entries are the raw material I work from.

Merita's diary, 28 August 2000

Kit was slow to dress the next morning. More bruises had appeared overnight. After taking another couple of painkillers, she put the packet in her handbag in case she needed more later. She pulled on a pair of fitted, navy pants and slipped into matching navy pumps. One of her ankles was painfully swollen after her fall down the stairs. Thankfully, when she tested her weight on it, she found that she could walk almost normally, without too much of a limp. She put on a white linen blouse, which buttoned up to the neck, and fastened it with a cameo brooch that she had inherited from her grandmother. She used a sparkly hair clip to pin a lock of hair back on her right side, leaving the left side loose.

    She had suffered almost as badly after some of her full-contact Krav Maga classes, she thought, trying to reassure herself that she had gotten through this before. Her mobile looked almost as battered as its owner; its screen was a spider's web of cracks. Angel had sent a message telling her to come in for a meeting with a VIP at nine fifteen a.m. Kit sighed. She was not in the mood for another meeting with Jacob Mueller, his assistants, or any of the visiting dignitaries. No doubt he would designate her again as notetaker. She had not gone to law school for all those years to take notes at meetings.

When she arrived at the office, Eva gave her a long, hard look but then apparently decided not to say anything before she called her into her office. Eva's morning coffee was sitting in the polystyrene cup with her cigarette slowly smoking beside it in an ashtray.

"Sit down," Eva said. "We have a surprise visitor this morning."

"Who might that be?"

"Visar Dreshaj, the Albanian-Kosovar politician, wants to talk about progress on the Staro Dorbi massacre investigation."

"Why is he coming here? Doesn't he normally speak to the head of mission or political affairs? Or Matt—I mean Major Petri."

"Normally, yes. With all the funny business going on at the moment, I'm not even going to ask him why or invite anyone else to the meeting. Call it prosecutor's intuition."

"Why do you think he's coming here then?"

Eva took a drag on her cigarette, got up, and looked out the window. She could see over the rest of the compound from that commanding position; officials walking from one building to the next, carrying files, OIDC vehicles coming and going, security guards swaggering about in uniform with guns at their sides.

"He must want something. I'm not sure what. Maybe information. He asked to speak only to us. He met us at the last meeting with Mueller, and perhaps it's because of your reputation after the conference." Eva turned around and smiled grimly at Kit.

"Okay, it's going to be interesting. I don't mind taking notes at our meetings, but I do object to taking minutes for Mueller."

"As I said, it's better to be in his good books than his bad ones. This isn't a battle I want to fight at the moment. It's a way to get into meetings and be better informed than we would otherwise be."

"Maybe that's how the Playboy bunnies look at taking drinks around the Playboy mansion," Kit said.

Eva laughed. "I'll draw a line if he asks us to dress up as Playboy bunnies."

"I'd like to see that," a voice in the doorway said. It was Angel. She put a small mobile on Eva's desk. "Click it on and press record just before he comes in."

Eva looked at Kit. "I thought it might be a good idea to record the conversation just to cover ourselves."

"Do you think he might try to compromise us?"

"You never know."

Kit went to get her notepad just before Angel called them to the meeting.

Eva greeted their visitor and offered him tea or coffee. Dreshaj accepted a cup of coffee with two sugars, while Kit asked for an Americano. She noticed there was a red light glowing on the recorder in Eva's tote. They sat around the small table in the unadorned conference room. Dreshaj was wearing a crumpled, gray polyester suit, a red tie, and had disheveled dark-brown hair.

"It's very kind of you to stop by, Mr. Dreshaj," Eva said. "What can we do for you?"

He thanked them for their time and said that he wanted an update on the investigation in private. "I know this is an unusual request, but given the importance of this case to my constituents, I hope we can have an off-the-record discussion."

"As I'm sure you're aware, Mr. Dreshaj, we're not in the position to discuss the ongoing police investigation."

"I think it could be mutually beneficial if communication channels could remain open between us. To be frank with you, I'd prefer to have open, confidential, and off-the-record discussions with you that do not go outside this room."

Eva took a cigarette from her box and held it between her fingers. Dreshaj pulled out his pack of Lucky Strikes and lit Eva's cigarette with his lighter. Eva looked at Kit, who had her pen poised. Eva shook her head. Kit closed her notebook and put down her pen.

Dreshaj nodded, then asked his questions. How long had Eva and Kit been in Kosovo? Did they have friends or family here? How did they enjoy it? Eva answered for them both, explaining that she had been in Pristina since the beginning of the OIDC mission, while Kit had only been there for a few weeks. She said that they enjoyed Kosovo, although they didn't have much chance to relax because they were very busy with work. She did not answer the question about friends or family.

"I hope you will excuse me for asking such personal questions," he said. "May I ask what you think about the independence of Kosovo and Serbia's claims over it?"

Eva took a long drag on her cigarette while she thought about the question. Kit thought Dreshaj was behaving as if he was a confidential informant. Perhaps he actually had information for them, not vice versa, and wanted to sound them out first about their views on Kosovo. She shook her head, which was getting too full of conspiracy theories. She needed to wait and see what would happen. Again the ideas of khash, Sergei's metaphysical system, came to mind, and she thought about strategies that might be applied by the players on this particular part of the chessboard.

What was her intention in this segment of the game? That much at least was clear. She wanted to help solve the crime, get justice for the victims, and prove herself in this new international scenario. She also wanted the best for her friends as well—Matt to be reinstated, Owen to be out of hospital, and while Blaku was not a friend as such, she hoped for a soft landing for her after she had given evidence in the case.

"You know the official position of this organization. We are neutral and aim to respect and assist both sides of the conflict equally," Eva said.

"I know the official line, yes. But what about you personally. You are Italian, no? You recognize Kosovo's legitimate need for existence and New Zealand too," he said as he nodded toward Kit.

"As you also know, Mr. Dreshaj, we're international civil servants and as such we do not take instructions from our home governments."

"I was hoping for a frank and open discussion."

"Do you have information to share with us?" Eva asked.

"That depends." There was a long pause. Dreshaj shifted in his chair and looked out toward the window through the glass conference room wall. Eva reached into her bag and turned off the recording device. She placed it on the table in front of them all, so he could see that it was off. "Of course, there could be other recording devices," Dreshaj said. "But I appreciate the gesture. I would like to say this … If certain confidential information came into our possession that could have a bearing on the case, and if we were able to share this information, I would like your assurance that you would use it to bring the chief perpetrators to justice without fear or political influence affecting your decisions. I would also like to know that it would not be given to the other side and the whole thing covered up for political reasons."

Eva listened carefully and paused for a moment before responding. "This is a strictly off-the-record discussion, Mr. Dreshaj. I believe you appreciate that. If anyone asks me, I will say that this meeting never happened. I give you my word that I will pursue any criminals to the utmost extent of the law. You probably know my reputation as an uncompromising prosecutor. That's how I achieved this position. I also believe my staff to be of the highest integrity and know that they would not be involved in any coverups or double-dealing that could affect the case."

"It seems that different people have different views on what makes a good prosecutor," Dreshaj said.

"I like to think of the standards set by former US attorney general Robert Jackson, who in a speech in April 1940 talked about the role of the federal prosecutor." She glanced up at a framed text Kit hadn't noticed before in the otherwise plain room. "He said among other things that citizens' safety lies in the prosecutor who tempers zeal with human kindness, who seeks truth and not victims, who serves the law and not factional purposes, and who approaches his or her task with humility."

Kit made a mental note of the quote. She was impressed and surprised that Eva was conversant with the thought of the US attorney general's words from 1940. She agreed with her boss and felt good to be part of her team.

"I'm impressed by your learning, Ms. Refazo. If only all justice officials thought like that. And what about your views on Kosovo?" Dreshaj continued. "Do you think we belong to Serbia?"

"I think it's clear that Kosovo belongs to Kosovo. There is, of course, a need to protect the rights of minority communities."

"Thank you, Ms. Refazo. That's what I wanted to hear. In case any such confidential information does come my way, I may contact you to discuss these things further."

Eva thanked Dreshaj and rose from the table. She shook his hand and explained that she needed to go to a court hearing and that her colleague would escort him out.

Kit escorted Dreshaj into the lobby before they made their way down the stairs. She exchanged pleasantries with the visitor until they were almost at the base of the stairs. Then she was distracted by a passing co-worker she hadn't seen for a while. When for a moment she wasn't looking where she was going, she overbalanced on her weak ankle and stumbled. Without thinking, she grabbed Dreshaj's arm to steady herself. He grasped her hand and pulled her closer to him.

"S-Sorry," she mumbled. "I twisted my ankle yesterday, and I guess I lost my footing for a moment. I'm sorry." Kit felt her face turn pink. They were close enough that she could smell his cologne. She looked into his dark brown eyes. They were kind. Kit was trying to present a professional impression and had failed yet again by placing herself in a vulnerable position.

"Are you okay?" Dreshaj asked with concern.

" Er … yes, I think so. I just lost my footing."

"Allow me to escort you down the next flight of stairs." Dreshaj smiled.

Kit appreciated his courtesy and relaxed. "But I'm supposed to be escorting you."

"Kosovo is a place where the unexpected happens," he said.

"I've noticed that."

When they reached the bottom of the stairs, a security officer walked up to them to lead Dreshaj to his car.

"Do you have a business card? Perhaps we could meet for a coffee next week. Maybe Wednesday, if you have time. I'd like to hear more about legal practice in New Zealand. My nephew's considering emigrating to Australia or New Zealand to study law. I'm sure he'd appreciate any information you could give me."

Kit handed him one of the business cards that she kept in her pocket and he gave her one of his. "Please call me Visar," he said.

"Alright, I will. Thanks, Visar. You can call me Caitlin," she said. They shook hands and he departed.

Kit went back to her office, grateful that as far as she knew no one had seen her embarrassing fall on the stairs. Initially, she had assumed that Visar was just being friendly with his coffee invitation, but then she wondered whether it might be a continuation of the discussion they had just had in the meeting room. She had the distinct impression that he might have confidential information which he wanted to share, perhaps relating to one of their cases. Most likely it related to the massacre. Even more disturbing was the fact that she had actually enjoyed taking his arm.

That afternoon, Kit stayed in her office and rewrote what she could of the summary she was preparing about international law and standards regarding conflict-related, sexual-violence law reform. Although now she probably wouldn't need it because of the news that the new task force leader, Major Petri, did not intend to prosecute the sexual-assault allegations against Raco. It could prove useful for another case though. Before she knew it, it was time to meet Sergei. Each time she met him, it seemed there was more and more to talk about. She was looking forward to seeing him. She also needed to see Matt to update him on what had happened. She send Matt a text suggesting they meet the next day.

The Gallery Bar included a stylish book station, a small art gallery which displayed the work of local artists. They often had live music, which added to the atmosphere. The bar was popular among young, local professionals, as well as internationals of all kinds. The decor combined post-industrial chic with steam punk that would be enjoyed anywhere from Pristina to New York to Auckland.

When Kit arrived at the Gallery Bar, Sergei was waiting outside for her as he tapped his mobile. His thick, dark-blond hair was perfectly groomed as usual, and he was wearing a well-cut linen suit, probably Italian rather than Russian. It struck Kit that he was something of a chameleon. He could look outstanding anywhere, charm anyone, and blend in whenever he wanted to. At the moment, he wanted to be seen. The gallery was surrounded by a fence with well-trimmed hedges. Instead of rushing toward him, she took her time.

He looked up at her and beamed as he clicked off his mobile and put it in his pocket. "Are you checking me out? Come, let's go inside for a drink." He walked closer to her and held out his hands before drew her in and kissed both her cheeks. "They make a great mango Siberian sunrise cocktail here. Why don't you try one? I don't think they realize that Siberia is actually in Russia."

Kit laughed and walked ahead of him through the wrought-iron gateway and along the path leading to the bar. "Do you think they have a ban on all things Russian here?"

"It wouldn't surprise me."

"But they're letting you in tonight," she said.

"Sometimes being in plain sight is the best way to hide." Sergei caught the eye of the waiter. With a nod, the waiter indicated the table he had reserved in a corner close to the book station, away from the main crowd at the bar and the music speakers.

Kit ordered a white wine spritzer, while Sergei ordered a straight vodka, chilled. "Keep them coming," he added.

"I think I'll skip the Siberian sunrise," she said. "I feel as though I need to keep a clear head these days."

"Why is that? How are you doing since we saw each other last?"

Kit looked up and smiled at the waiter as he delivered her drink. She took a long, slow sip and enjoyed the refreshing coolness.

"Where to begin? I think the last time we spoke was in Prizren, wasn't it?"

"Yes."

Kit paused, unsure how much she wanted to tell Sergei. She didn't want to relive the episode in the mountains. Although something about it nagged at the back of her mind. If he hadn't made her take the taxi home alone, perhaps it wouldn't have happened.

"My apartment was burgled. I surprised the burglar, but she snatched my briefcase and ran off with it."

"My dear, that's terrible news," Sergei said as he reached across and put his hand over hers. "Are you alright?"

"Yes, I suppose so. I gave her a run for the money, but in the end she was faster than me. That reminds me. Do you know where I can do self-defense training?"

"I can make some enquiries. I noticed that you were limping and …" He reached up, brushed aside her hair, and revealed the bruise blooming on her cheek.

She pushed away his hand and sat back. She didn't want to be touched or comforted. She picked up her glass.

"I don't want to talk about it anymore right now. Tell me more about khash. How would a practitioner have reacted in such a situation?"

"We can discuss that, but first I want to know how you really are. Has something else happened to upset you? Do you think the thief was a regular thief or was he after something in particular?"

"She was after something in particular—she's one of our suspects in a case. There's no doubt she was looking for confidential notes that I might have taken during the interview with her and her co-conspirators."

THE MISSING DIARY

"Do you keep these confidential notes in your apartment?"

"I guess she thought that was a possibility, but no, I don't." Kit wasn't about to admit to losing the translation of Shala's diary.

"And you said the burglar was a woman. Did you report it to the police?"

"Yes, she is a KLA operative and former police officer, so she's pretty tough. No, I didn't report it to the police. I thought it wouldn't change anything, and I didn't want to be interrogated about what happened."

"Probably wise—most of the local police are KLA sympathizers, as we are well aware. I might be able to put the resources of the Russian Liaison Office at your disposal to help protect you. We could even move you into a safe house in one of the Serbian villages. We could make sure that you're safe there and also away from all the other trouble going on."

"What other trouble?"

"I don't know, you just mentioned that there were other things that were troubling you. I don't like to see you so tense and upset. Let me help."

"Thanks, I really appreciate the offer, but I'll be fine. I don't think she meant to harm me. When she couldn't find anything, she just grabbed my briefcase and ran. There … there wasn't anything special in the briefcase." Her lie came out naturally without her having to think about it. In a way it was true; the translation was poor, and they had another copy. "My boss offered me protection, but I turned it down. I don't want security officers following me."

"You know best, but remember I am just a phone call away. You can always come to my apartment or even to the Russian Liaison Office where we will provide you with protection. You have my word." He raised his chilled vodka shot glass. "To our friendship," he said and knocked it back. He put the empty glass on the table, and a few moments later the waiter passed by and replaced it.

"I see they know you here," Kit said as she indicated the refreshed vodka glass and smiled.

"You know, in my country we believe that vodka is a cure for all ills."

"I don't know about curing all ills, but I'm sure it makes you worry about them less."

"I can't disagree with you ... As to how a khash practitioner would deal with your issue, I can't give you a simple answer. We tend to think strategically, so probably the best approach would be to avoid the situation before it happens, or try to use it to advantage somehow."

"How could I use the situation to my advantage?"

"I don't know. Maybe ... for example, by having a tracer in your bag, you could then track the location of the thief."

"I don't possess a tracker."

"A mobile will do. They can be traced."

"I'll keep that in mind. Look at the mess she made of my mobile." She put the battered Samsung on the table.

"My offer of protection is still there. Perhaps this job is too dangerous for you. Although I don't want you to leave Pristina yet. For my own reasons."

"What reasons?" she asked and immediately wished that she hadn't. She wasn't sure she was ready for a frank exchange about the feelings between them. She was still feeling shocked and upset by what Xander had said and done. She didn't feel strong enough to tell Sergei about that.

He looked at her and raised an eyebrow. "You must feel the energy, the affinity, between us? I felt it as soon as we met. This is rare in a friendship. We need to get to know each other better … and that takes time. I have another suggestion. I could arrange accommodation for you in an apartment block where some of our liaison office staff live. That way, I could make sure that you're safe."

"I do appreciate the offer." This time it was her turn to take his hand. "I'll keep that in mind … If things get more difficult, I might just take you up on it."

"The offer is open. I wanted to talk to you about something else. You've shown such an interest in the khash philosophy, and I think you have the makings of a gifted practitioner. A group of us meet at least once a year to hone our skills. This year we plan to meet in Ljubljana. We do intensive training, learn to visualize our preferred scenarios, and fine-tune our intentions so we can implement this into our lives."

"Who's the teacher? Or do you teach each other?"

"We teach each other, but we also have a mentor or spiritual director. I think you would like him. Father Akadi comes from a family who has been linked to the Orthodox church for several generations. He's also a friend of Father Peter who we were going to meet the other day at Prizren. It's not a religious retreat as such though, because some of our group profess to be atheists."

"Does all this go back to your founder, the one that you mentioned?"

"You're very perceptive. Generally, we don't like to say his name in public because there has been so much misinformation about him. But yes, you're right. There is a tradition that the line of priests who are linked to our group come from the son of Rasputin. He wasn't recognised as such, since our founder was not married to his mother at the time."

"So it's kind of informally attached to the Orthodox Church."

"That's a good way to put it," Sergei said. "While the group prefers to work with as little publicity as possible, prominent families in Russia often seek our help. A number of the wealthiest oligarchs are among our clients. Their donations help with the upkeep of the church and help fund our retreats and other things."

"How would you overcome the difficulties of oligarchs in Russia?"

"I mean by providing spiritual support, prayer, counseling—teaching them how to move toward their best possible outcomes."

"I'd love to learn more about this. Can you give me more info closer to the time? I've heard about Ljubljana. I understand it's one of the most beautiful cities in Europe."

They sat for a while longer, listening to the live jazz group which had started playing. Sergei downed another shot of vodka before he showed Kit around the art gallery. Then they left the bar and headed into the ramshackle streets of Pristina. Kit had to watch her step on the uneven footpaths. She was grateful that Sergei escorted her safely back to her apartment.

She had only prepared for a kiss on the cheek before saying good night, but when he wrapped his arms around her, she stayed there with her head resting against his

The Missing Diary

chest before she hugged him. His warmth was reassuring, and the freshness of his cologne intoxicated her senses.

"Let me walk you back to your door to make sure it's safe," he said as he brushed her ear with his lips.

Even though the voice in her head screamed no, she acquiesced.

It was quiet and dark inside the foyer of her building. She had a sense of trepidation as she wondered if any of her stalkers would be waiting for her inside her apartment. They caught the elevator up, and as soon as they emerged, she looked from side to side, checking that there was nobody lurking in the shadows. She moved swiftly toward her apartment door but stopped short with surprise. Her briefcase was on the floor outside her door. Shala had obviously left the briefcase there. Kit quickly opened the door, picked up the briefcase, and went inside.

"What's that doing there? Is that the briefcase the intruder took?" Sergei asked.

"Yes, it looks like she brought it back."

She turned on the lights, afraid that there might be someone waiting inside. There wasn't. She opened the briefcase, riffled through the contents, and found that the original contents were still there, except for the translation of the diary. In its place was a small card with a flower and a smiley face drawn in red ink. That woman was incorrigible.

"I'll check later to see what's missing. All the documents seem to be here." The lie came easily.

"She probably took copies of what she needed."

"Probably," Kit said as she slipped the briefcase into the utility room and shut the door. Out of sight, out of mind.

"Can I offer you a drink?" she said.

Slowly and deliberately, Sergei closed the door behind them. "The only drink I want now is you," he said.

She turned to him. Her breath came faster and heat filled her chest … her heart … her mind. Her palms burned with the need to touch his skin. It seemed that they were back on that precipice overlooking Prizren. She looked into his molten, predatory eyes. Now there was no holding back. She fell, and there was no one to catch her.

CHAPTER EIGHTEEN

The key to understanding a person is to know who they associate with. Our friends can kead us to success or failure. They can bring us down faster than our enemies. I'm starting to wonder who my real friends are.

Merita's diary, 30 August 2000

Early the next morning, Kit rolled over and extended her arm. She expected it to rest on Sergei's muscular chest, but there was only an empty bed. She came awake slowly as she registered the fact that her passionate Russian lover from the night before had already disappeared. She sat up and checked the time. It was five thirty a.m. She pulled on a robe and padded around the apartment to check whether he was still there. She found a note on the kitchen table thanking her for last night and saying he had to meet someone at the airport—early. She dashed to the utility room and breathed a sigh of relief when she found her briefcase still there. Why had she thought Sergei might have taken it? Although he had said that any thief could take photographs of what they needed. He could have done the same.

It was disappointing to find him gone, although it was a relief that she had her place to herself. She leaned over. A trace of his fresh cologne still lingered, a silent testimony to their night together.

She checked her phone and found a text from Matt asking her to join him for a jog in Gërmia Park this morning.

He picked her up at seven a.m. outside her apartment in his Ford SUV. He didn't want to drive his official EUFOR vehicle, which could attract too much attention. Kit wore a comfortable pair of track pants and a T-shirt. Matt wore army running shorts, a camo T-shirt, and running shoes. Kit had never seen him so informally dressed. Carrying a small bottle of water, she opened the car door and slid into the passenger seat. "Hi, how's it going?"

"Pretty good for someone who's only semi-employed."

"They're still paying you, aren't they?"

"Oh yes, but that's not the point. I've decided to use some of my newly found spare time to get fit now that I'm no longer leading the task force."

"Good idea. I've been thinking the same thing. Been meaning to join the gym for a while now. I've got a home gym set up, but it's not the same."

They chatted as Matt drove to Gërmia Park, one of the few parks near Pristina of any size. It included picnic areas, cafes, and paths through the wooded lower foothills of the Rhodope mountains. Once he'd parked, they set off up the hill into the park at a leisurely pace.

"I want to talk to you without being overheard," Matt said.

"I was thinking the same thing."

"You go first."

THE MISSING DIARY

Kit outlined briefly what had happened the night Shala had broken into her apartment. She also mentioned the approach by Visar Dreshaj.

Matt comment about Shala's possible motivations.

"I thought there must be important evidence in that notebook. I have a copy of both translations back in the office. In the safe. And, you say, she returned the briefcase minus the translation—very kind of her. I suspect that someone may have tampered with the translations and substituted nonsense. Judging by her behaviour, I don't think Shala arranged for someone to steal her diary from the evidence room."

"My thinking exactly."

As they stopped at the top of the hill, Matt indicated that they should take the wooded path to the left, which followed a meandering, beaten path through the forest and upward to a small rise.

"I didn't see any police reports about your burglary. Did you report it?" Matt asked.

"No, I didn't. In fact, you're the only person I've told about it." *Except for Sergei.* "I have problems at work. They're querying my attendance. I've had nothing but trouble since I came to Kosovo. I don't want to be associated with more drama at the moment."

"I understand, but are you sure you shouldn't tell Eva about it?"

"I don't want to draw attention to the fact that I was carrying a translation of the diary. Also, after the business with Raco, they're threatening—or offering—to assign me close protection. I don't want security trailing around after me all the time. I don't think Shala will come after me. She got what she was looking for."

"Thanks for telling me about it," Matt said as he stretched out his leg on a tree stump. "By the way, you will be pleased to hear that Owen is out of hospital. The doc says he's going to make a full recovery."

"That's a huge relief."

"That brings me to what I wanted to talk to you about. Brussels is really messing us around with this task force. They want to show that they're integrating the countries from the Eastern Bloc—political machinations that have nothing to do with law enforcement."

"Was that the reason that they took the task force leadership away from you?"

"Yes. I think Petri is playing a political game, and I'm not prepared to let it go."

"But what can you do about it?"

"I've discussed it with London. They're okay with it. I'm setting up our own task force under the radar. We can't accept what they're doing with this massacre. Petri intentionally let Raco escape. And he's been running interference ever since I convened Task Force Capture. If the massacre goes unsolved, it's going to cause ongoing tensions between Belgrade and Pristina and severely undermine peace efforts."

Kit stretched her legs as she admired the rising sun coming over the mountains. "How would that work?"

"The cooperation of Eva as chief prosecutor is essential. Our task force would provide her with evidence to support prosecutions. We would effectively short-circuit whatever political game Brussels and Romania are playing."

"I think she'd be willing to do that. She basically told Dreshaj that she would prosecute without bias or political interference. I'm sure she means it."

The Missing Diary

Matt nodded and produced a pack of cigarettes from his pocket. He lit up and looked thoughtfully into the distance. Kit was about to comment on the inconsistency of trying to get fit through running and smoking, but she decided to let it go. He was a grown man.

"So, how do you think this would work?" Kit said.

"We'll continue to do our own investigations but keep the information away from Petri and his group for as long as possible. I've got contacts in the Kosovo Police, and I think they'd help if we ask. Owen's on board. I thought of approaching Don Edison, with the canine unit. He's a former marine, and he's a good man. That would get the Americans onside. If your boss is willing to support us, perhaps we could use your office assistant for some logistical backup if necessary."

"Interesting idea. Do you want me to approach Eva about it? Or maybe set up a meeting where the three of us can discuss it? By the way, I'd prefer you don't mention Shala breaking into my apartment, because I haven't told her about it."

"Yes, please set up a meeting with Eva—away from the office. Don't worry, I won't mention the break-in. I think those translations are most likely forgeries anyway. We can arrest Raco with the help of the Kosovo Police and make sure that the information your office needs goes directly to Eva. I think you should also speak to Dreshaj and find out what he has to say."

Kit tightened the headband holding her ponytail in place and started jogging on the spot. "You've got my support. I'm in enough trouble at work as it is, so I don't think this will make any difference. If they don't extend my contract, I'll go back to New Zealand—no problem.

We'll follow up on the witness relocation program for Blaku as well."

"I haven't forgotten about that. London is in direct contact with New Zealand authorities, and they're planning to issue her with a new identity there. They're also willing to offer her cousin safe passage out of Kosovo if she's interested."

"I'm thinking of going to the safe house to see her," Kit said. "Do you think that would be a problem?"

"It should be okay, but just make sure that you're not followed. We might have to arrange for you to have some counter-surveillance training. You've already been followed twice by suspects."

Kit led off down the path. "This is going to be brilliant. I feel really excited about the idea. It's a pity I can't put it into my official work plan since it's going to be off the record. One last thing. What are we going to call the task force?"

"What about Task Force Eagle Eye?"

"That's good enough, until we think of something better." Kit smiled. "And where are we going to meet?"

"I know of a new apartment block that's renting penthouses at a good price. They've got ample underground parking. I'm thinking of taking a new apartment there as cover, and a second penthouse apartment to run operations out of. I can give all our task force members a card key for access."

"What about security?"

"The building owner is a friend of mine. He's an American who came to Kosovo with the US Army, married, and decided to stay. His property manager is a bodybuilder. His fixer, Granit, can also help us out at a pinch. There shouldn't be problems with security as long as we're discreet."

"Let's see how things go and we can always reassess. You're the commander, of course."

"Of course," Matt said as he accelerated down the path.

Task Force Eagle Eye was meeting for the first time. The six members sat at the round, wooden table on functional office chairs. The designer penthouse was light and airy with a view over Pristina. There were skylights and windows that looked toward the hills to the east. The working area had a whiteboard and a wall unit with reference books and maps. The room had a scattering of Oriental rugs from Matt's collection from his international deployments in Turkey and Afghanistan, plus a few local antique Kilim designs. On one side of the room was an area to make coffee, with a small bar next to it. Don Edgson was in attendance, and Max lay placidly under the table. Bambino kept his distance from the other dog and lay in a pool of sunshine on an Oriental rug.

On one side of the table sat Kit, Eva, and Angel, while on the other sat Matt, Owen, and Don. The coffee corner had already been put to good use. Each had helped themselves to a cup. Matt welcomed them.

Eva told the assembled group said that since Major Petri had taken over, there had been no further official contact about the case with the Office of the Chief Prosecutor, let alone any coordination or sharing of information. "We need to be discreet about this, obviously," Eva said. "I'm willing to accept any suitable evidence that can be used in court. As far as I'm concerned,

Matt, you're still our main focal point with the EUFOR Police. No one has formally advised me differently. And even if they had, I reserve my right to review any evidence presented to us."

"I propose that we all leave any information relating to the work of Task Force Eagle Eye here. Except anything we have to provide to the Office of the Chief Prosecutor or the Kosovo Police. I don't want any of you to become a target for people looking for information on sensitive cases." Matt looked briefly at Kit and then looked away, remembering his promise not to talk about the break-in at her apartment.

"It looks like a really great HQ for our task force, Matt," Kit said. "How well equipped is it?"

"There's a combined media and computer room, a kitchenette, and storage facility. It's wired with the latest high-speed, digital-cable service. I still have a few more enhancements to make."

"Like bulletproof glass?" Owen said.

"It's good to see you back on your feet again," Don said, nodding to Owen.

"I see why you're preoccupied with bullets at the moment," Kit said. "How are you doing, Owen?"

Owen grinned. "To tell you the truth, I was getting bored lying around in bed all day. I feel a lot better now, thanks. It was a shock, though, to find out that we'd been taken off the lead of the Staro Dorbi case. Big mistake."

"I agree," Matt said. "That's why I've asked you all here today. I hope you're ready to work on this informal task force. I hasten to add that I have informed London about it. They prefer us to be in charge of the investigation rather than our Romanian colleagues." He looked around the table and noted the nods from each person.

The Missing Diary

"So, where are we on the evidence?" Eva asked.

"Raco's house was a treasure trove, particularly the basement. We've got a match from ballistics on several guns—the Kalashnikovs and pistols—and the cartridges at the massacre matched the bullets used by those guns. Plus the DNA evidence from the cigarette butt matched DNA found in Raco's house. The suspect we arrested might be willing to cooperate in return for a reduced sentence. So, I'm pretty sure we can prove Raco was at the massacre. What we don't know is the full extent of the conspiracy. Who are the other members of the group who committed the murders? Were they acting alone or on orders? Are there links to other crimes such as organized crime or drug running?"

"What about the guy you arrested—and the one who shot me? Can't he tell us who else is involved?" Owen asked.

"We're not sure yet what he'll tell us. Who he might be willing to implicate. Merita Shala, the KLA soldier, was uncooperative. It would be useful if we could locate her diary. Someone stole it from the evidence room. We have two translations, but both appear to be inaccurate."

"Who would have taken it?" Owen asked.

"That's what I'd like to know. Maybe the same people who let Raco escape."

"You mean Petri and co?"

"Could be."

"How would you describe Merita Shala?" Eva asked.

"What would you say, Kit?" he said and continued. "She's tough, arrogant, noncooperative. She was a police officer before joining the KLA. She knows police procedure and what she can get away with. Early twenties.

Our confidential witness, Vasha Blaku, said Shala knew she was being held hostage but didn't do anything about it. They seem to think that because Blaku had been dating a Serb, she deserved punishment."

"You mentioned that there's no intention to press charges against Raco for the sexual assault," Kit said. "This is one of the reasons we need to take action of our own rather than relying on the Task Force Capture to do anything."

"Blaku can provide evidence of Raco's conspiracy to import arms, but it doesn't seem that she knows who's responsible for the massacre at Staro Dorbi," Matt added.

"She's been directly threatened by Raco and was abducted twice and abused," Kit said. "I want to sound her out about witness relocation and see if she's ready to make another formal statement, preferably on video."

"I'm going to need to review all the witness statements," Eva said. "And also all the evidence from the crime scene, the postmortem reports, and also the two house searches. Did you get any further evidence from Shala?"

"No, but we have her phone under surveillance. Owen, give Eva copies of our evidence files. Don, please put Shala under surveillance for a week or so. Let's see what she's up to."

"I've had a look at the phone surveillance records. She hasn't been using the phone much. I think she knows we've got her under surveillance. She made calls and then hung up quite a few times. Probably a code to meet someone," Don said.

"Let's try to match the calls with her meetings." Matt said.

"What would you like me to do?" Angel asked.

Matt looked at Eva. "If it's okay with your boss, you could help with logistics and coordination from here. Could you check with Dr. Prabhu at Pristina Morgue to see whether she's finished the postmortem reports yet? We need to make sure that all the ballistics and other evidence has been analyzed."

"We need to put in an appearance at the office occasionally," Kit said dryly. "I'm already being given grief by the personnel section for my attendance records."

"Well, we do need to have quite frequent meetings away from the office for court findings and appearanccs. I can justify your attendance," Eva said. "Let's see how it goes. Matt, do you think our group will continue operating after Raco's arrest? Is there a need for it?"

"I'm keeping options open," Matt said.

The team got up to begin their various tasks. Angel went to the table in the corner where the phone and computer were located and started checking documents. Don made a phone call. Owen looked through SMS transcripts and phone call records. Eva signaled to Matt and Kit that she wanted a quiet word with them. They went into one of the smaller breakout rooms and closed the door.

"I just wanted to mention that I've been having problems of my own," Eva said. "According to our budget office, there might be some job cuts coming up. I heard a rumor that my position might be cut. The head of mission is not supportive. He keeps trying to discuss cases with me."

"What's wrong with that?" Matt asked.

"He hasn't said anything directly, but he often talks in code. But if I understand him correctly, he wants to influence me either to press charges or drop cases. That's not his role. My office has to be independent. He has the political overview, but that's all."

"How many cases?"

"Three at the moment. With these budget cuts hanging over my head, there's an unspoken understanding that if I play his game, I get to keep my job."

"I can't stand that guy," Kit said. "The bad news is getting worse and worse."

"Is there anything more I should know?" Matt asked.

"Not really. Let's try to get a good result for this case at least. Who knows what the future holds."

"Maybe we'll all be out of jobs soon," Kit said.

CHAPTER NINETEEN

My number three male friend is from Germany. Maybe a nice international man will make a good change. He wants me to go home with him. Things are getting so hot here, maybe it's not a bad idea. I'm not sure whether I can bear to be parted from my warrior brothers though. But perhaps this way I can make sure I'm there to support them in the future.

Merita's diary, 1 September 2000

"Can you give me a lift tonight? I'd like to tell Vasha Blaku the good news," Kit asked Angel as they exited the elevator into the underground car park. "We should be able to get her into a witness protection program. I want to make sure she's comfortable with that idea." The building was a new one, and the car park was only partially full. The fresh paint and building materials still smelt fresh. The OIDC white vehicle was parked a short distance from the elevator.

"Sure. What time?"

"Around nine p.m. I don't want to draw attention to the safe house." Kit looked at the OIDC vehicle. "That looks obvious here, doesn't it?"

"Now you mention it, yeah. We should use a private car to come here in the future or a taxi."

"So tonight, could you drop me a block away and pick me up later?"

"You mean so we're not too obvious if someone is watching?"

"Yes, I'm not used to this cloak and dagger business. I thought I'd be lawyering here, not skulking around safe houses."

Angel rummaged in her bag and produced the key. "Do you wish you were home?"

"Yeah, I do. My mum and …" She was thinking about Xander, but her feelings weren't as they used to be. Things were getting complicated. "I'll tell you later. Things aren't going well."

"It's good to be away from home sometimes. It helps you to clarify things in your own mind. What you want out of life, not someone else's agenda."

Kit opened the four-wheel-drive's passenger door and climbed in. "Too right." This was what she wanted to learn about with Sergei's help. Maybe Xander was also helping in his own way.

That evening as the dusk was deepening, they set off in a northerly direction. They drove past a shopping mall and turned up a side road into a nondescript residential area. It was close to the edge of town before open fields and homesteads. Kit had never been in this part of Pristina before.

"I've got the address, thanks. Can you drop me off here and come back in forty-five minutes?"

THE MISSING DIARY

"Will you be okay? Did you check that Blaku's there?" Angel pulled over to the side of the road and turned off the ignition.

"Yeah, she's there. Where else could she be? She can't move around freely at the moment without risking being seen by Raco and his clan. I'll be fine." Kit tried to brush away Angel's concern. Kit had to believe everything would be all right and that she didn't need anyone else's help.

"Maybe I should go with you. You know . . . for backup or safety."

"It's okay, thanks. Everything looks quiet. I'll go now. If you don't hear from me, please come back here in forty-five minutes." Kit felt that if she moved quickly and decisively toward her goal, nothing could stand in her way.

She didn't wait for Angel to reply; she opened the door, got out, and tossed her black hobo bag over her shoulder. Her baseball cap hid her face from any curious looks. She waved to Angel and set off around the corner toward the safe house.

The dusk grew even deeper as a flight of crows wheeled over her head. Shadows were lengthening around the ramshackle apartment blocks and houses that rose up on both sides of the road. She didn't know the neighborhood. There was an absence of streetlights, and of the few that there were, most were not working. The lamp she was walking toward flickered and went out. She looked ahead to where she knew the safe house should be. All the curtains were drawn, but small slivers of light escaped. Maybe she had been reckless in not allowing Angel to accompany her; not that Angel would've made much difference in case of an armed attack. As she hurried along, she rummaged in her bag to check the address.

As Kit approached the safe house, a burly figure appeared from the overgrown hedge. In one smooth motion, the well-muscled form of Dasham Raco stepped up behind her, slipped a black hood over her head, and clamped his hand over her mouth so she couldn't make a sound. Her world went black. She kicked and struggled and tried to scream. Her muffled sounds were loud in her own head, but she knew they would not carry into the night.

Raco picked her up and carried her away. As he bundled her into the trunk of the black SUV, her bag was pushed into the corner. When he'd taped her wrists and ankles, he shut the trunk. His nephew Enver, who'd helped him escape the police search, was driving. Enver was pale and slim with short, dark hair.

Raco leapt into the car. "*Drejto!*" he said.

Enver hesitated for a moment, then obediently drove out onto the empty street.

Kit lay on her side with her wrists and ankles tightly bound as she struggled to breathe with the hood covering her nose and mouth. As the car bounced over potholes, it jarred her bruised and battered body. She felt alone and afraid. Her confidence and bravado had not helped at all. The movement of the car and her dire situation made her nauseous. She gagged. She didn't know if she would survive the ordeal. She thought about what Blaku had suffered at the hands of this killer—that was the minimum mistreatment she could expect.

She had no way of contacting anyone. Angel would return and find that she wasn't there. Only then would they start searching, and by that time, no doubt Raco would have taken to her to a location that would be extremely difficult to find. He had already been hiding somewhere for days, and even with a warrant out for his arrest, the police had been unable to locate him.

Kit took deep breaths to steady herself and think logically. Could anything give her a clue about where they were going? How long had they been driving? What could she hear? What could she feel? The smell of petrol was overwhelming, as was the smell of something else. Who knew what Raco transported in this vehicle. Maybe animal carcasses, guns and ammunition, dead bodies? All her efforts to calm down and think rationally were hopeless. All she could do was wait until her captors took her out of the trunk and did whatever they were going to do.

After what seemed hours, the vehicle pulled off the road and drove onto an even rougher surface. Kit guessed that probably about fifty minutes had passed, perhaps long enough for Angel to realize that she was missing. She had the impression they were driving down a long driveway somewhere in the countryside. She was in complete darkness—perhaps darker than she had ever been in her life. Her predicament was overwhelming. Her throat convulsed, and she let out a sob.

Finally, the car stopped. She heard the two doors open and slam shut and the sound of boots slowly crunching over gravel. When the trunk opened, she heard the two men talking in Albanian, which she couldn't understand. It sounded as if Raco was giving an order. Then two rough hands took hold of her, and she was lifted her out of the trunk and set on her feet. She heard a ripping sound as the duct tape was removed from her feet.

"We're here. Walk," a heavily accented voice said in English.

She made a muffled sound in protest as she tried to scream.

"Just walk." When Kit felt something pressed into the middle of her back, she knew it was a gun. She stepped forward and kept moving. She was blind, and her hands were still bound. Her martial art's training was useless. Raco was physically much stronger than her and would overpower her if she tried to resist. Adrenaline made her heart race as her mind tried to think of something, anything, that might help her. If she could get him talking and establish a rapport, perhaps he might not abuse her. Given his track record, however, that strategy seemed unlikely to succeed.

"Steps," Raco said gruffly. Kit paused and stepped forward and upward. Then she moved forward again, tripped, and almost fell. She heard the door close behind her, and then he removed the hood from her head.

Kit looked around the large, almost empty room. It could have been a room in an old farmhouse, or perhaps it was an abandoned military building. Her eyes were already adjusted to the darkness, and she looked at two lanterns which provided light, although the light was only in shallow pools around a table and a counter. The younger man moved to light a candle on another table across the room. The room was dusty, and the few pieces of furniture in it were battered and in disarray. Raco pointed to a simple metal chair close to one of the lanterns. She sat down.

"You've put me to a lot of trouble," Raco said.

"Not nearly as much trouble as you've caused." Kit tilted her chin upward and looked at him defiantly.

Raco stepped forward and slapped her hard across the right side of her face. Her head flew to the side and jerked backward. Her ears were ringing and her cheek stung. Blood filled her mouth. She spat it out.

"No one is going to help you. Enough of your smart talk. Do you know who I am? What I do?"

Kit looked at Raco; her eyes were streaming. She nodded.

"You're going to answer my questions about the police investigation. Tell me, how much do they know about the killings and about me and my group?" He stepped back and looked her up and down, evaluating her.

Kit shuddered. She preferred the blow across the face to the predatory way he was looking at her, as if he was devouring her body with his eyes. Her skin crawled, and sweat trickled down the back of her neck.

"It's been a while since I had a redhead to play with."

Kit looked at the floor. She wasn't going to give him the satisfaction of seeing dread on her face. "You tried to run me off the road the other day. Why?"

"That was supposed to frighten you off the case. It didn't work apparently."

"Supposed to? Who told you to do that?" Kit pressed. But he wouldn't be drawn.

"Your accent, it's different. Where are you from? England? Canada?"

"New Zealand. Know where that is?"

Raco shook his head impatiently. "No idea. It doesn't matter. You're an international working for the EUFOR Police."

"I'm a lawyer; a civilian, not a police officer. I'm from New Zealand, a small country in the South Pacific. We're friends of Kosovo. Why are you doing this to me?"

"You and your friends made life difficult for me. I saw you when they tried to arrest me. You must know that during the war we had to do things that we wouldn't normally do. There are always casualties in a war." He turned and spat on the floor.

"The war is over."

"That's what they say—but Serbia hasn't given up on Kosovo."

"Is that why you killed those Serbian farmers? They weren't soldiers. That's a war crime."

Raco recoiled. In spite of his bulk, he moved with the fluidity of a snake as he struck the left side of her face.

"What do you know about Kosovo and Serbia? All the politicians are corrupt, all take whatever they can. The Europeans are just as bad. They take as if they're an occupying army, but they do nothing to help Kosovo in the long-term."

Kit probed her bottom lip gingerly with her tongue; her lip was split. "Maybe I can help you put your case."

He moved away out of the light toward the darkness. Kit became aware that the younger man was watching in silence from the other side of the room, where there was an old kitchen sink.

Raco came back toward her; his eyes were black in a room full of shadows. "We cooperate when we have to—even with the enemy."

Adrenaline had given Kit mental clarity. She kept her head tilted toward the floor but watched him as carefully as she could by angling her eyes.

"What do you mean? I thought you hated the Serbs."

"Don't make such stupid comments or you'll make me hurt you again."

THE MISSING DIARY

Kit said nothing. She heard the other man rustling about in the kitchenette. When a message came through on his mobile, Raco read it before he punched redial and walked back to the darker side of the room. He exchanged a few words with whoever was on the other end and clicked off.

"We don't need to hurry this," Raco said. "You'll be our guest for a few days. Don't think about being rescued. No one will find you here. I'll continue with our informative discussion later. I need to go out now. Enver will keep an eye on you while I'm away. He might even have a bit of fun."

"Who was it?" Enver asked.

"The Inspector wants to discuss the next delivery."

The young man stepped forward and looked at Kit hungrily. She shuddered again as she remembered that Blaku said she had been abused by more than one man.

"On second thought, save the first time with her for me. Give her some water or something to eat if she needs it. We'll continue when I get back." He looked at Enver, who looked down. "Understood?"

Enver nodded.

With that, Raco turned, picked up his car keys, and walked toward the door. He hesitated briefly and cast a glance over the shoulder.

Kit had not moved, but she watched him as he left the room.

"Sorry about that. Uncle has a bad temper," Enver said.

"No shit," Kit mumbled as her tongue felt the swelling on her lip.

"Would you like some water?"

"Yes." Kit looked toward the small, dusty kitchenette. She wondered what condition the water was in. He filled a mug from the tap and held it to her mouth. She took several sips.

"Uncle says that it's time for me to start thinking about getting married."

Kit shot him a look. Where was the conversation heading?

"You're a beautiful woman, but we prefer to marry Albanian women. You know—keep the family together. He said that he'll help me try different girls to see how I like them."

Kit wasn't sure how to respond to that comment either. Enver seemed to be in another world, where violent abuse of women was normal. She wondered whether he had the mental capacity to understand what was going on. Perhaps he had been traumatized during the war.

"Maybe I'll discuss it with uncle later. You've got beautiful red hair," he said as his callused, filthy hand caressed her ponytail. Everything inside Kit made her want to pull away in disgust; yell at him to get away from her; scream for help. But she knew that no one would hear her, and it could provoke a violent reaction from him. Perhaps it was a better idea to keep talking.

"I'd be really grateful if you could take the tape off my hands and feet. It's so tight." That much was true. Her hands were turning blue because the circulation was being cut off.

"You must think I'm stupid. If I did that, you'd run away, like you did before in the mountains. Then uncle would be very angry with me."

"No, I don't think you're stupid. You could undo my hands and then I could drink by myself. My feet would still be bound, so I couldn't run away."

"Would you give me a kiss if I took the tape off your hands?"

Kit couldn't bring herself to say yes, but she nodded and extended her hands. Enver found a serrated steak knife in the kitchen and brought it back with another cup of water. He sliced the tape away from her hands and offered her the glass of water. She rubbed her hands with relief as her circulation returned. She began to calculate her chances of overpowering Enver. They were reasonable, but her feet were still bound, and he was carrying a knife. She decided to bide her time.

"And how about my kiss?" He presented his unshaven face. She leaned forward and pecked him on the cheek.

"I can see that you'd like more," he said. "But you heard what uncle said. We'd better wait until he gets back." He placed the knife on the table behind her and took the glass and the mug back to the kitchenette.

"Where has your uncle gone?"

"He has a business meeting."

"What kind of business is he in?"

"This man in town, he's quite prominent, he arranges jobs for us—guns from Albania. You know, for protection in case the Serbs come back."

"You say he's quite prominent. Is he a politician?" Maybe she could get some useful information out of the young man. He seemed naïve, and maybe he would speak openly.

"I'd better not say. Uncle told me I shouldn't talk about it. If you're very nice to me later maybe—maybe—I might tell you more." Enver smiled at her.

What planet had this man come from where he thought he could flirt with a woman who was being held hostage? "Okay, let's see what happens." It seemed like a safe, neutral reply.

"Uncle will probably be an hour or so, but then he'll probably want to stay up late. Maybe we should both get some rest," Enver said.

"Whatever you think is best," she said. She had read about hostage negotiators who recommended trying to establish a rapport with the offenders to avoid further harm and perhaps make escape easier. It seemed to be simpler with Enver than with Raco. The older man had violence bubbling just below the surface, waiting to explode, while the younger one was naïve, perhaps even traumatized. That made him a little bit easier to deal with.

"I'll just go and sleep over there," he said as he pointed to an old mattress in the opposite corner of the room. There were two mattresses. Kit shuddered to think what they had planned for later. "Don't try to get away though; I'll be watching you." He turned and went over to lie down.

Kit sat quietly for a moment. She desperately needed to regroup her thoughts. This could be her only chance to escape before Raco returned. With his brutality and strength, she did not like her chances of getting away from him, whereas the young man seemed willing to believe she liked him and that she didn't mind being held hostage. She heard his breathing start to deepen. Her hands were free, and she needed to see if she could reach the knife on the table. She didn't want to take the risk of waking him though. If she could reach it. then she could quickly cut her feet free and then, armed, with her speed and agility, she hoped she'd be a match for him.

She needed to clear her mind. She thought of Sergei and the little that she had learned of his philosophy. She imagined him speaking to her. In her mind, she heard him saying, *Katarina, you must think of the best possible outcome, project and imagine it coming irresistibly into the world. Do not think of what might go wrong, only what will go right. In that moment you will take your opponent by surprise and he won't be able to stop you. You're a natural. Don't doubt yourself.*

In her mind's eye, Kit saw the image of herself free from her bindings, heading for the door, opening it, and walking outside. But when she turned, in the lamplight she saw Enver lying in a pool of blood. She didn't like that part of the visualization. She would rather escape without harming him. She was sure Raco would beat him soundly when he came back and discovered she had escaped. Also, she didn't know where she was. She was certain they were somewhere in the countryside; plus, she didn't have her mobile. By now Angel would have told Matt and Eva that she was missing, but they wouldn't know where to look for her. No, she mustn't think like that; she must only think about what would go right.

The dread in the pit of her stomach went from nervous fluttering to a sense of excitement. Adrenaline flooded her body, and she felt hyperaware. She heard every breath Enver took as he slid deeper and deeper into sleep. Slowly she began to turn in her chair, alert to any sound she might make. When the chair creaked she stopped and watched Enver carefully, but he didn't react. She stretched out her arm. The knife was a foot out of reach. Try as she might, she could not reach far enough behind her. She would have to stand up.

She decided to try to use the power of visualization that Sergei had taught her. She visualized herself quickly and silently rising to her feet, turning, then shuffling with her bound ankles toward the table. When she reached the table, she'd pick up the knife, and in one movement, she would release the tape around her feet. The room blurred as she moved from intention to action. She allowed her body to fall into the pattern of visualization she had set in her mind. *This will work. This is working. I am free. I am free!*

She stood up slowly as she kept watch on the man sleeping in the corner. Using what little slack there was in the tape around her ankles, she shuffled forward until she was close enough to reach the knife. Scarcely daring to breathe, she picked up the black-handled knife and sawed through the tape around her ankles with its serrated edge. She felt the pleasure of release as soon as she was able to move her feet. There was no time to lose, and she moved as quickly as she could without making a noise toward the door on the other side of the room. She had just reached the door and was about to grasp the handle when she heard Enver stir.

"What are you doing?" he asked.

Kit didn't answer and grasped the handle. She was too slow. He sprang to his feet and put his body between her and the door. She turned the handle, but he slammed his full body weight against the door and slammed it shut.

"What are you doing, Red?" he said as he looked at her with panic in his eyes.

"I'm leaving. Don't try to stop me." She wrenched on the doorknob. Still he continued to block her exit.

"You know I can't let you go. You heard what uncle said. You like me, don't you?"

"Get away from the door now. I'm serious."

"Get back to your chair. I have to tie you up again," he said as sweat broke out on his white forehead. He grabbed her left arm and forced her away from the door. Kit knew that it was now or never. She had to get out before Raco returned. Adrenaline surged through her body, and she struck at Enver with the knife. She felt sick as the knife penetrated the young man's ribs. It was easier and softer than she might have imagined. Her martial arts training came to the fore, and with her other hand, she pushed against his chin and forced him across the room. He stumbled and fell onto the filthy mattress. Blood was seeping out of his wound. In a flash, Kit recognised that this was what she had seen in visualization. She hadn't liked it, but it had a compulsion of its own. She had a pang of regret leaving him gravely wounded, but she knew that her survival depended on putting as much distance between her and this house as possible. With one glance backward at the figure moaning on the mattress, she opened the door and bolted through it.

Stars were out, and the night felt clear and fresh. Kit wiped the blood off the knife on the grass and tucked it up her sleeve in case she needed it again. There was enough moonlight to see the access road. Before her were dilapidated farm buildings which stood close to the hills on the edge of a forest. She set off jogging along the gravel driveway that she was sure led to the main road. She had to be careful because of poor visibility and avoid the potholes.

She couldn't afford to fall and twist her ankle again. But even less could she afford to be there when Raco returned.

As Kit entered the road which ran off the driveway, she realized that she had no idea where she was, or how to get back to Pristina. The terrain was elevated and close to the hills; lights were sparkling in the distance. That was probably Pristina or another town where she could find help. She decided to keep moving. That was her priority. As adrenaline continued to surge through her body, her aches and pains didn't seem so bad. She sucked in the fresh scent of pine trees and the surrounding countryside as she ran for her life.

She turned left. Her memory told her they had turned right shortly before reaching the farmhouse. Fifteen minutes later, she came to an intersection and crossroads. She had lost her sense of direction and could no longer work out the direction of the lights. She bent over to catch her breath as she tried to decide which way to go. She couldn't stay where she was, and taking any road would be better than taking none. Yet again she thought about the khash philosophy and imagined that she was hovering above the crossroads as she sought to discern the correct direction to take. But all she could see were roads heading in several directions, except the one that she had come from. Movement to her left caught her eye. A fox was sitting beside the road. It looked at her. She was momentarily startled, but then she smiled. After her experience in the cave, she felt comforted by its presence and stood there looking at it for some moments. The animal stared at her. She was afraid to make a sudden move for fear of frightening it away.

"You look like you know this area well. Which way should I go?" she whispered. The fox licked its paw, almost catlike, before it turned tail and nonchalantly trotted back along the road. She took that as a sign, and it was enough to prompt her to decide which road to take. It was then that she thought about Enver. There was something innocent about him in spite of his involvement in the crimes of his uncle. He seemed to have genuinely wanted to make a connection with her but had gone completely the wrong way about it. She had acted in self-defense. It was the first time that she had seriously wounded another person. Kit's breath caught in her throat as she considered the possibility that the wound could be fatal.

After ten minutes of walking briskly along the empty road, she saw headlights approaching—the first that she had seen since leaving the farmhouse. The height of the lights suggested that it could be an SUV, quite probably Raco. The fox had disappeared when it dived into a ditch and vanished into the shadowy undergrowth. Kit clambered over a patch of brambles and hid out of sight of the road. She kept her head down as she tried to see if it was the black SUV. She was almost certain that it was Raco when the vehicle turned in the direction of the farmhouse. Afraid that her pale skin would be reflective the headlights and not wanting to draw unwanted attention to herself, she pulled back. In that instant, she saw that it was a white OIDC jeep.

As Kit scrambled across the ditch, she scratched her hands and scraped her knees on the rambles, but she felt no pain, only relief. Owen was driving, and Matt was in the front passenger seat with Angel in the rear. Kit waved her arms desperately as the vehicle went past. It came to a halt a few meters away. She ran toward the car. Her chest was heaving as she sobbed with relief.

Angel opened the car door, got out, and ran to meet her. She was carrying a blanket, which she wrapped around Kit before she led her to the vehicle and helped her in.

"Are you okay? What happened?" Angel asked.

Kit gave compressed details about her ordeal as Owen drove away. "You have to call an ambulance for Raco's nephew. I had to stab him to escape. Raco went out, but I'm sure he'll be back soon. They were holding me at a farmhouse not far from here."

"Did he hurt you?" Angel said with an anxious expression on her face.

"Mainly my dignity. He wanted to know everything I knew about the police investigation. But they were planning something for later." Kit shuddered. On the verge of bursting into tears, she bit her lip.

"You did well to get away," Matt said. "Don't worry about the young man. I'll call for an ambulance now and Kosovo Police so they'll arrest Raco when he gets back. Are you up to taking us to the farmhouse?"

"I think so," Kit said, although, in fact, it was the last place she wanted to go. "Raco is so dangerous. He's going to be looking at murdering me when he finds that I've escaped. Are you armed?"

"Yes, I've got my service revolver and we have a rifle," Matt said. "I propose that we take up a surveillance position outside until backup arrives."

"How did you find me?" Kit said as she wrapped the blanket tightly around her, more for comfort than warmth.

"We followed your mobile signal," Owen said. "It led in this direction, but then it moved away. We thought that following it to the location where it stopped was our best lead."

"I dropped my bag with my mobile inside in the trunk of Raco's SUV when they transported me in there. They taped my hands and feet so I couldn't retrieve it. Check the signal again; maybe it's coming back now."

"Don's been using the police frequency to track the phone and he's updating me. We guessed it was probably in the vehicle that abducted you."

"Did you think to call Task Force Capture?" Kit asked.

"No," Matt replied.

They waited until the police unit and an ambulance arrived. However, there was no sign of Raco. After Kit had been checked over by a medic, they drove back to Pristina.

CHAPTER TWENTY

Razor says there's a drop under the third bench in Gërmia Park where he gets instructions … I'm uneasy…

Merita's diary, 3 September 2000

Kit stepped into the shower, closed her eyes, and let the hot water sluice over her. She turned so that the warmth reached every angle, curve, and crease in her body. She had to wash away Raco's touch.

Enver was out of a critical condition in hospital. She was relieved because he wasn't fully responsible for his actions. Raco had set him a bad example. Even though Enver was creepy, Kit didn't want to be his killer, even if she acted in self-defense. She could easily imagine how Vasha Blaku must have felt after weeks of degradation at their hands. Kit scrubbed and scrubbed as she slathered on shower gel until she was sore and almost raw. Her need to reclaim her body was enormous. Kit knew she had overcome him for the time being.

The police were only able to implicate two suspects from the shooting at Staro Dorbi. Merita remained an enigma, but her diary must contain crucial evidence. Kit had to make sure the grandparents of the slaughtered mother and child knew their killers had been punished so their daughter and granddaughter could rest in peace. In New Zealand, she had considered herself a liberal, but having seen what happens when evil runs rampant and the innocent are victims, she had gained a stronger desire for justice and, beyond that, retribution.

She still planned to meet Visar Dreshaj to hear what he had to say. When Kit checked her phone messages, there was one from Angel, asking how she was.

Kit texted back. *Okay, thanks. I hope Dreshaj doesn't just want a date. I'm meeting him later tonight, hoping for new info.*

I'll wait for your text and keep Eva informed. Call if you need backup, Angel sent back. Kit put down her mobile and thought about Angel's message. Before she had wanted to act alone and succeed no matter what. But now, she needed the team close.

Can you and Owen get a table at Club Europa 50? Just to be on the safe side, she texted to Angel.

Will check with Owen. Should be okay. What time?

6:30 p.m.

Unless you hear otherwise, we'll be there.

Refreshed at last, Kit blow-dried her hair and applied a little more makeup than usual. Her black dress fell to her knees; a discreet length but figure hugging. Even if Dreshaj had no romantic notions, it might put him into the frame of mind to share more information. She eyed two wigs sitting on stands on top of the dresser —one a glossy brunette bob, and the other a layered dark blonde that reached her shoulders. Ever since she was a young girl, she had enjoyed dressing up with her sister and pretending to model clothes, even though they didn't fit properly. They had the best fun when they were allowed to try on their aunt's wigs. Her aunt had alopecia and had collected several natural hair wigs to suit her mood, which delighted the girls. Still, Kit occasionally liked to wear a wig out to feel as if she was becoming someone else. She briefly considered wearing one now, but that could defeat the purpose of becoming a trusted confidante for Dreshaj.

Once she put on a pair of stilettos, Kit tossed an emerald cashmere wrap over her shoulders. After she selected a matching handbag, she ordered a taxi. Just before leaving, as an afterthought, she put on her New Zealand greenstone pendant for extra luck. As she turned to walk out, her eye caught a glimpse of the vanity mirror. She barely recognized herself. She had changed so much since arriving in Kosovo. She wasn't sure if it was a good thing or a bad thing. She could feel her strength and the confidence in her voice when she spoke to Dreshaj or her co-workers. It was as if she had been born again.

The club was only about half-full when Kit arrived. Angel and Owen were seated towards the back. Angel's dark-blonde hair shone under a spotlight. She nodded in their direction and then relaxed. She needed to focus on Dreshaj. If he felt a genuine connection, he was likely to be more forthcoming.

A few moments later, an Albanian-accented voice spoke behind her. "Caitlin, how kind of you to meet me. How are you?"

Kit turned, smiled, and reached out her hand to Visar Dreshaj. His dark hair was in a classic tapered cut, if a little messy on top. He wore a well-fitted jacket and sharp Italian loafers, and Kit smelt an enticing hint of sophisticated aftershave. He was all politician.

"It's good to see you. I can't complain. How are you?" She flashed him a smile while her eyes darted to the back of the room where Owen and Angel were watching. Angel was texting— probably to Matt or Eva.

"In need of a drink," Dreshaj said as he caught the attention of a waiter who led them to a table in an alcove over the opposite side of the room, behind the central bar. Her friends were out of sight.

Dreshaj pulled out a chair for Kit before taking a seat across from her. He passed her the cocktail menu, and she chose a whiskey sour. If it was strong enough, it might deaden the pain of her injuries. Dreshaj ordered a local beer called Birra Peja.

"Aren't you having something stronger?"

"Not so early. Perhaps later." He took out his cigarette packet, opened it, and extracted a cigarette. "May I?"

"Be my guest."

"We're not supposed to smoke in bars and restaurants, but it's a hard habit to break. Usually people start after midnight when the police give up enforcing the no smoking rules."

"But you'll take your chances."

"I don't think they'll throw me out. My cousin is married to the owner."

"Nice for some." Kit reached for her whiskey sour and took a sip. "This is deadly."

"Would you like me to order you a different cocktail?" Dreshaj said with concern.

"Where I come from that means it's excellent."

Dreshaj leaned back in his chair and took a drag on his cigarette. He scrutinized her through the smoke as they exchanged pleasantries, and Dreshaj asked Kit about her family origins and religious affiliations.

"How would you describe your religion?" she asked.

"Like many Kosovars, I'm a Muslim on paper. But for us, our Albanian heritage and family are more important."

"I was born in New Zealand."

"There are not many New Zealanders in Kosovo, although we have seen a few Australians helping with the EU mission." Visar drank his beer.

Kit waited. If he planned to provide some sensitive information, it would be soon.

"I wanted to share something with you. This has to stay off the record. At least as far as where you got it from."

Kit looked at him, her blue-green eyes highlighted by the jade pendant at her throat. She reached for a cigarette and held it forward for him to light.

"Tell me more," she said.

"An important piece of evidence in a case you are dealing with has come my way. I can't tell you how I got it, and I don't want anyone to know that this came from me."

"I'll do what I can, but the final decision is not mine. You've met Eva, though. She's fair."

Kit glanced up. Owen and Angel had moved to a different table. They were ordering tea and coffee. She, on the other hand, welcomed the opportunity to relax with a cocktail, which should also help Dreshaj feel more at ease.

"I know you can't make any promises, and I'm taking a risk by doing this." He reached into his jacket pocket and pulled out a manila envelope, put it on the table, and pushed it toward her. Without opening it, she took the envelope and slipped it into her bag.

The Missing Diary

"What's inside?"

"Something you've been looking for. Keep it with you at all times."

"I can guess what it is. How did you get it?"

"Sorry, I can't tell you."

"You got someone to steal it from the evidence room."

"You think so little of me." Dreshaj glowered at her. "No, I found out about it indirectly. Then I made it worth the while of the person who had it to give it to an intermediary, who procured it for me. I want justice as much as you do. I can't let this incident destabilize Kosovo as it was intended to do. We're clinging to a fragile peace."

At that moment, Dreshaj's phone rang, and he spoke for a few minutes in his native tongue. "You must excuse me. That was the prime minister. He wants a word. I have to go, but your colleagues over there will no doubt escort you home."

"What?" Kit looked around. How had Dreshaj known they were nearby?

He smiled as he put money on the table to cover the drinks.

"Why are you giving this to me?"

"You're new here, and you don't have a vested interest. Sometimes family members or friends do things they shouldn't. We can't always confront them without bringing disgrace on everyone. But I'm giving you the chance to do something about it. This will make your career … or break it. People see their dreams trampled into the ground in Kosovo and end up selling their souls to the highest bidder."

"I'm humbled by your trust. I'll do my best."

"Trusting you is a gamble." He stood up and reached out his hand. "Let's meet again for pleasure, not business. My family owns a chain of casinos." He took her hand in his, drew her close, and kissed her on both cheeks, then paused. "If I take you to a casino, would you wear that dress?"

"I can do better than this dress, but I don't think your wife would appreciate it."

"She knows to keep out of my business," he said and smiled. Then, nodding slightly towards the envelope in her bag, he added, "I've included a translation of the important parts into English. A good one."

After acknowledging Owen and Angel, Dreshaj strode out the club. Three men waiting for him at a nearby table escorted him to a waiting limousine.

Kit went over to Angel and Owen. "Let's go," she whispered.

Angel and Kit walked out first, while Owen followed behind.

"What did he give you?" Angel asked.

"I don't know. Documents I think. I want to take them home to read, and I'll report to the task force tomorrow morning. You know—our task force." Kit guessed what the document was, but she wanted to read it first in privacy.

"What's in there?" Owen asked.

"I prefer not to speculate," Kit said. "Something that Visar thinks will get him a date with me at a casino."

Angel giggled. "Really?"

"Yes. He didn't seem concerned when I mentioned his wife."

"You won't take him up on the offer, will you?" Owen asked.

"Oh, I don't know. I'll see what happens. It might be worth it for the information."

"You could go undercover," Angel said.

"It's not fantastic cover when everyone knows I'm a prosecutor."

They walked together along the dilapidated lane leading to the car park. The call to prayer from the mosques mingled in the evening air with the barking of feral dogs, the sound of car horns on the street, and music blasting from a CD shop.

Angel drove, and while she waited outside Kit's apartment block, Owen escorted Kit to her door. Since the break-in, Kit had had the locks changed and a security-monitoring device installed at the entrance.

She went inside and locked the door.

Her hands trembled with anticipation as she pulled a brown, hard-backed diary out of the white envelope, together with a handwritten English translation, perhaps prepared by Dreshaj himself. She went to the kitchenette and switched on the coffee machine. She wouldn't get much sleep, but she was excited about reading Merita's diary.

> It's odd, but everyone is taking orders from the same hidden chief. Even my brother warriors and Raco. Because of this, the near miracle has happened, my Kosovo Albanian brother is going on the same mission as my Serbian sweetheart. The stakes are high. They want to discredit the international presence in Kosovo, for their own reasons. A small Serbian village will be the sacrificial lamb. This fake peace will not hold.

Kit took a deep breath and put down the piece of paper. Merita implied that the group responsible for the massacre included both Kosovo Albanians and Serbs. Everyone assumed that a Kosovo-Albanian group had attacked the Serbian farmers of Staro Dorbi for revenge.

Before she carried on reading, she checked her mobile for messages. There was a message from Sergei saying he arranged for her to go to the workshop at Ljubljana with his group of philosopher friends. He had even booked a flight for her. She was excited by the prospect. It would be a welcome relief from the pressure in Pristina, which was extreme. The easy schedule of her life in New Zealand seemed as if it belonged to another lifetime. There was another message from Xander. She was about to delete it but stopped as her fingers hovered over the phone. Had she been too hasty with Xander? Perhaps she should at least read what he has to say. After she's finished reading the diary.

Once she'd taken a sip of the hot, bitter coffee, Kit read on.

> Razor says there's a drop under the third bench in Gërmia Park where he gets written instructions. I'm uneasy. The Russian liaison officer has a similar way to communicate with the Serbs through Mitrovica North. He tells them to avoid the telephone or internet as much as possible.

What the hell?! With a growing sensation of ice in her core in spite of the hot coffee, Kit was jolted upright and shook her head. "No, it can't be," she whispered and read on.

> Razor said Sokolov was busy with his wife visiting from Moscow, but the operation has to go ahead anyway before the peace becomes too settled. I prefer not to kill civilians, but Razor said it's important to our long-term goals. Or Sokolov's long-term goals to keep the conflict alive. Plenty of people on both sides, both Serbs and Albanians, profit from war. That's why a joint squad will hit Staro Dorbi, made up of fighters from both sides.

Kit was disoriented and dizzy as she gripped the side of the sofa to steady herself. At the back of her mind she suspected it but refused to let her suspicions blossom into the full flower of distrust. Sergei was married. She had been so sympathetic when he told her that he had lost his wife years ago. How naïve she was to believe his lies. She stifled a cry as the full horror of the deception began to dawn on her. Did he also have a family in Moscow? A son or daughter? Or both? He was cultivating her as an asset by asking about her work. All that philosophy—what a lot of bullshit! At least it was consistent with his philosophy to use whatever means were effective to create confusion for his adversaries and to dominate whatever scenario was playing out like a chess game. And he had played her. Now her old boyfriend Xander looked like a safe haven in a storm of emotion and hurt.

Kit stood up and walked toward the floor-to-ceiling windows and looked out over Pristina. Her heart pounded, and her body tensed as a new wave of adrenaline washed over her. Raco had been the brutal, sharp end of the operation, but Sergei was the malevolent mastermind behind it.

"Oh my God," she whispered. "He's got diplomatic immunity." But maybe his government would waive it so they could prosecute him for this abhorrent crime. That was unlikely though. Perhaps the instructions had come from Moscow. In the morning, she would talk to Matt before anyone else. Assuming all this was true; Dreshaj could have falsified the record. Merita had described the location of the drop Sergei used to give instructions; she should go there to check whether he had left any incriminating messages that could be traceable. She felt humiliated to think how vulnerable she had felt with him; how he had romanced her. Her skin crawled at the thought of their night together.

She returned to the couch and put the translation next to the original to see they corresponded by checking words that she understood. The diary looked original in its handwritten form. An entry described how Merita had met a German man who worked for an international organization, and how she planned to marry despite her attachment to her two warrior brothers. Through him, she would be able to get a visa to move to Munich and leave this mess behind.

If that was true, she owed Dreshaj a vote of thanks. She needed to think about how to manage the situation. Her first impulse was to confront Sergei immediately, but perhaps that was not the best idea. She needed to discuss it with Matt first and mention that she'd had coffee with Sergei a few times and downplay the extent of her involvement. It would be good to get a warrant to search his accommodation, but since it was part of the Russian liaison compound, that would not be possible. All this talk about how his mother had sent things from Moscow.

More likely, his wife had sent him the gifts. He had been manipulating her, which was why he lied about his marital status. Kit balled her hand into a first and hit the couch. Part of her wanted revenge so badly. How could she entrap Sergei into further incriminating himself? If this was the missing diary, she had evidence pointing toward Sergei's involvement. Even if they couldn't prosecute him because of diplomatic immunity, they could close the case and prosecute Raco and his confederates with the evidence they had discovered in his house.

What Sergei had done to her was worse than what Raco had done, or tried to do. She felt violated to her core, not just her body.

Kit had had a safe installed in her apartment after the break-in. She would put what Dreshaj had given her in it, but first she would photograph everything.

Once she'd done that, she put the documents and the memory card from her camera in the safe and locked it.

Chapter Twenty-One

Kosovo, my love. You're broken, fragile, and volatile, yet passionate, loving, and strong. For you, it's all or nothing. Your answer to every question is "Let's go for broke!" Loyalty above all and keep our word. I hold you in my heart, and there, we are healed. The future is yours to create or destroy.

Merita's Last Diary Entry, undated

The next morning, Kit found Matt in the garage of his Sunny Hill home. He was working on restoring a vintage Fiat convertible.

In khaki overalls and old shoes, he was leaning under the hood, tinkering. Around him was a jumble of tools, old nails, and pieces of furniture. Kit could smell automotive oil and petrol.

"Hey, chief," she said with forced cheerfulness. "How's it going?"

Matt looked up and grinned. He stood up and wiped his hands on a dirty handkerchief.

"Hi. You caught me at one of my favorite hobbies. They have some nice, old Fiats here in the former Yugoslavia that you can buy for a song."

The Missing Diary

They were interrupted by a blonde woman in her mid-thirties, with her hair clipped up. She had navy-blue eyes and wore jeans and a T-shirt. A toddler with similar straight blond hair was clinging to her leg. She carried a tray with a mug of coffee, a sugar bowl, and a spoon.

"Here's your coffee, hon," she said in a London accent.

"Thanks. Sylvie, this is my colleague Caitlin Chase from the Chief Prosecutor's Office. She's stopped by to discuss some work issues."

Sylvie regarded Kit with an appraising glance. "Can I get you a mug of coffee? It's only instant coffee, I'm afraid."

Kit stepped forward; the two women shook hands and Kit greeted the toddler. "That would be lovely, thank you. Nescafe is fine."

Matt explained that his wife Sylvie and their son David were visiting from London where she worked as a nurse in a hospital. While Sylvie wasn't able to get over to visit Matt in Pristina often, he had found a house where she and their son could stay.

"It's the first time I've seen something of your private life," Kit said. "You've got a nice setup here. Good to meet you, Sylvie, and your lovely son."

Sylvie put down the tray and returned to the house.

"I'm sorry to disturb your weekend, Matt," Kit said. "I need to talk about something important that's come up."

"What is it?" Matt looked up and scanned Kit's face.

"I've got the missing diary. Dreshaj gave it to me last night. He was very uncomfortable with its contents and wanted to hand it over to law enforcement. He's afraid to give it to someone who might have a vested interest. Since I'm new in Kosovo, he thought I'd be a good choice. He doesn't want to be named as the person who gave it to us though."

"Where is it?"

"There's a copy in the safe in my apartment. I've got the originals here."

"Show me."

Kit pulled out the envelope from inside her denim jacket and offered it to him.

"On second thoughts, keep it for now. My hands are covered with oil at the moment. Tell me about it."

"Dreshaj has provided a translation of key parts of the diary." Kit spoke evenly, trying to keep any inflection out of her voice that might show her emotions. "So, while Raco led the assault team in Staro Dorbi, the person who directed it appears to be the Russian liaison officer, Sergei Sokolov. Also, the assault team who killed the Serb farmers included both Albanian and Serbian Kosovars, not just Albanians as we assumed."

"Sokolov? Does that make sense?"

"According to the diary, Shala seems to think the massacre was intended to destabilise the international peace in Kosovo. That would keep the possibility open for Serbia to reclaim territory here. Criminal groups on both sides would benefit from that and from weapon sales and other organized crime."

Matt thought for some moments and then slowly nodded. "It makes sense. Russia has been an expert at misinformation campaigns and asymmetrical warfare for some time. The massacre stirred up hatred on both sides. Let's get a warrant and bring in Sokolov for questioning."

The Missing Diary

"I don't think it'll be that easy. He'll claim diplomatic immunity. There was something else. The means of communicating between him and Raco, and perhaps others, was to leave a message under a seat in Gërmia Park. The third seat going up the hill. It could be useful to look there."

"You're right about the diplomatic immunity, but you might have cracked this case open." Sylvie arrived with another tray, another mug of coffee, and more shortbread.

"I don't know if our visitor will have time to drink all that, love," Matt said. "We need to investigate some evidence for a case."

Kit picked up the mug and a cookie. "It's been a long time since I've had real British shortbread. And I haven't had breakfast."

"All right then," Matt said. "You have your coffee and I'll contact the rest of our task force. We should drop these documents at a secure location and then go to the park."

He disappeared for ten minutes while Kit ate two pieces of shortbread and drank half a mug of coffee. She looked around the well-organized garage. The drywall was minimally finished, and against it stood rows of receptacles filled with nuts and bolts, wire cutters, and different-sized axes. On the other shelves storage boxes, toolboxes, and small bins lined the shelves. Workbenches stood against the wall on which wall hooks and magnet bars kept the tools tidy and within reach. Several windows provided ventilation. At the back of the garage sat a generator and a large can of diesel in case of power cuts. That was like Matt, she thought. Always prepared for the unexpected.

"Let's go," Matt said when he came out the house.

They drove toward Gërmia Park. "I was looking for some insights into your personality in the garage," Kit said.

"Did you find any?"

"I discovered that you're married with a son. I didn't know."

"I've been planning to host a small office barbecue one of these days. You'd have met them then."

"And apart from that, I can see you're well organized and you like restoring vintage Fiat cars."

"I prefer the Ford SUV for everyday use. I'm planning to drive the Fiats back to the UK and sell them for a good profit."

"Sounds like a plan." The banter helped to distract her from the lingering sense of betrayal by Sergei, which was offset by a curiosity about what they might find. It was best to get everything else in the open.

"I had coffee with Sergei a few times. He seemed like a nice enough guy, and I never suspected …"

Matt changed down a gear as they drove out of the city and into the more wooded and grassed areas leading to the park, which was one of the few recreational areas in Pristina. It was always busy on the weekends during summer, and the traffic was building up.

Matt glanced toward her for a moment and then focused back on the road. "This might put those conversations in a different light. I'll debrief you on that when we get back to the task force HQ. Perhaps he was trying to get information out of you. But for now let's concentrate on checking this drop."

"I wondered about that. Naïvely, I thought he was just being friendly."

"Diplomats always have an agenda."

"Especially the Brits," Kit said.

"Especially them." Matt smiled. "I remember where that seat is. It's close to the entrance, so I'll park just outside Gërmia. There might not be anything under the seat. It wouldn't mean he hasn't used that drop before. He might have others and alternate between them."

"True, and we need to get a proper translation of the whole diary. I only have edited highlights," Kit said.

"I won't let that damned diary leave my sight. And I'm not going to tell that bastard Petri about it either," Matt said as he pulled into the parking lot before the controlled entrance to the park. An attendant charged drivers a few cents, but pedestrians could enter for free. Benches were distributed at intervals up the gravel trail. Mothers with strollers and toddlers wandered, while other children played on swings and slides. Families sat at tables and benches, enjoying picnics. Venders of novelty items peddled their wares—mostly balloons and toys. On either side of the road, the trees had changed color from green to rusty orange.

Kit and Matt reached the third wooden bench up the hill and sat down.

"This is it," Kit said. "Let's take a look."

Matt checked the top of the bench and behind the back. Kit pretended to drop her wallet a short distance away and knelt to pick it up. A note was wedged into a metal bracket supporting the wood. She extracted it from the seat, sat down, and opened the note.

Boom Boom Room 12:30 a.m., she read.

"Ever been there?" Matt asked

"No, what is it?"

"A nightclub in this centre of Pristina. Internationals and well-connected locals go there. I went once or twice with police colleagues when I first came to Kosovo."

"That name's not subtle."

"It is what it says on the box." Matt smiled. "A lot of boom boom of various kinds goes on there."

"It doesn't give a date, but it could mean tonight. If that's the case, we should get out of here before the intended recipient comes to pick it up."

"If we had more notice, we could have staked out this location. But I agree; let's go. The task force meeting I arranged is in half an hour."

When Kit and Matt arrived at the apartment, the others were already there. Eva was supervising her dog, who was yapping at Max, while the Tervuren ignored him. Don was stretched out on the couch leafing through a newspaper. Angel was preparing coffee and laying out pastries from the local bakery. Owen was on the computer checking the Interpol database for updates on red notices for suspects. Matt convened them around the meeting table and invited Kit to brief everyone on the recent developments.

Owen whistled and swore under his breath. "Who'd have thought it?" he said.

"It's tricky," Eva said as she reached for a cup of coffee. Ignoring the pastries, she toyed with her cigarette packet. "Sokolov has diplomatic immunity, which his handlers will invoke. I'd like to prosecute him though. It's possible the Russians might waive the diplomatic immunity if we can find convincing evidence of a crime. It doesn't look great for their office otherwise."

The Missing Diary

"I agree," Kit said. "We need to take this investigation as far as we can. We should go to the nightclub. Owen, can you run a forensic analysis? Let's see what we can learn from the scrap of paper. In the meantime, we should make a duplicate note and return it to the seat in the park where the person it was intended for can find it."

"Let me take care of that," Owen said. "I'll make a copy and drop it back at the park if you can tell me where to put it. On the way back, I'll give the original to our forensic lab. Make sure they report to us, and keep that bastard Petri out of the loop." Owen retrieved a sealable, plastic bag from his bag and placed the note inside with a pair of tweezers. Then he cut a small piece of paper and made a duplicate message. Kit explained to him where to place it on the park bench.

"Before you go, Owen, let's agree who'll go to the Boom Boom Room tonight, alone or in pairs," Matt said.

"I'm going," Kit said. "I want to talk to Sokolov before he's brought in for questioning."

"Are you sure?" Eva asked. "There's a good chance that Raco or one of his associates might be there."

"I've been thinking about that," Kit said. "My hair draws too much attention. I'll fix it so they don't recognize me straight away."

Chapter Twenty-Two

Kit lead the way into the nightclub, accompanied by Owen and Angel. Don and Matt waited outside in the Ford Explorer. Kit wore the brunette wig, styled in a bob. Her stirrup black slacks were topped with a sequinned tank and embroidered denim jacket.

"I don't know how you're going to balance in those stilettos," Owen said.

"Practise. You should try it sometime."

"Ha! Ha! Not my style."

"So, what are we going to do?" Angel asked.

"I'm looking for Sokolov. You keep an eye open for Raco and any of his associates. If we need backup, call Matt and Don."

The Boom Boom Room lived up to its name. A band played a driving beat; couples danced, while others sat at tables along the edges. Groups of people linked arms in a circle or lines and moved backward and forward.

"That looks simpler than the way we dance at home," Owen said.

"It's a kind of Balkans line dance," Angel replied.

Kit headed to the bar and ordered a straight scotch. She knocked it back quickly and grabbed the attention of the bartender, who had brown, shoulder-length hair tied at the nape of his neck and a broad Scots accent.

"Have you seen a Russian guy around tonight? He owes me a drink," she purred. Her voice, although quiet, cut through the background noise of the club. "Thirties. So high." She waggled her hand in the air in an approximation of his height.

"Yeah, out the back." The bartender indicated a door behind him. "We have all sorts here. Even Russians. Where are you from?"

Kit smiled as she moved away from the bar and made her way toward the door. "I'm an international," she tossed over her shoulder. She turned the door handle with determination and thrust open the door. Inside was a separate lounge area furnished with couches and chairs grouped in a horseshoe around a low table, while a small bar stood in one corner. Sergei sat in the middle of the coffee-coloured couch. On his left sat a woman with long, blonde hair and on his right was a younger man. Across from them sat two other men. It looked to Kit like a business meeting.

Sergei looked up. He was startled at the interruption, although at first he gave no sign that he recognized Kit. "Could you give us a few moments please." His voice was cool and calm.

"Who the fuck is this?" drawled the woman sitting next to him.

"Could you give us a few minutes—please—alone," he repeated.

The woman—who was wearing skin-tight jeans, boots, and a cropped T-shirt—got up, shot Kit a poisonous look, and left.

"Is everything alright?" asked one of the men in a thick Russian accent.

"*Da*," Sergei said and nodded without taking his eyes off Kit. He got up and walked toward the bar. "Can I get you a drink? Scotch or vodka?"

"I'm a whiskey girl, as you know," she answered with ice in her voice.

"I've never developed a taste for it." He poured two glasses, a vodka for him and straight whisky for her. He handed her the tumbler.

"Apparently you're not going to remark on my appearance?" she said.

"You startled me for a moment, but then I recognised you. Are you on an operation?"

"You could say that, although I think lawyers can drink on duty."

Sergei said nothing but, still holding the bottle of vodka, sat down again and raised his glass.

"There's no easy way to say this, Sergei. I need to speak to you."

"Did you get my message about the study course in Slovenia? I booked two air tickets."

"Is your wife coming?"

"I told you she's dead. What do you want to talk about?"

"That's a lie. She's alive and lives in Moscow."

"Says who?"

"I can't say."

Sergei considered for a moment. "Alright—technically I do still have a wife. After she had a horrible car accident, she had a personality change and we don't get along any more. She couldn't have children. For me it was as if she's dead. It seemed easier to describe her as having passed away rather than explain this complicated situation."

"Well, it was a lie. And you are a liar. I'm so disappointed in you. How long had you been planning the massacre in Staro Dorbi? It must've been hilarious for you to return to the scene of the crime and see my naïve reaction to the whole situation. And you … pretending to be helpful when I fainted. Pretending to give me support. Pretending …" She curled her upper lip into a sneer.

"What are you talking about? Who has filled your head with such nonsense?"

"I can't tell you where I got this information. But I want to hear what happened. Did you plan that massacre of innocent Serbian farmers? You let us suppose that Raco was the guilty one. But he was just carrying out your orders as a gun for hire."

"Katerina," he said in a soft voice. "You've been under a lot of stress. I heard about the abduction by Raco. I hope he didn't hurt you. He was only supposed to warn you off the case for your own safety and find out what you know. We didn't expect that you would jump out of the moving taxi. I'm afraid that you are … unwell. And while I find your outfit very becoming, it's not necessary to dress up in such a disguise."

"Don't worry about my outfits or my state of mind. Just answer my question. Did you plan the massacre? Were Raco and his joint Albanian and Serbian team acting on your orders?"

"Well, my dear, now it's my turn to make no comment." Sergei pulled out his mobile and sent a text message before he walked over to her, took her face in his hands, and gazed into her eyes. "I want you to know, I meant everything I said to you. I was sincere about all that happened between us—as sincere as I can be in the circumstances. I believe you are a natural strategist and would contribute greatly to our team of philosophers. My invitation to you is genuine and remains open. In this game we play, it's not always possible to be one hundred percent transparent about our plans. But I sincerely want to help you." He leaned forward and kissed her firmly but gently on the mouth.

If that had taken place a week ago, she might have responded warmly. There was something in her that responded, but she was too angry. She slapped his face. "You bastard. I'm not buying any more of your bullshit." Her body tensed, and her voice shook with fury. "By the way, was that Faberge egg real? Is anything about you real?

Sergei chuckled as he rubbed his reddening face. "Not much gets past you. The egg was real, yes—an excellent copy of the Faberge egg in Moscow. And I am also real, as are my orders from Moscow."

Kit shook her head, speechless for a moment.

"Remember what I taught you. Try to take an overview of the situation. Use chaos and the unexpected to your advantage. It's because of me that you were able to work all this out. Try not to be too angry. You'll cool down soon enough and get a better understanding of things."

"Don't worry, I already have a better understanding of things. And stop calling me Katarina, and I'm not your dear … anymore." She slapped him again on the other side of his face.

"As part of our training with the FSB, we're taught to withstand beatings during interrogation. So you might as well stop hitting me. It has little effect. Unless you're suggesting we incorporate this into our bedroom play."

"I'm furious with you," Kit hurled the words at him.

"I love your passion and determination, your fearlessness. I mean everything I say. You're a woman of incomparable quality. But I've got to go now. My driver is waiting outside."

"That's right, just walk out. No accountability right to the end. I'm downright disgusted with you. You're a murderer, nothing more. Your philosophy counts for nothing." Kit was panting. Her head swam with memories of the people who had been murdered, lying in the field like battered mannequins, or like a doll in the case of the young girl.

Kit hadn't noticed the other door when she entered the room. It was probably part of their standard operating procedure to use rooms with more than one exit, she thought with the part of her mind that was still analysing the situation.

Kit got out her mobile and called Matt, whom she assumed was with Owen outside the club. At that moment, a noise erupted from the room outside. The music stopped, and there was a sound of breaking furniture, followed by a short burst of gunfire.

Sergei turned in front of the exit. "You should leave too. I can drop you home, or you could come with me."

"Bloody hell! You didn't hear a word I said did you, or perhaps you couldn't care less. There's no way I'm going with you."

"As you wish." With that, he left the building through the rear entrance, where a black diplomatic limousine was waiting for him in the alley. He slid into the rear passenger seat and closed the door. The car drove away into the night.

The ruckus in the other room built to a crescendo. Women screamed and men yelled. More shots were fired, and wailing sirens approached. Matt hadn't answered her call. "Raco," she whispered.

Kit opened the door leading into the main bar and was struck by a scene of pandemonium. The power had been cut and only the weak, orange emergency lighting was working. The door stood open, and while one or two people ran out of it, most of the club goers had taken shelter behind upturned tables and sofas. The band had left their instruments on the stage and were nowhere to be seen. Windows were smashed, as was the mirror and some of the bottles behind the bar.

Kit looked around but couldn't see anyone that she recognised. There was a lull in the action until another shot broke the stillness. The bullet hit the wall—a foot away from her. Someone was shooting at her, and she had a good idea who that would be. She took shelter behind the bar next to the barman. "Did you find your Russian?" he asked.

"Yeah, I did. Thanks."

"I hope he bought you a drink."

"He gave me a drink, yes. But he's no gentleman. He's left the scene already."

"I don't blame him. It's like a gangster land here sometimes. I think the police are coming."

"I've got friends here. I'm going look for them. I think that last bullet was meant for me."

The bartender gaped at her—lost for words.

"Maybe this isn't a safe place in case he comes after me," she said.

"He's a friend of yours?"

"He was very friendly, although it wasn't reciprocated. I'm Caitlin by the way." She extended her hand and he shook it.

"Gavin."

"Pleased to meet you. And now, as much as I like your bar, I think we need to leave."

He pointed to a shotgun and a baseball bat behind the bar. "If anyone comes over here and tries anything, they'll come off second best."

Kit shrugged, scooted behind him, and peered out from behind the bar. If Raco was shooting at her, he would probably come after her. She had to move. Or maybe it was just crossfire. Across the other side of the room, Angel was crouching behind a couch. She raised her hand and started counting on her fingers. Kit understood that she should run. She trusted Angel's judgement and made a break for it when the countdown got to zero. At that moment, Owen appeared and started shooting as he provided cover for Matt, who had tackled Raco.

Just then the wailing sirens stopped, and two police cars and a van pulled up outside the building. Their blue lights flickered across the club through the windows. A scuffle broke out on the other side of the room. In the low light, Kit recognized Raco's massive bulk, his muscular arms pumping as he exchanged blows with Matt and dominated him with his heavier build. Owen joined Matt and tackled another man in Raco's group. A revolver skidded across the floor. Kit dove to the floor, scooped up the Glock, and checked it. There was a bullet in the chamber. She flicked off the safety so it was ready to fire. She wished for a moment that she'd had weapon training. After realizing that she wasn't going to use it—there were too many people around, and she was untrained—she adjusted her grip and turned the weapon from a gun into an improvised club. It felt like a lifesaving move.

Kit's pulse was beating rapidly as the room swam before her eyes. Don and Max were outside with the Kosovo Police, briefing their commander. Kit felt so much pent-up rage at Raco—on her own behalf, on behalf of Vasha Blaku, and even more, on behalf of the mother and child she had seen heartlessly slaughtered on the killing field of Staro Dorbi. Her body was tight with energy and tension. Every muscle was corded and quivering, her heart was pounding in her chest, and her vision was blurred with red. Ignoring the possibility of further gunfire, she stalked across the room and delivered a stunning blow with the butt of the Glock to the base of Raco's skull. She felt the satisfying crunch of bone under the impact of the blow, and he collapsed, stunned.

As Raco slumped on impact, Matt heaved the man away from him, turned him on his stomach, and cuffed Raco's hands together.

Raco lay motionless. Kit wanted so much for Raco to be convicted and to give evidence against Sergei. Matt helped Owen with his assailant as he grabbed the other man from behind and pulled him back, but not before Owen had delivered a last punch to his jaw. Kit stood in a moment of stillness before sound and movement burst in on the scene again. Her mind swirled, trying to process what was happening. She could hear the police officers running and shouting as they poured into the building. She placed the Glock on the ground and stepped away from it. Her eyes met Matt's, and she saw the relief and pain in his face. A fleeting smile played on his split lips. They had finally captured Raco.

CHAPTER TWENTY-THREE

As the members of Task Force Eagle Eye sat around the table, the air was thick with tension. Each was nursing a mug of coffee or tea, and the only sound was the clinking of cups against saucers and tapping on the computer. A plate of freshly baked pastries and another plate of flaky *burek* sat in the middle of the table, but no one seemed interested in the food. Matt and Owen both had bruises on their faces, and Owen was favoring his arm. He was still recovering from being shot and hospitalized, and the fight at the night club meant the wound had to be restitched. Kit had her hair in her signature ponytail; the bruises on the side of her face were fading. Eva sat on the arm of a chair by the window, smoking, with Bambino quietly at her feet. The group was silent, each person lost in their own thoughts, until finally Angel came in with several newspapers and put them onto the table.

"We made the news," she said. She spread open the newspapers, some local and others international. News of the arrest of Raco and his associates was plastered all over the papers. Local and international news outlets were quick to report on the story, with many giving credit to the Kosovo police commander, although he did mention cooperation with international police.

"It's fine with me," Matt said. "We don't need to be mentioned by name, and it's probably better if we aren't. Let the locals take the credit. My commander knows what happened, and I've been reinstated as the head of Task Force Capture. Now it's a matter of finishing the paperwork."

"My office will be taking it from here," Eva said. "We're preparing the indictments."

"More work for you?" Matt said as he looked at Kit.

"I'm coming to the end of my contract here. I'm not sure what I'm going to be doing. I'm going on holiday for a couple of weeks and then maybe back to New Zealand."

"I want to talk to you about that," Eva said. She opened her briefcase and pulled out a folder. "If you'd like to stay, I can offer you a contract extension for a year."

Kit looked around the table. She felt torn. On one hand, she loved her work, but on the other, she didn't know if personnel would be willing to extend her contract.

"I thought personnel was starting disciplinary action against me for bad timekeeping."

Eva smiled and stubbed out her cigarette. "We've sorted that. Mueller told them to stop the crap. He gave you an excellent evaluation for your work on this case on my recommendation. This looks great for the organization. We want to keep you on board."

"The head of mission backed me up? I thought he hated me."

"He said we need more dynamic younger people on the team. People who can think outside the box and get things done. People like you."

"That's a joke," Kit said and grinned.

"Don't look a gift horse in the mouth. I'd like you to stay. I need your help on our next high-profile investigation with the police."

"What's it about?" Kit asked.

"I call the file *Corruption in High Places*. I'll tell you more later," Eva said.

"We might need another task force. Task Force Icarus. The members remain the same," Matt added.

"Icarus—isn't that the Greek myth about the talented inventor who made his own wings and flew too close to the sun?" Owen asked.

"That's the one," Matt said.

Kit laughed. "I'll be a part of that task force too, if I stay."

"I was thinking you'd take a leading role on Task Force Icarus," Eva said.

"Me? I'm not a police investigator," Kit said. Her relationship was showing cracks already, and if she didn't go back to New Zealand, she didn't know how long it would last.

"You're our star problem solver," Matt said. "You'll be the lead investigator on this task force, police officer or not. That's why we need you to stay in your current job."

"We value your work," Eva said.

"I'd love to stay," Kit said. "Life was never as interesting."

"Some kinds of interesting we could do without," Owen said.

"True," Kit said. "But all's well that ends well."

"Interesting," Don said. "Any need for a canine unit?"

"I'm not sure yet, but I'd like your expertise on hand, Don. The work will be interesting, no doubt about it. It will also be challenging and potentially dangerous" Matt said.

"You remember that attaché from the Russian Liaison Office?" Matt said. He looked at Kit. She said nothing but bit her lip. "I contacted the Liaison Office, and they told me he's left for Moscow. His ambassador said that any investigation against office personnel would be met with a claim of diplomatic immunity."

"Sokolov was behind the whole thing," Eva said as she stabbed the paper with her pencil. "But proving it is another matter. I'm planning to issue an indictment against him on principle. Let them assert diplomatic immunity. We might be able to get some information out of Raco."

"Good luck with that," Kit said. "I hope I didn't hurt him too badly the other night." She had acted on impulse, and on reflection, she thought that cudgelling Raco with the pistol had not been the wisest course of action. After the confrontation, she feared his lawyer might bring charges against her for assault or, worse, unlawful killing.

"You should have hit him harder. He's recovering in hospital and will be moved into detention tomorrow," Owen said. Kit flashed him a smile. His support felt reassuring.

"We have the diary, but unless we can call Merita Shala to give evidence, I'm not sure how useful it'll be in court," Eva said. "No doubt defense counsel will dispute the evidence. The gap in the chain of custody when it got lost leaves us open to challenge."

The Missing Diary

"Shala claimed that her diary entries were all a fantasy. But it gave us the information we needed to make the arrest and find out who was behind the killings," Kit said.

"I've checked with Immigration and it looks as if Shala has left Kosovo. She's got married and gone to live with her new husband in Munich. I doubt that she would come voluntarily to give evidence at the court hearing," Owen said.

"Let's review all the evidence and see what we can do," Eva said. "We have an abundance of evidence against Raco and his gang on multiple offences, including two counts of kidnapping, assault, sexual assault, and gunrunning. We have the forensic evidence that puts them at the scene of the massacre. But as for Shala, I'm not sure we can extradite her, and I don't think we can go behind the diplomatic immunity for Sokolov. I'm going to try though. We can request the waiver of his immunity."

"The Russians will never waive his immunity," Matt said.

"I know, but let's try to make the point," Eva said.

"Is that my new contract?" Kit said as she pointed toward the documents in Eva's hand.

Eva nodded and pushed the documents toward her.

"One year, renewable," Eva said.

"I'm going to sign right now. When can I start?"

"Personnel told me that there needs to be a break of the month between ending one contract and beginning another."

"That'll work in well with my plans. My mum is coming from New Zealand with my fiancé and another friend. We're meeting in Dubrovnik. Xander might hire a yacht so we can sail around the Croatian coast."

"Sounds perfect," Eva said.

"Your fiancé is coming?" Angel asked, raising an eyebrow.

Kit shrugged. "He said we had a misunderstanding and wants to make a fresh start. I guess I'll give him a chance."

CHAPTER TWENTY-FOUR

Kit walked through the historic city of Dubrovnik. A UNESCO cultural heritage site, the medieval ramparts, massive city walls and historic buildings make the city a cultural and historical gem. Kit recognized the architecture from several popular historical and fantasy TV shows. It was late summer and the cobbled city squares were packed with tourists from cruise ships. She was dressed like a tourist, her hair pulled back under a red cap and wearing a T-shirt, leggings and trainers.

Dubrovnik was a couple of hours flying time from Pristina with a transit through Vienna. She had just checked in at the Hilton Imperial, the grand dame of hotels in Dubrovnik. Her mother and Xander were already there. Charles, her mother's friend, had come from New Zealand, partly for a vacation and partly to meet Vasha Blaku, who was joining New Zealand's protected witness programme, arranged through Matt and Charles's shared contacts in London. Vasha and her cousin were sharing in a room, and Charles had a room in the same small hotel on a lower floor. Charles would escort Vasha to New Zealand with her cousin and assist her through immigration.

They had arranged to meet for lunch at a seafood restaurant by the old marina.

Kit was excited at the prospect of seeing Xander again. He had called to apologize for his last phone call and explained that nothing had come of his friendship with university tutor. He had just wanted company because he was missing Kit.

Kit had rolled her eyes and sighed upon hearing this. "Okay, hon, let's meet to see if we can sort things out," she'd said. She had wanted to put the whole sorry incident with Sergei behind her.

She was almost running when she caught sight of the restaurant's outdoor seating area which overlooked the sea. When her mother saw her she stood up and waved.

"It's so good to see you," Kit said to her mother, who was looking every bit on holiday wearing sunglasses with nautical style slacks and a stripped linen tunic. Kit's breath caught in her throat when she turned to Xander. Dressed in khaki cargo shorts, and a smart-white polo shirt, he looked better than she remembered him. He was more mature but also there were more signs of stress around his smiling brown eyes. His curly chestnut hair was trimmed short. Lean at the best of times, his tall physique now tended towards wiry, from the sailing, she guessed. They had both changed, matured. She wondered if that was enough to make things work between them.

Kit searched his eyes, before letting herself be wrapped in his arms. "I've missed you," she murmured as she raised her face for a kiss. Extracting herself slowly, she greeted Vasha and her cousin. Vasha was a different woman, much more relaxed than she had been in Pristina, and smiling broadly in her bright yellow sundress and matching shoes. The bruises from Raco's assaults were long gone. Her cousin, a younger, shorter woman with straight dark hair was wearing blue capri pants and navy T-shirt with a matching-silk scarf, shook Kit's hand with a friendly smile.

Charles, a man in his late fifties, hugged Kit warmly. "Good to see you again, kid," he said.

Charles had a thick, bushy beard sprinkled with silver. His kind eyes sparkled as he smiled at Kit. A solidly built man in his late fifties, Charles had been a body builder in his younger days.

"Not so much of the kid now, thanks," Kit said standing tall and grinning at him. "Wait till you hear the stories I've got to tell."

"I hear you busted a serious crime case wide open."

"There are still one or two loose ends." She looked across the brilliant blue Adriatic Sea. "But we've got a solid case with the help of our confidential informant."

They ordered the salmon salad, seafood risotto, tagliatelle and grilled prawns, followed by crème caramel. The table looked over the sea and was next to the old city wall. While gentle jazz played in the background, Rosalyn brought Kit up to speed with developments back in Auckland.

"Guess what," Xander interrupted their chat. "I've hired a yacht so we can sail from Dubrovnik to Split."

"Wow! Tell me all about it," Kit said as her face lit into a brilliant smile. She sat down at the table and Charles poured them all a glass of Grk the famous white wine from Lumbarda on the island of Korčula.

"I've rented it for two weeks—you can just about see her berth from here," Xander pointed to the rows of yachts and other pleasure craft moored nearby. "She's big enough for all of us. Then we're flying back together to Auckland," Xander said.

"Um … " Kit squinted into the sun that was behind him. She raised her hand to shade her eyes and hesitated for a moment. "Didn't I mention that I'm staying on in Pristina for a bit longer?"

"No, you didn't. Bloody hell! I thought we'd had this conversation. You're coming home. It's better for you. And it's better for us."

"Sorry about that. I thought it would be easier to explain in person. My boss renewed my contract and I'll be in Kosovo for a few more months. She needs me to work on another case."

"What case?" Charles asked. "I know you can't go into details. But in general terms, what's it about."

"I don't know exactly. Eva's going to brief me when I get back. I think it might be about white-collar crime."

Xander stood up, left the table and went to the railing overlooking the sea. "I don't know why you insist on working in that godforsaken place. You proved the point that you could succeed at criminal law abroad, didn't you?"

Kit got up, stood next to him and placed her hand on his arm. "Please try to understand. They need me at OIDC. Even the head of mission said so. They need someone like me who can get things done."

"We support you, love," Rosalyn said. "But we'll be looking forward to you coming safely home to New Zealand. How long do you plan to be away?"

"Another few months," Kit said. The lie came easily. "It's a great team too. I used to think I could go it alone, but now I realize the importance of teamwork."

"Except when it comes to us," Xander said in a sour voice.

"If I could say something." Vasha's voice rose up from the table. "I'm so grateful for everything that Kit has done to help me. If it wasn't for her, criminals would be walking free today. Serious criminals, violent in ways than you can't understand."

The others turned to look at Vasha. No one spoke until Kit went over to Vasha and touched her shoulder. "I understand."

"I know you do." Vasha put her hand over Kit's. Her voice cracked, and a tear spilled out down her cheek. Vasha's cousin took her other arm and gave her a hug.

"Alright, let's see what happens. Maybe I could look for work in Pristina," Xander said after studying them for a moment.

Kit flashed him a smile. "You're more than welcome. I know my mission in life. I'm bringing more justice to the world with my team. How about you?"

Xander's silence was filled by the arrival of coffee. Just then, Kit felt her mobile vibrate. She got up and turned to face the sea. With her back to the others, she checked the message from an unknown number. *Don't forget about Ljubljana, S.* She took a moment and stood looking out over the marina.

"What is it, love. A message from work?" Rosalyn asked.

She couldn't hide much from her mother. Kit turned around. Xander wasn't paying attention; he was talking to Vasha's cousin.

"Nothing really," Kit said as she came back to the table. "More work. An interesting case that might be something to look forward to."

As she read the text from Sergei about their upcoming trip to Slovenia, she felt a wave of guilt wash over her. She wanted to be tough and not feel anything, but it was hard. Part of her knew that she and Sergei still had unfinished business. But right now, she had to try and move on with Xander.

Although her emotions were in disarray, she looked forward to going back to Pristina and getting started on Eva's case. She was eager to uncover the evildoings of the corrupt and bring them to justice.

THE END

The Crime Scene Kosovo series continues in *The Price of Justice*.

Kit Chase is an international lawyer, determined to uncover the truth of a massive money laundering scheme. After a whistleblower's corruption investigation points to senior officials within her own organization, she discovers that the legal system she trusts is not enough to protect her.

From Kosovo to Albania and Slovenia, with each step of the investigation, Kit is dragged deeper into a web of corruption and deceit, facing off with old enemies yearning for revenge. As dark secrets are revealed and sinister plots are uncovered, Kit must use her knowledge of the crypto-currency world and espionage tactics to stay one step ahead of those who wish to silence her.

Meanwhile, Kit's personal life is thrown into disarray as an old flame rekindles their past romance and her father makes contact after twenty years absence. With danger lurking around every corner, Kit must find a way to stop the criminal masterminds behind the money laundering scheme or risk losing her freedom—or worse—for good.

Coming soon in ebook and print formats.

More Books by Tasmin Turner

Thanks for joining Kit in this adventure. If you enjoyed the book, a review on your favourite platform would be much appreciated.

The Crime Scene Kosovo books will include the following:

The Missing Diary #1
The Price of Justice #2
Explosive Reprisals #3

You can sign up to be notified of new releases, giveaways, and pre-release specials at www.wish-books.com

ABOUT TASMIN TURNER

Tasmin Turner is the author of the Crime Scene Kosovo Series, which is based in the early 2000s in post-conflict Balkans. Tasmin lives in the heartland of New Zealand, after two decades living in Europe and the US. She's passionate about writing and enjoys frequenting cafes.

Author's Note

Information About Kosovo

The series Crime Scene Kosovo is set in a fictional post-conflict Kosovo, with fictitious characters, organizations and events. The information below is a brief account of Kosovo's real historical background.

Kosovo is a self-declared independent country in Europe's Balkan region. Although many nations—including the United States and several members of the European Union—acknowledge its 2008 declaration of freedom from Serbia, Russia and some other countries, including some EU states, do not recognize Kosovo's independence. Most inhabitants are Albanian, and the minority are Serbs, together with other ethnic minority groups. The official languages are Albanian and Serbian.

The name Kosovo is derived from a Serbian term meaning "field of blackbirds." After serving as the heart of a medieval kingdom of Serbia, Kosovo was governed by the Ottoman Empire from the mid-fifteenth century to the early twentieth century. This was an era when Islam grew in importance and the number of Albanian speakers in the region grew. Then in the early twentieth century, Kosovo was incorporated into Serbia (later part of Yugoslavia). By the second half of that century, Muslims of Albanian origin outnumbered Eastern Orthodox Serbs in Kosovo, leading to frequent inter-ethnic tensions in the province.

In 1998, an ethnic Albanian-led secessionist rebellion escalated into a global crisis, resulting in NATO's 1999 air bombardment of Yugoslavia, which at that time was a remnant state comprised of Serbia and Montenegro. Peace was restored afterwards, and Kosovo was administered by the United Nations and supported by several other international and regional organizations during post-conflict times.

A landlocked country, Kosovo is flanked by Serbia to the north and east, North Macedonia to the south, Albania to the west, and Montenegro to the northwest. About the same geographic size as Jamaica or Lebanon, it is one of the smallest countries in the Balkans, with a population of less than two million people in 2021, predominantly of Albanian descent. The capital, Pristina, is also the largest urban area. Albanian and Serbian are spoken languages, with most Kosovars adhering to Sunni Islam.

The information in this description is drawn from the following source: Allcock, John B. , Young, Antonia and Lampe, John R.. "Kosovo". Encyclopedia Britannica, 8 Nov. 2022, https://www.britannica.com/place/Kosovo. Accessed 16 January 2023.

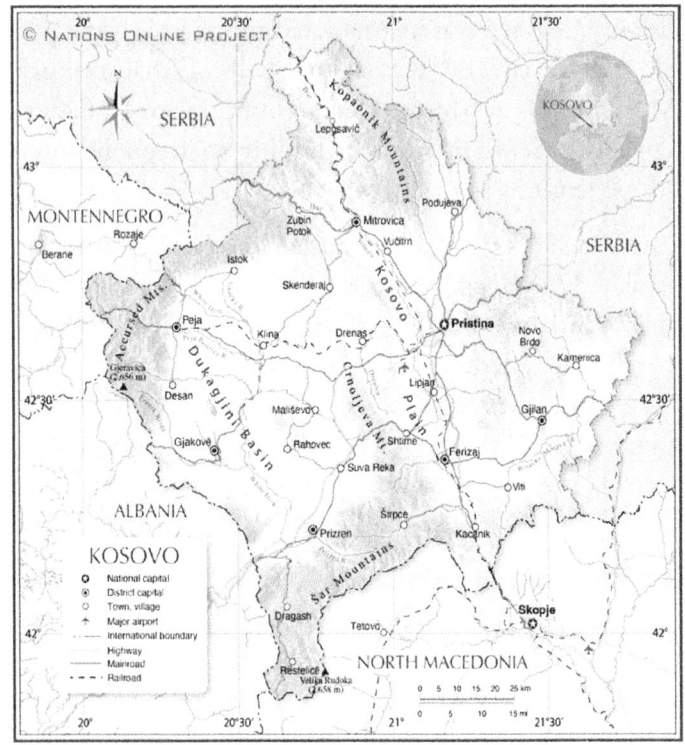

Map of Kosovo

The source of the map is Nations Online Project accessed 10 January 2023
https://www.nationsonline.org/oneworld/map/Kosovo-map.htm

Made in United States
Orlando, FL
28 May 2023

33581023R00173